D0002908

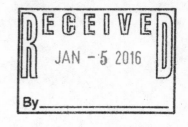
ONLY
THE STONES
SURVIVE

BY MORGAN LLYWELYN
FROM TOM DOHERTY ASSOCIATES

After Rome
Bard
Brendán
Brian Boru
The Elementals
Etruscans (with Michael Scott)
Finn Mac Cool
Grania
The Horse Goddess
The Last Prince of Ireland
Lion of Ireland
Pride of Lions
Strongbow

THE NOVELS OF THE IRISH CENTURY

1916: A Novel of the Irish Rebellion
1921: A Novel of the Irish Civil War
1949: A Novel of the Irish Free State
1972: A Novel of Ireland's Unfinished Revolution
1999: A Novel of the Celtic Tiger and the Search for Peace

ONLY THE STONES SURVIVE

Morgan Llywelyn

A TOM DOHERTY ASSOCIATES BOOK

NEW YORK

ONLY THE STONES SURVIVE

Copyright © 2015 by Morgan Llywelyn

Designed by Mary A. Wirth

A Forge Book
Published by Tom Doherty Associates, LLC
175 Fifth Avenue
New York, NY 10010

www.tor-forge.com

Forge® is a registered trademark of Tom Doherty Associates, LLC.

ISBN 978-0-7653-3792-4 (hardcover)
ISBN 978-1-4668-3654-9 (e-book)

The Library of Congress Cataloging-in-Publication Data
is available upon request.

Our books may be purchased in bulk for promotional, educational, or business use. Please contact your local bookseller or the Macmillan Corporate and Premium Sales Department at (800) 221-7945, extension 5442, or by e-mail at MacmillanSpecialMarkets@macmillan.com.

First Edition: January 2016

Printed in the United States of America

0 9 8 7 6 5 4 3 2 1

FOR ERIU,

who saved me when I was broken

The distinction between history and mythology might be itself meaningless outside the Earth.

—C. S. LEWIS, *Out of the Silent Planet*

ONLY
THE STONES
SURVIVE

❧ PROLOGUE ❧

Concealed within the stones are frozen fires.

Borne on vast waves of polychrome gas that attracted, discarded, formed, and reformed patterns of infinite complexity, the living sparks had taken their allotted places. They were burning before the beginning. They will burn after the end. Their fire is impervious to time.

Time is a human concept. Creation is on a different scale.

Every spark was a syllable spoken into silence, a miniscule portion of the great Word that became a roar of limitless power and exploded to create a universe.

From chaos, cosmos.

The Word defied understanding. There was no need to explain that which was everywhere and everything.

Before us.

❧ ONE ❧

WHEN IT WAS OVER and the soil had drunk its fill of
blood, the slaughtered Túatha Dé Danann lay amid their tattered banners. Their weapons of bronze had been no match
for the cold iron brought by the invaders.

The most recent battle had reached its inevitable conclusion.

Day was dying too. A low winter sun could not warm the
bodies scattered across the plain. Their garments were all
the hues of the rainbow; their faces were the color of death.
The tarnished sky above them would surrender to a blaze of
stars, but for the dead, beauty and brilliance were canceled.

Near the center of the battlefield a man lay curled up like
an infant. His blood-soaked garments concealed any sign of
life. His shield was shattered, its princely emblazonment
unrecognizable. The victors had kicked the ruined shield
aside but paused long enough to strip him of his weapons.

The spark within him refused to die. Hot and stubborn,
it smoldered with a will of its own. His slow return to
consciousness was not pleasant. His mouth and throat

were parched with thirst. A thousand angry bees were buzzing in his ears.

Me.

I.

Am alive. Yes.

Dizzy, very dizzy.

But alive.

Without opening his eyes, he knew his wounds were deep. The brain in his battered skull struggled to function. At first he could only manage a single thought at a time, but each led to another, like stepping stones across a river.

This is not the end.

No.

The invaders cannot destroy the Children of Light.

No.

They only want our land.

Our sacred land.

The taste of bile flooded his mouth; his stomach cramped in revolt. He lay very still until he was sure he was not going to vomit. A fastidious man, he did not want to die in a puddle of vomit.

He was not ready to die. Not now and not like this, with so much time still ahead of him like a banquet waiting to be enjoyed.

My time, our time. Together.

Yes.

He fought to throw off the pain that held him captive.

Terrible wounds can be healed. We can summon the power. Through the ancient ritual.

We?

Are there enough of us left . . . for the Being Together?

When he tried to raise his head and look around, fresh

waves of agony washed over him. He was being torn and twisted—he was pierced and bludgeoned!

Before he could draw breath to scream, the torment ceased. The abrupt shock was almost worse than the pain.

Opening his eyes meant another shock. He was staring into a void, the total absence of anything perceptible to the senses. No sight, no sound.

Nothing. Nullity.

Is this what death is?

No. No!

He tried to move; his body would not respond. His limbs seemed to be detached from the rest of him. There was no longer any pain, but he would have welcomed pain. Pain would mean he was still alive.

Like trapped mice, his thoughts raced around inside his skull.

No way out, no way back.

Go forward, then.

But how?

He was as helpless as a child waiting to be born.

Born into what?

Part of him longed to crawl into a corner and cower there, gibbering.

No. That is not who I am.

I am me!

As if in response, the void gave way to an impenetrable blackness. Like ebony. Or was it onyx? His frantic mind sought reassurance in definition.

Black means it is . . . something.

He clung to the thought as random streaks of colored light began to spangle the darkness, warmly radiant lights that appeared both immeasurably distant and close enough to touch.

He reached out to them.

The result was unsettling, as if he were falling upward.

His body responded with a violent start.

Instantly, he was cocooned in a thick mist as comforting as a mother's arms. Through the mist came the chime of distant bells.

Fear gradually faded into acceptance. His worries ceased to weigh upon him. His damaged body was a burden he need not endure. It would be so easy to let go; he could just drift away and . . .

No! He concentrated his entire will, his formidable will, on that word. The denial of surrender.

The little strength he retained was just enough to repel the mist. The cloud dispersed reluctantly, fading to a grainy half twilight. He began to see huddled shapes lying near him. Forcing his eyes to focus, he recognized the fallen fruits of battle, left to spoil.

None of those dead bodies belonged to the woman he loved. His relief was greater than his pain had been. She must be somewhere on his other side, then. During the final assault, he had placed himself between his wife and the enemy. When he twisted around to look for her, something tore inside him, but he ignored it. He must hurry to find her; they had a long way to go.

He tried to call her name, but his voice failed. His throat locked on the syllables his heart had sung for years.

Rolling onto his belly, he used his elbows like oars to row across the earth, dragging his wounded body after him. Moving hurt; even breathing hurt. No matter. His agonized efforts were forcing the circulation back into his limbs. His arms and legs tingled as if a thousand bees were stinging them, but he had learned his lesson: pain was good. He scrabbled his way across the broken and bloody ground un-

til he had enough strength to get to his feet. He stood sway-
ing, assessing his condition. Back, shoulders, arms . . . *Yes!*
He would be able to carry her if she was injured.

But she was not injured; she was waiting for him. Just a
few more steps. He would find her soon. Her spirit was calling to his, guiding him. She was at the core of his being; he
had never doubted they would grow old together.

Until he found her.

His throat opened then.

The cry he gave was enough to shatter the canceled stars.

❧ TWO ❧

YOU CAN CALL ME Elgolai na Starbird. That is not the name I was given when I was born; it is who I am now.

It is what I have become.

On the day of my birth, I received a lengthy title that referenced past generations of the Túatha Dé Danann, identifying the nobility, the heroes, and the scholars and the artists among my ancestors. Every member of our tribe inherited a similar record of lineage, which was to be a source of pride and a guidepost for character. The infant's personal name was added to the end of the long list.

An invisible chain connected the newest Danann to those who had gone before; thus another of the Children of Light was secured in history.

My personal name, chosen by my parents before I was born, was Joss. Joss had the strong yet jaunty quality that Mongan and Lerys wanted for their son.

Naming is an act of creation.

I was born in the season of leaf-fall. To balance their long life spans, my people had a low birthrate; the arrival of an infant was a great event. Because my father was a prince of the Túatha Dé Danann, my birth was celebrated for seven days and nights. During that time, all debts were canceled and misunderstandings forgiven. Gifts in my name were given to every member of our clan, my extended family.

My early life was a happy dream. As an only child I had the full attention of my parents. The sun always shone, or so I think now, and when the sun was not shining the moon and stars were. Rain, if any fell, was soft and warm.

The clothing I wore was fashioned by my mother from the shimmering fibers of many colourful plants. My fitted tunic was soft and comfortable, cool in sunseason. My hooded cloak was as light as thistledown, yet kept me warm in dark-season.

Our house was almost indistinguishable from the forest around it. Branches more slender than the arm of a Danann were inserted in the soil and bent like basketwork to form the walls and roof. The outside was covered with thin strips of grassy sod. Ferns and leaves were woven into elaborate patterns and fastened to the interior walls with stems. They could be changed according to the seasons—or my mother's mood. A family might live in one place for three generations, then decide they wanted to be closer to the music of a water-fall and move the entire structure in a single day.

As the seasons passed, I became aware that there was more to life than childhood. I asked my parents when I would become an adult. My mother laughed, but my father said, "You will become an adult when you begin having adult thoughts, Joss."

"What is an adult thought?"

Still laughing, my mother told me, "An adult thought is one which is not about yourself."

But everything was about me. In the dawn of life children

assume they are the center of the world and happiness is the normal condition—until they see its other face.

The Great War, when it came, was an awakening. Reminders of better times grew too painful. Titles extolling past glories fell into disuse. By the end of the war I was simply Joss.

The name I bear now is an oddity. As am I.

The event that would change everything was not recognized as a war, not at first. Like a tiny crack in a stone, it needed time to widen into malevolence.

The annual Being Together of the Túatha Dé Danann was held at the Gathering Place. The locale had been sacred to our tribe ever since we came to this island, and it was sacred long before we arrived, sacred even Before the Before. Place does not need people.

Before the Before stretched into an unimaginable past, as incapable of limits as the stars in the sky.

There were limits on our tribe, however, determined by the size of the land we occupied. The sacred island must always be able to feed us. We could not take more than we gave back. Our festivals were ceremonies of thanksgiving and promises of future generosity on our part.

The Túatha Dé Danann comprised a number of clans, each one an extended family tracing its origins from a common ancestor. Every clan had unique physical characteristics and patterns of thought. This made the connection between them vitally important. We were more than a tribe; we were a community: people and place wedded together. As long as the community survived, the Túatha Dé Danann would be immortal.

Looking into each other's eyes, my people saw themselves reflected.

From the blue mountains and the whispering forests, from the silver shores and the fragrant bogs and the hidden places of the heart, the Dananns flocked to the Gathering Place in response to the yearly summons for Being Together. Kings and queens and all the nobility, the elders of the tribe, the makers and builders and artisans, those who worked with the land and those who worked with the sea. None were excluded. The Children of Light were a single entity.

The youngest children did not attend the Being Together, however.

When my parents invited me to accompany them it was a tacit recognition of my approaching maturity. The ceremony was an important rite of passage, the initial step into the mysterious world of the adults.

I was more interested in the opportunity to meet people of my own age.

Although the Dananns inhabited the entire island, their numbers were relatively small. Their emphasis on family and kinship, their peaceful nature and strongly pastoral but self-sufficient society had produced a scattered pattern of settlement. Their dwellings reflected their surroundings, whether forest or mountain or seaside. If you did not know what to look for, you might never see them.

Several families of our clan lived within half a morning's walk of our home. Their children were younger than I was. On the occasions when I met these cousins, such as harvest time, we had little in common. I thought of them as babies. I do not know what they thought of me; it did not matter. Then.

For the Being Together an elderly couple joined my family on our journey to the Gathering Place. The Dagda and his wife, Melitt, lived at the other end of our valley. Originally he was simply Dagda, but over time his name had become a title of respect. The Dagda was the oldest member of our clan—and also the oldest of the Túatha Dé Danann, a man of such experience and wisdom that generations had called him king. When the task of tribal leadership finally became too arduous for a person his age, he had passed the kingship on to three brothers of royal birth. One man by himself could not have equaled the service the Dagda had rendered the tribe.

Relieved of the burden of authority, the Dagda had turned to teaching.

During darkseason I went to him to study or he came to me, more often the latter. Refusing to acknowledge his age, he would come striding down the valley with the energy of a younger man.

I must have been quite young when the pattern was set because I do not recall its beginnings, but I know I resented the time it took away from my play. The Dagda always had a lot to say and seemed to take forever to say it, droning on while I pretended to pay attention to wax tablets inscribed with numbers or to maps that he drew on the earth with a pointed stick.

The Dagda was inclined to say important things, lessons I obviously was meant to learn, when I least expected them. For example he might suddenly announce, "At birth we receive a gift of days, Joss. No person can say how many are allotted to him, but even if they number in the thousands, not a single one should be squandered. Our days are the greatest gift we are given."

Why did he tell me that when I was happily engaged in daydreaming?

Occasionally I did listen—if he was answering one of my many questions. Such as, "What is time?"

The Dagda's reply did not enlighten me. "Time is an illusion with a purpose."

Much, much later, when I realized the question I should have asked next, it was too late.

While I respected the Dagda's age and immense knowledge, I was genuinely fond of his plump, rosy-cheeked wife. Melitt was a merry little woman who baked delicious bread with summer fruits inside, like clusters of jewels.

As the five of us walked across the countryside, my mother chatted with Melitt and the Dagda, discussing old friends in common and days gone by, topics in which I had no interest. Fortunately, I was not expected to take part in their conversation. My father was busy preparing me for the event to come.

"The Being Together is the perfect occasion for making and renewing friendships," Mongan explained, "giving us the opportunity to exchange ideas, tell of our joys and share our sorrows. With singing and dancing we express our pleasure in living, and we reward the generous earth for supporting us with gifts of thanksgiving. But there is another purpose for the great gathering. An annual meeting of the clans is essential because we are so few in number.

"As you will see demonstrated if the need arises, Joss, when the Túatha Dé Danann unite in common purpose, we can achieve more than any single individual can do alone. Within our combined power is the summoning of wind, the distribution of clouds, the taming of storms, the redirection of rivers, the enrichment of soil, the raising of hills, the opening or sealing of caves, the purifying of pools, the ritual of healing, and more besides. Almost any deed you can imagine can be accomplished by our acting together."

We . . . *my people* . . . could do all those things! How thrilling!

The adults were walking with the sedate, gliding gait that characterized our race, but I began to skip uncontrollably. Prompted by something the Dagda recently said to me— "Live your life in the expectation of sudden joy, Joss"—I turned handsprings; I laughed aloud. No butterfly dancing on the air could be more giddy.

My people cherished childhood and usually made no effort to curtail it. Why should they, when we lived so long? A Danann childhood could last for more than twenty sunseasons, followed by the responsibilities of adulthood for another eighty sunseasons. Only then could one become an elder, a person whose acquired wisdom was counted as part of the tribe's treasure.

Unfortunately, my childish behavior on the morning of the Being Together brought a stern rebuke from my father. "Calm yourself, Joss! When we reach the Gathering Place you must be sedate and well-behaved. Listen instead of talking. Be mindful that you have nothing to contribute yet; it is enough for you to be there."

I promised; I would have promised anything on that bright morning. The future was a splendid Unknown, and I was eager for it.

I would approach it differently now.

At high sun we came to a pathway beaten by the passage of countless feet over countless seasons. The grass on either side of the path was so thick it tempted my bare feet to stray. The air was a heady perfume. We were immersed in life: leafy woodlands and lush grasslands and fern-fringed pools where predator and prey drank together.

Before us lay a meadow thickly starred with flowers. At home my mother could fashion almost anything from stems and leaves and blossoms. A flick of her fingers could create a wreath for the brow or a platter to hold bread.

I was stooping to pluck an armful of color and fragrance when she stayed my hand. "You must take nothing away from this place, Joss. Not ever." Her rebuke was gentler than my father's, but it went deeper.

The Dagda added, "Do no damage here, young man. Anyone who does is destined to die roaring in pain."

I swallowed hard and kept my hands at my sides.

The green land rolled before us in waves like the sea that embraced our island. I had not yet been taken to the coast to see the white-crested waves that were the manes of Manannan Mac Lir's horses, but someday I would. I would see and do many, many wonderful things. It was part of my heritage.

I was Danann.

The path we were following began to slope toward a distant hill. Our small group soon was enlarged by a trickle, then a stream, then a river of people dressed, as we were, in their brightest clothes, with more flowers in their hair. Cheerful strangers surrounded and enfolded us. Kinfolk I had never met called out my names, my many impressive names, and told me theirs.

My parents were congratulated on the simple fact of my being.

I thought myself a very fine fellow indeed.

When we reached the hill it did not appear very high; it was a long, grassy ridge crowned with timber columns, outlining halls. The halls were roofed with thatch but open on all sides to light and air. Instead of climbing up to them, the Dagda led us around to the sunrise slope, where we sat down on springy grass and warm earth. A vast crowd—or what looked like a crowd to me, who had never seen one before—was spreading out along the flank of the ridge.

All were careful to sit down without crushing the flowers.

So was I.

While we waited for the ceremony to begin, the Dananns sang. Mindful of my father's admonition, I stayed quiet and listened. It was just as well; I did not recognize any of the words. Rippling, floating words like a trill of birdsong or a stream burbling over pebbles. My mother leaned over to murmur in my ear, "We are singing in the old language, Joss. This is a song of welcome."

I didn't even know we had an old language. Yet when I listened closely, I observed that every unfamiliar word found its allotted place in the music. One could not be separated from the other.

Like the Dananns from their land.

Was that an adult thought? I must ask my father.

The singing ended abruptly, rising into one pure note of aching sweetness that took me by surprise.

How did they all know to stop at the same time? I must ask him about that too.

Before I could voice my questions, several splendidly attired men and women stood up in front of the crowd and began to make speeches of welcome. My father whispered their names to me, identifying them as members of the ruling family—who were related to our own clan. The audience warmly applauded each one in turn. "They are much loved," my mother said proudly.

At that moment I began to love them too. My kinship to these radiant beings did not have to be explained; I could feel it welling up in me. As if responding to a silent command, the assembled Dananns broke into song again. The music celebrated what we were all feeling—even me, who didn't know the words. I wanted to stay there and feel that way forever.

The joyous atmosphere was short-lived. It faded when

one of the princes—a man whom my mother identified as her uncle Aengus—made a sobering announcement. "I regret to say that the tribes which our ancestors subdued are no longer content with the peace imposed upon them."

I had only the vaguest idea what he meant. I knew that great battles had been won by our race long ago, led by a hero called Nuada of the Silver Hand, but I had never paid much attention when the Dagda was relating the details of history. The stories were not about *me*.

"Men of the Iverni recently tried to assault a child on the brink of adulthood," Aengus continued, "the girl who is called Shinann." This provoked expressions of shock from some of his listeners and angry muttering from others. Shinann herself was not present, but many of her kin were. Aengus raised a hand for silence. "She is unharmed, I assure you, but it was not the only such incident. One of our craftsmen seeking copper ore in the mountains was threatened by a party of the Velabri. He tells us they were carrying weapons that were not shaped for hunting animals. To make matters worse, the dark-spirited Fír Bolga are now openly skirmishing with our shepherds in the borderlands."

When he finished speaking, the elders took turns addressing the issue, then invited comments. Most people agreed that while none of these incidents posed a serious threat by itself, taken as a whole they were disquieting.

The Dagda pointed out that any unusual disturbance, such as a vortex in a normally quiet pool or a sudden leaping of birds into windless air, could be a dark portent. "This behavior among the formerly pacified tribes might signal the first twitch of rebellion," he warned. "Their numbers are greatly diminished, but their primitive instincts remain."

A rebellion! In a vague way I knew what that meant: a

chance for real excitement. I had been quiet for long enough this morning. Youth and sun and strength were coursing through me. I was eager for action.

Sitting cross-legged beside me, my father placed his hand on top of my head as if to hold me down. "Stop fidgeting, Joss. We are not playing games now."

But my mother gave me a tiny wink. Lerys was younger than my father; she and I often were confederates in small acts of naughtiness.

I winked back at her.

The discussion was becoming heated. One of the younger men jumped to his feet and shouted, "Unbury the Earthkillers!" Another promptly cried, "We need the Sword of Light and the Invincible Spear! They will remind the savage Fír Bolga where the real power lies!" A third added, "We must strike before they attack us and try to seize our treasures."

Earthkillers? Sword of Light? What were those? I had never heard of them before, but the very names made my heart race.

My father lifted his hand from my head and stood up. "You all know me," he announced in a ringing voice unlike any he used at home. "I am Mongan na Manannan Mac Lir, heir to the wisdom of my forebears. Their experience as leaders—and yes, as warriors too—is part of me. Therefore I warn you: the treasures we possess were not acquired through war, but war could destroy them."

"Impossible!" shouted a voice from the crowd.

Others hotly contradicted him. The argument grew more passionate. Every person present seemed to have an opinion about the Earthkillers—whatever they were—and was determined to express it without listening to anyone else. Tempers

flared. Men and women who had been laughing and singing together only moments before shouted furiously at each
other.

I sat small between my parents, hardly daring to breathe.
An event that had begun as a celebration had turned
into . . . what?

Something dangerous had been set loose in the Gathering Place.

THREE

AT LAST THE GREAT QUEEN, whose eyes were old when the world was young, stood up. Everyone's attention went to her; she had that power. When Eriu spoke the crowd fell silent. No bird could rival the music of her voice. "How can you accuse the Fír Bolga of being savage in one breath," she asked in a reasonable tone, "then want to turn the Earth-killers against them in the next? Is that not the ultimate savagery? As you well know, we have ample means at our disposal to discourage violence without committing it ourselves. We can repeat the techniques we have used before to call upon the resources of the sacred island."

In support of her sister, the queen called Fodla the Wise counseled, "Beware how you cry for war, my people. When there is keening on the night wind in the halls of the Iverni and the Velabri, there will be wailing likewise in our own halls."

Dos na Trialen na Barinth, Prince of the Lakes, was next to speak. "What Eriu suggests may be the obvious solution," he told the Dananns, "yet I warn you there are drawbacks.

Such a response might require little effort, yet we cannot be sure of the results. Our powers are broad but not precise, and one mistake could erupt into war very quickly.

"Let us consider some alternatives. I propose we visit the disaffected tribes in person and seek to resolve their problems through negotiation. For example, they should be amenable to an offer of additional grain. The elders have predicted the weather will be unusually harsh during the next dark-season."

Greine, titled MacGreine, the Son of the Sun—and also husband of Eriu—stood up next. There could be no doubt of his right to kingship; his face and form exemplified Danann nobility. He spoke slowly, leaving space between his phrases so his listeners had time to think about them. "Discouragement is practical. Negotiation is wise. But if there is a revolt anyway . . . and I'm only saying if . . . we must be able to defend ourselves. It might be prudent to consider our weaponry in case anything untoward does happen."

Greine's two half-brothers, MacCuill, the Son of the Wood, and MacCet, the Son of the Ancient One, were nodding in agreement. But Banba the Brave, youngest of the three queens of the Túatha Dé Danann, drew the sunlight into herself until it burnished her coppery hair. "Let us forget this talk of Earthkillers and put our trust in the bronze swords and spears forged by our ancestors!" she cried in a clarion voice. "Every one of you must have some stored away in honor of the past. Those strong old weapons will serve us well with no risk to the land."

A man halfway between youth and age leaped to his feet. "I agree with Banba! I propose that we can form companies and begin weapons practice at once. Sippar, Rodarch, Agnonis and Ladra, you can join me."

His enthusiasm took hold like fire in dry grass, scattering

sparks. The men who were eager to fight became more eager; the ones who wanted negotiation grew more determined. Those who supported Eriu's way were mostly the
elders, whose voices were not strong enough to outshout anyone else.

Greine waited. From time to time he exchanged a look
with Eriu. I had seen my parents exchange that look; it said
more than words ever could.

I turned to see what the Dagda thought of all this. The
old man was sitting as he had been from the beginning, with
an impassive face and his arms folded across his chest. He
had passed the rule of Ierne to a newer generation and would
not interfere.

Was he right or wrong? I still do not know, though I have
asked myself that question many times.

Even the Dagda could not see the future.

Finally, Greine raised his arm. In his fist he held a staff
carved of white ash, the symbol of regal authority. When he
spoke he did not shout, yet his voice went everywhere. "The
responsibilities of a king are heavy," he intoned. "None is
heavier than that of making a decision when his people
cannot agree among themselves. My wife has laid out a
straight path, but when alternatives were suggested that
path seems to have lost support. We now come to a fork in
the road. We are in danger of losing our direction. Therefore, this is my pronouncement."

The listening Dananns held their collective breath.

"I decree that the Earthkillers remain in the ground as
Eriu wishes," Greine soberly intoned. "I shall not order their
use. Our ancestors brought the gifts from the stars when they
came here, but the time for using them has long passed. We
have become a wiser people. The Túatha Dé Danann will
enforce peace on this island with simple swords and axes.

The other tribes are primitive but not stupid; the sight of so much weaponry in our hands should discourage them from further violence."

I expected someone to argue with him, which would have been exciting, but nobody spoke up. The air was filled with his words and his words alone.

When the last echo died, Greine announced, "Now we must invoke the Stone of Destiny to seal the agreement." He reached out to take the hand of Eriu, and they began climbing the ridge. The entire crowd followed them, a moving blaze of color. It was steeper than I thought. From where we were sitting, the ridge had appeared to be a low hill, but when we reached the top I saw to my amazement that the land was spread out below us from mountaintop to mountaintop.

A king's view.

At the crown of the ridge was a grass-covered mound like a burial cairn, together with a single pillar of gray stone sunk into the earth. The exposed part of the monolith was taller than a man and rounded on top. I thought I saw tiny flashes of color peeping from its rough surface.

The stone was watching me.

A shiver danced across my shoulders.

Greine went to one side of the pillar, Eriu to the other, while the Dananns formed a circle around them, spilling back along the ridge and blocking my view. The sun was warm, but a cool breeze was blowing across the hill. The sweet, damp air smelled of life, of green and growing things. A corncrake uttered its grating cry from its nest among the grasses. Far overhead, an eagle circled.

The Stone of Destiny stood at the center of the Túatha Dé Danann.

Throwing back his head, Greine lifted both his arms and

brandished the ash wood staff. "Lord of wind and flame!" he exhorted. "Lord of the boundless curve! You alone know my people's destiny. If we have chosen wisely, support us. If we have chosen wrongly, protect us. This I ask for the Tribe of Danu, the Children of Light."

Then he waited.

When nothing happened, I tugged at my father's arm. "Is the stone supposed to do something?"

Mongan looked down at me. "Not now. We do the doing. The Stone does the knowing."

This made no sense to me. Was this not an ordinary piece of rock? "Where did it come from?"

"We brought it with us, Joss. Before the Before."

Greine backed six paces from the Stone, then turned and walked away down the ridge. Every person he passed saluted him by saying, "Elgolai."

"Is that the old language?" I asked my father.

"It is," he confirmed. "Elgolai means, 'He goes out,' which is a term of the highest respect. Life is extended by the going, not by the staying. Greine is a direct descendant of those who had enough courage to go out Before the Before."

I had thought myself capable of thinking adult thoughts. Apparently I still had a long way to go.

❧

Later in the sunseason, an unfamiliar fleet appeared off our southern coast. The clans that lived along the shore assumed they were traders. The Sea People were known to sail great distances in order to buy and sell copper and tin and olive oil, silk and amber and rare perfumes. As restless as fleas, they were always going somewhere else. One of their trade routes passed between our island and the rising sun.

We too had come from somewhere else. Before the Before.

The lures of the Sea People did not attract the Túatha Dé Danann. We had what we needed. What we did not have we did not want. Preferring the steady glow of serenity to the destructive tarnish of commerce, whereby everything was bought and sold and nothing was ever enough, we had long since developed ways of avoiding traders.

Unfortunately, the fleet from the south penetrated our usual defenses. This had happened before; my people were not alarmed. They habitually greeted any unwelcome visitors with courtesy and sent them on their way with confused impressions designed to discourage further contact.

This time would be different.

FOUR

SHORTLY AFTER SUNRISE, Éremón thought he saw land. An irregular shape floated on the horizon, startlingly green against the blue of the sea. The husky Gaelic warrior had been keeping watch in the prow of his galley for most of the night with two of his hunting hounds at his feet while he alternately strained to see something that was not there and struggled to stay awake in case it ever appeared.

Then there it was.

Éremón blinked. The vision vanished. He blinked again. The miracle he sought glowed like a green jewel in the light of the rising sun.

Kicking one of his hounds aside, Éremón turned toward a thin, swarthy man awkwardly draped across a pile of rope. "Get up quick, Sakkar! Look where I'm pointing. Is that Ierne out there?"

With a groan the Phoenician dragged himself to his feet. He had hoped to eke out a few more moments of rest before the work of the day began. Every part of his body ached. He was no longer young, and coils of rope were no substitute for a comfortable bed. It could be a long time before he enjoyed a bed again. "I may see something," he conceded. "Perhaps . . ." He shrugged his left shoulder. "At this distance it could be anything or nothing. You'll have to go closer."

Éremón glowered at the smaller man. "I have to go closer, Sakkar? And risk running aground? Need I remind you that I am responsible for the future of the Míl's entire tribe? All these lives depend on *me*!"

Éremón was the youngest son of Mílesios—respectfully titled the Míl—the recently deceased overlord of a large Celtic tribe in the northwestern corner of the Iberian Peninsula. The clans comprising the tribe were known collectively as Gaelicians, or the Gael. The dominant clan preferred to be called the Mílesians after their chieftain. The fleet was laden with iron implements and weaponry and carried all six of the Míl's princely sons—even though one of them was mad.

As Sakkar was aware, Éremón was claiming a prerogative that was not his alone.

The Phoenician would not dream of contradicting him.

Sakkar had been an orphan, one of the countless ragged little beggars who thronged the crooked streets and malodorous alleyways of the ancient seaport of Tyre, on the Middle Sea. A scrawny child with dark, almond-shaped eyes and nimble fingers that could slip a coin from a purse without being discovered.

Deference to authority had been beaten into Sakkar from an early age, but from some unknown ancestor he also had inherited a stubborn pride. He refused to spend the rest of his life begging—or stealing.

As soon as he was big enough, he had apprenticed himself to a Tyrian shipbuilder. "I'll do anything," he insisted. His new employer promptly assigned him to carry timber that weighed almost as much as he did.

Sakkar was short but wiry, with iron muscles and boundless stamina. In the beginning, nothing more was required of him. The work was exhausting, yet he thrived on it. For the first time in his miserable life, he was sure of a meal at the end of the day and a dry place to sleep at night. He took great pride in being able to earn his living.

After a few months he began to look for other jobs around the shipyard. On his own, he taught himself to straighten bent nails, to braid rope, even tried his hand at patching sails. Such skills came easily to him. Before long, his efforts were observed—and approved. The more he could do, the more he was given to do. In time, Sakkar was offered better food and slept on a pallet instead of the floor.

Within a year he understood how a ship was constructed, down to the smallest detail. In another year he could have built one by himself.

A decade had passed, during which Sakkar absorbed knowledge like a sponge, observing everything that happened around him and listening intently to more experienced men. In this way he had mastered several languages and a handful of dialects that were common among those involved in commercial trade. He also acquired the gestures and manners that set an educated person apart from a common laborer. Only a portion of what he learned was of any apparent value; some of it was merely trivia that stuck to his brain the way barnacles stuck to the hull of a ship.

Barnacles have their uses too.

On the day when Sakkar was promoted to shipwright, he had thought a special star shone over him. This was confirmed a few years later when he met a wealthy trader called Age-Nor, who required an outstanding shipwright to accompany his fleet and supervise the inevitable repairs needed on long journeys.

Sakkar had demonstrated a full and impressive range of skills, and the position was his. He abandoned his original employer without a second thought. Age-Nor promised that after their first voyage together, Sakkar would be able to afford a house of his own and an obedient wife instead of waterfront prostitutes with bad teeth and worse diseases.

Except all had gone terribly wrong. Which proved one could not trust the stars.

Ruefully, Sakkar rubbed his crooked right shoulder. The smashed joint had not healed properly and never would; he was left with a useless arm and damaged nerves. Gradually, the fingers of his right hand were contracting into claws. There was nothing to be done about it. At his age, whatever that might be, structural changes to his body were permanent.

Éremón growled, "Well, Sakkar? Either that's your famous 'island in the sunset' or it's not. If you've tried to deceive us, you'll regret it."

Sakkar's bright black eyes were as innocent as a child's. "Who would dare incur the rage of Éremón the warrior, champion of every battle?"

Éremón smiled; he never could resist flattery. Perhaps it was a weakness, he told himself, but he had so few weaknesses this one was rather endearing.

"As I explained to your late father, I never visited Ierne myself," said the Phoenician, "but in the harbor-front taverns of Tyre and Sidon it was often mentioned. Late at night, when sailors have drunk too much, they speak of strange things. I have heard it said that Ierne has wealth beyond measure, more gold than in all the treasuries of the East. Some even claim it contains the secret of eternal youth."

Éremón grunted encouragingly; he liked that part the

best. His stocky body was revealing the first hints of a possible rebellion in the future.

"No two descriptions of Ierne match," Sakkar went on, "but all agree it is one of the Pretanic Islands in the ocean-river at the edge of the world. With my own two ears I have heard Greek navigators describe its position in relation to the tin mines of Albion and"—he hesitated, reluctant to put stress on something he knew to be unreliable—"and the stars above. Those are the guideposts that have brought us to this place. So it must be Ierne."

"Let me remind you . . ." Éremón began again.

Sakkar interrupted, "I would never endanger the family of Mílesios, great prince. May Melqart, god of Tyre, strike me down if I am lying."

Éremón tensed instinctively.

Both men glanced up.

No bolt of fire shot from the sky.

More relieved than he wanted to reveal, Sakkar said, "Let me remind you, Éremón, that after I was injured in a shipwreck on your coast and abandoned as useless, your family took me in. Among my people, such a deed confers a powerful obligation. When Mílesios happened to mention Ierne, I realized what the gods intended. Your gods and mine," he added hastily. "It was in my gift to tell your father what I knew of Ierne, but more than that; I was the perfect person to design these galleys for your people and supervise their construction.

"You Gaelicians stake your honor on your hospitality. My people stake theirs on fulfilling obligations. Therefore, I can assure you these ships are as safe as any seagoing craft can be. There is no danger of running aground prematurely; you can sail close enough to have a good look. If you are satisfied with what you see, have your men lower the sail and row as far as the shallows, then wade ashore."

Éremón's voice cracked like a whip. "Are you trying to tell me how to command my fleet?"

Sakkar pressed his hands together and gave a slight bow, just enough to show respect but not enough to admit subjugation. "I would not be so presumptuous, great prince. You know how to proceed in these matters far better than I could."

Éremón was never sure if the Phoenician was mocking him or not. Sakkar's aquiline features were like a closed box. Éremón's brother Amergin was fond of him, though—which was enough reason to be suspicious of the former shipwright. Amergin was the chief bard of the Mílesians, but in Éremón's opinion he was no judge of people. That was proved by the fact that Amergin never said anything unkind about anyone.

Of all his brothers, Éremón found Amergin the most difficult to understand. Amergin was not only a bard—reciter of histories, keeper of genealogies—but a druid. Among Celtic tribes, the druids comprised the intellectual class, men and women whose abilities were of the mind rather than the arm. Their high prestige derived from the esoteric disciplines they practiced, sometimes in private and always beyond the comprehension of their less-gifted kin.

As far as Éremón was concerned, Amergin was a riddle on two legs. He preferred people to be uncomplicated, like himself. Éremón said exactly what he thought without any druidic misdirection. If he disliked a man, he told him to his face, then cheerfully hit him in that face if a fight was offered. This did not apply to women, of course, but nothing simple applied to women.

Éremón pulled his mind back from the dangerous subject of women. His wife Odba had been one of those who stayed behind when the fleet departed, but he could not be sure he had escaped her forever. Odba might have a touch of the druid herself, the way she could hear his most private thoughts. When he had first mooted the idea of taking Taya as a second wife, Odba had pounced on him like a cat on a rat, and there had been bitter war between them until the day he and the rest of the fleet set sail for Ierne.

At least their sons had chosen to come with him, Éremón reminded himself. Moomneh and Legneh were old enough to realize they could not expect any inheritance without their father.

Three of Éremón's brothers, Donn and Ír and Éber Finn, were the proud possessors of obedient wives who had joined them on the voyage without complaint—or at least without any complaint that Éremón knew about. Éber Finn even had three wives and an impressive swarm of children crowding the deck of his galley. They seemed to be as happy together as a litter of puppies. How, Éremón often wondered, did Éber enforce such domestic harmony?

And what did a young woman like Taya see in a man like Amergin?

Éremón was almost as tall as Amergin. Among the Mílesian princes only yellow-haired Ír of the Long Legs was taller, but Ír was no competition. His mental instability put him in a class apart. Éremón believed himself to be the most handsome of the brothers. In his opinion, Donn and Colptha were as plain as mud. Neither looked impressive; they could be anybody.

Only Éremón and Éber Finn had inherited the ruddy coloring and heroic torso of their father. Strangers sometimes mistook the two for twins. As was traditional with warriors of the Gael, they sported flowing moustaches that hung far below the jawline. The vitality of their moustaches symbolized the vigor of their manhood.

Bards, on the other hand, were clean-shaven.

Their mother, Scotta, had once described Amergin as "the one dark leopard in a litter of golden lions." How could any woman desire a black-haired, lanky druid who went around with his bare face hanging out? Taya deserved much better. Pretty Taya with her plump white arms and level eyebrows, like a line drawn with a sooty finger. Her round hips and full bosom that a man could lose his face in . . .

Whenever Taya crossed Éremón's mind, he found his thoughts wandering.

The entire tribe knew that Taya had shamelessly pursued Amergin at one time. Yet Old Irial, chief druid of the Gaelicians, claimed that druids dwelt alone in an inner winter. And bards were preoccupied with memorizing histories and genealogies and preserving them in great swathes of poetry. From this Éremón concluded that Amergin's only relationship was with his harp. He could not begin to compare with the lusty physicality of a chariot warrior.

Fortunately for Éremón, Taya had realized this before she made a grave mistake.

When they were settled in the new land, Éremón was going to build a splendid dwelling for his second wife. He would shower Taya with the luxuries that Odba would have enjoyed if she had treated him better and joined him on the journey. The riches of Ierne that Sakkar had so casually mentioned would be Taya's: three colors of gold, masses of silver and copper, amethysts as big as a man's fist. Even chypre, the nauseatingly heavy perfume that women loved and was made from sandalwood. Surely there was sandalwood on Ierne? If not, Éremón would import it.

Soon he and the other sons of the Míl would be able to forget the misfortunes that had befallen them. Éremón did not like to think about such things, but they were always at the back of his mind, like awareness of a rotten tooth.

The prosperity of the Mílesians had depended on two factors: their vast herds of black cattle, and the surface tin mines in their territory, which was located in the northwestern corner of the Iberian Peninsula. The cattle provided the Mílesians with quantities of rich milk and supple leather to exchange with neighboring farming tribes for basic agricultural produce. The Mílesians were a warrior race; they looked down on people who dug in the dirt.

Copper alloyed with tin was the basis for bronze. Once supreme among metals, bronze was being replaced by iron, which was stronger. However, bronze retained its high prestige for ceremonial use and ornamentation. For centuries, the tin trade had provided a very high standard of living for the ancestors of the Mílesians. From the great port cities of the Mediterranean, the Phoenicians had brought a cornucopia of undreamed-of luxuries to Iberia to exchange for tin. The Sea People had offered gold from Ophir, silver from Ethiopia, amber from the Baltic, fragrant cedar from Lebanon, and fine cotton from Egypt.

After several generations, such opulent items had become necessities.

Mílesios and his clan dressed in silk embroidered with gold thread and wrapped themselves in woolen cloaks as soft as clouds. They wore so much jewelery that they clanked when they walked. Gold neck rings, ear rings, arm rings, finger rings, sword hilts and clothing fasteners and horse-harness ornaments, even silver trinkets for favored servants. They hunted wild boar in the forest with great shaggy hounds crossbred from dogs imported from Egypt and the deserts of Arabia.

With the assurance of those born to wealth, the Mílesians had assumed their resources were infinite.

They were mistaken.

Seven years of unprecedented drought had all but wiped out their herds. Producing enough tin to satisfy the demands of the traders finally had exhausted their mines. Almost overnight, or so it seemed, the splendid garments of the Gaelicians grew shabby. They had nothing to offer the Sea People in return for more bright silks and fine linen. Without enough cattle to trade with other tribes, the adherents of the Míl were reduced to exchanging jewelery of the finest workmanship for real necessities such as beans and barley. At the summer market, their nearest neighbors, the Astures, gave them one sack of mouldy wheat for two massive gold arm rings and went away laughing.

Astures! Men who stooped to plant seeds in the earth! Éremón still shuddered at the remembered humiliation. And the cruel barbs Odba had slung at him when he returned home with so little to show for his efforts. She did not even prepare a welcoming feast for him—and Éremón was a man who loved his food. He was famed for eating right- and left-handed.

Mílesios, his immediate family, and his far-flung dependants were all desperate to regain their lost prosperity. In common with people everywhere, they accepted myths as historic truth. One of these, related long ago by a patriarch called Bréoghan, involved an island he had glimpsed from the top of a watchtower at the harbor. He had claimed to see a lush green island of incomparable beauty floating on the northern horizon, a rich sweet land of honey and harvests where gold glittered in the streams.

Bréoghan's own people did not believe him, but the Phoenician traders with whom they did business believed. A few even claimed to have visited the island. Yet they were reluctant to go into any detail about the place they called Ierne. They spoke of it in hushed tones and insisted they would never go back. Their reaction added a delicious shiver of fear to the tale, which was repeated from one generation to the next until Ierne became little more than a tale to frighten children.

Yet when the pangs of poverty bit deep, the Míl and his kin began to speculate in earnest. What if Ierne was real? A land like that would offer the opportunity they needed, if only they could reach its shores and start anew.

Centuries earlier, a branch of the Celtic race had undertaken a similar migration, leaving the dark forests of northern Europe in search of a better life. Known as the Gael, they had dispersed along the western edge of the continent. The Gaelic ancestors of the Mílesians had even crossed the Pyrenees on their way to their current homeland.

What sort of courage, Éremón had asked himself, did it take for men to pack up their families and all they possessed and journey into the unknown?

Now he knew. Not courage but desperation.

And Sakkar had appeared at just the right time. Unless of course they were mistaken about the Phoenician and he was a harbinger of disaster . . .

Again Éremón reined in his wandering thoughts. His eyes were still fixed on the image on the horizon. Why was he finding it so hard to concentrate? The riches of Ierne would not be denied to him . . . putting two fingers into his mouth, he gave a shrill whistle. He raised his other arm and pointed toward his discovery. The gesture was intended for those on board the other galleys and the accompanying flotilla of hide-covered coracles. The two best-appointed galleys carried the families and possessions of the sons of the Míl, together with the brehon judges whose heads contained the laws of the tribe. Members of lesser Gaelician clans were in the other two galleys, crowded among crates of supplies and sacks of grain for planting.

Freemen of the laboring class—often prisoners of war—were relegated to the round boats.

Pushing Sakkar aside, Colptha the sacrificer thrust his face into his brother's. "What do you think you're doing, Éremón?" Colptha hissed. Even Scotta, who loved all of her sons, said talking with Colptha was like talking with a snake.

"I'm taking us to Ierne, of course."

Colptha's sardonic smile revealed a wide gap between his front incisors. In secret, he sharpened the teeth framing the gap to heighten their effect. "Éber Finn's the one taking us to Ierne," he said. "Look to your right; Donn's ship has already turned in the new direction, and I'm sure it's at Éber's direction. See him standing in the prow? On this voyage Éber has proved to be a better pilot than you or even your Phoenician; would you not agree, Sakkar?"

Sakkar knew better than to answer him.

Colptha enjoyed setting people against each other.

The sacrificer was a druid, like his brother Amergin or his cousin Corisios the diviner. Theirs were special gifts of the spirit that had been born in them. A druid might be a healer, a teacher, a judge—someone with a thirst for learning who was in touch with a world beyond the five senses. They spent years mastering their talent and gave their gifts freely to the tribe in return for its support.

Colptha offered sacrifices to the spirits who inhabited the unseen world. He was keeper of the sacred grove and representative of the trees. The Mílesians would not think of cutting timber without getting permission from the spirits of the

wood. Otherwise, the logs they used for building would rot
and their firewood refuse to burn.

The sacrificer might not be a likable man, but his services
were indispensable.

Éremón tried to think of a sharp retort for Colptha, but
the cleverness he sought eluded him. Amergin could command words; Éremón had only his sword. Waving his arm
emphatically, he shouted for his crew to hurry and take over
the lead.

The blur of green became more distinct as the fleet approached. Éber Finn's wives and children crowded the rail
of Donn's galley, excitedly pointing out the island to one
another and to Scotta, the widow of Mílesios.

Ír, who had begun the voyage with Éremón, capered
along the deck of Donn's ship too, laughing and careening
into his fellow passengers. Éremón had insisted that Ír
change galleys after the incident when the madman claimed
he saw a god. According to him, the giant fish that had leaped
out of the sea in the Bay of Biscay was an immortal being
with a special message just for him. His wild talk unnerved
not only the other passengers on the galley but also his
own wife and children.

In the presence of solid, phlegmatic Donn, Ír behaved
better. For a while. Until the island appeared on the horizon.

Colptha had taken the place of Ír on Éremón's galley, at
Scotta's request. "I want our family evenly divided in case
something happens to one of the galleys," she said.

From Éremón's point of view, the new arrangement was
only a slight improvement. "I have exchanged a madman for
one who is barely human," he confided to Sakkar.

Éremón's ship also carried Amergin—who did not in-
volve himself in the petty power struggles between his brothers. Amergin would not have captained a ship even if he

were asked. His gifts were those of the mind, not of the muscles. From the beginning he had placed himself amidships, where he could view everything that happened and store it in his capacious memory. For the rest of his life, Amergin could be summoned by any of the Mílesians to recite in detail the history of their great voyage.

Propped against the bard's leg was the leather case he had designed to protect his harp from dampness. He liked to keep Clarsah close by. To him the harp was alive, with a name and a personality. When Éremón's ship swept past Donn's and into the lead, Amergin raised Clarsah in salute to his brother.

Donn was the firstborn son of the Míl, yet Éremón had been given command of the expedition while it was still being planned. Donn was steady and reliable but lacked the fire that animated his brother. Éremón loved fighting as much as he loved eating and more than he loved women. Mílesios had said he was exactly the sort of man needed to conquer a new land.

The great chieftain was dead, but his word still carried weight. His sons would respect it.

At least until they made landfall.

❧ FIVE ❧

IN THE CLEAR LIGHT of a summer morning the approaching fleet resembled four fat geese followed by a flock of goslings. Fisherfolk along the shore, drawing in nets laden with the night's bounty, stopped work to stare. They observed that although basically Phoenician in design, with a high prow and brightly painted square sails, the timber galleys were not ordinary trading vessels. They had a large covered area amidships and rode exceptionally low in the water. Every bit of visible deck space was occupied by people and war carts and livestock.

By contrast, the small round coracles that accompanied them hardly even looked seaworthy.

The fishermen squinted in the sun. Eyes used to detecting the slightest ripple caused by a shoal of fish quickly noted the presence of women and children aboard the galleys. Traders never traveled with children. These were strangers, then—strangers whose intentions were unknown.

The fishermen turned their attention from bass and gray

mullet to a more urgent situation. Word must be sent immediately.

Birdsong; the rustling of leaves; the breath of the wind.
All carried the word. The message reached the ears for which
it was intended. And was understood.

There was no need for another Being Together to make
decisions. The Túatha Dé Danann knew what was expected
of them.

೪ჰ

Under Éremón's orders the Mílesian galleys lowered their
sails. The men took up their oars and prepared to row into a
natural harbor sheltered by a curving arm of land. Little scal-
lops of white foam ran in from a calm sea. Wading birds
stalked the shallows, feeding on tiny crabs. It was a lovely
summer's day. Everything was perfect, a dream come true.
Éremón shouted for the piper to blow the signal for going
ashore. The dogs responded with a volley of excited barking.
The women on the galleys began gathering their personal
items and marshaling their children.

But it was Amergin who meant to be first on land. Amergin who had observed the green shape on the horizon even
before his brother did and clasped the secret to himself like
a lover. Amergin, the bard who had dreamed for as long as
he could remember of . . .

"Ierne, Ierne," he whispered. With pounding heart, he
made ready to vault over the rail of the ship and drop into
the hissing surf.

He was unaware of the shimmering fog until it envel-
oped him.

The fog descended on the Mílesian galleys and the coracles laden with servants and surplus baggage. Voices cried

out in alarm. As if summoned by their shouts a wind came out of nowhere. It did not dissipate the exceptionally thick sea mist—if it was sea mist.

The treacherous wind began pushing the fleet away from the harbor. The oarsmen struggled to resist, but they were helpless against a rising gale.

And suddenly the tide was going out instead of coming in.

⁊❧

A party of the Túatha Dé Danann had assembled on the arm of land that embraced the bay. Their grace and bearing identified them as belonging to ancient nobility. Three queens were crowned by narrow diadems of gold, piped with copper wire. The oldest of three kings wore a belt of twisted gold set with chunks of amethyst.

The weapons they carried appeared more decorative than dangerous. Elaborately fashioned bronze swords, polished to a golden gleam, the hilts set with jewels. Knives of shiny black obsidian whose delicate edges were so sharp as to be nearly invisible. Throwing spears with shafts wrapped in gaily colored ribbons; thrusting spears with animal figures engraved on the spearheads. These examples of the metalsmith's art seemed more appropriate for a pageant than for war.

The Dananns were not anticipating a pageant. Some of them had reported troubling dreams recently, and others described a growing sense of disquiet for no apparent reason. Now this: strangers approaching in unfamiliar vessels.

Hands lightly caressed sword hilts. One or two men hefted their throwing spears as if to test their balance. The Dananns stood erect and relaxed, confident of their ability to deal with anything. The elegant bronze weapons were only one element of their armory. They had others.

~

The voyagers on the treacherous sea began calling out to one another. Anxious cries rang from galleys and coracles, trying to retain contact. In the circumstances, it would be easy for one vessel to become separated from the others.

Their speech was distorted by the unnatural fog. Cold and thick, it poured like liquid into their open mouths. They shouted louder. They cursed the fog and the sea and one another but their words were unintelligible.

Increasingly frightened, the women added their voices to those of their men until all blended into a bleat of panic.

The guardians of the island waited patiently. Watching. The strange thick mist did not impede their vision. A light rain fell, but they did not need shelter. When the sun returned, they smiled and chatted pleasantly, retelling the old stories to one another. Laughing a little, sometimes. Making a gentle jest.

Meanwhile, the glimmering fog crouched over the fleet like a ravenous animal, blotting out the rest of the world. Cloaking, shrouding, unnerving. Stroking terrified faces with icy fingers. Light and dark were indistinguishable.

Time spiraled back on itself, past and future flowing together.

Piteous cries came from the people in the boats.

Mongan remarked to the Son of the Sun, "There was no need to excite ourselves about this after all. The tried and true methods still work."

"By the time the strangers gain control of their vessels, they will be lost on the open sea," Greine predicted.

The ageless beauty who stood beside him made a tiny sound of distress. "I have no desire to cause them harm."

"No one wishes them harm, Eriu," her husband assured her.

Their son Cynos added, "We have not touched them in any way, merely denied them approach to our land. They were able to find this place, so they should be able to find a safe harbor on Albion."

"What if they don't?" asked a young woman whose shining ringlets framed a heart-shaped face. "The sea can be rough, and there are children on those boats."

Mongan put an arm around his wife's shoulders. "My Lerys has a tender spirit," he said fondly.

"And we have a son!" she snapped. "How would you feel if our Joss were lost on the open sea?"

At these words Cipir na Cassmael na Hasis, the Windweaver—who had a young son himself—ceased the gestures he had been making in the air.

The force of the wind dropped.

Greine looked in Cipir's direction. A silent order was passed from king to prince. Cipir's hands busied themselves again.

The wind howled until the sea roared in reply. Yet the fog remained.

Lerys was the first to hear the music. Cocking her head to one side, she listened with parted lips. A single plangent note rose above the wind. It permeated the fog, transforming the opaque mist into the living voice of melancholy, the embodiment of unbearable longings.

Lerys tugged at her husband's arm. "Oh, do listen, Mongan!"

He raised a quizzical eyebrow. "That strange sound? Where is it coming from?"

"Out there in the fog. Someone is playing a harp. Listen, everyone!"

Cynos said, "I never heard a harp like that, Lerys."

"There has never been a harp like that before," she told him.

While the Dananns strained to hear, the unfamiliar music fought the wind and the sea for supremacy. "Could it be a eulogy for a fallen warrior?" Mongan wondered aloud.

The harp, if it was a harp, added other themes. The music, if it was music, gave voice to sunshine. And moonlight. A woman's exultant cry as she bore a child. The clashing antlers of rutting stags. Hope and fear and courage.

Underlying all was an insistent beat like the thud of a mighty heart.

Deeply moved, Greine told his companions, "That is more than music; it represents an entire world."

Fodla whispered, "A world almost too beautiful to bear." Her husband, Cet of the Laughter, nodded agreement.

Banba the Brave dropped her hand to the hilt of the obsidian blade she carried in her belt. "What you hear is a trick," she pronounced.

Ladra and Samoll, the king's ceremonial spear carriers, immediately took up defensive positions on either side of Greine. He waved them away. "I see no danger yet. Wait until I summon you."

"Children," murmured Eriu. "There are children on the boats." She turned her luminous gray eyes on the fog, the luminous gray fog that swelled and shifted above dark, cold water capable of swallowing an entire fleet. Without hurrying, she began to follow the muffled sounds of the fleet as it drifted along the coast.

The rest of the party followed her.

❧

"The fog is lifting!" cried a hoarse voice aboard one of the galleys. The voice that had been shredded by hysteria as the fleet drifted blindly through the mist. Perhaps days had passed; no one could tell. Amergin had the disturbing sensation that time was being held in abeyance. In a bid to force its return, he had taken Clarsah from her case in spite of the humidity that could damage her strings. His strong, sure fingers had strummed an insistent rhythm. The rhythm of days and nights, of seasons and years.

The fleet had remained together by following the sound of the bard's harp.

Now the fog was blowing away like a bad dream. When the voyagers caught glimpses of land ahead, they shouted and cheered. Some of the women began to weep with relief.

"I told you I would bring you here," Éremón stated repeatedly. "I *told* you." But no one was listening. All attention focused on the radiant island emerging from the mist.

The clear light of a summer's afternoon illumined a fretted coastline heavily populated by great flocks of puffins. The endearing, comical faces of the seabirds seemed to smile a greeting to the newcomers.

A flock of delighted children grinned back at them.

The fleet drifted closer to shore, where rocky cliffs descended toward the mouth of a river. On the far side was a long beach of firm sand and shingle, and beyond that a sloping upland crowned with forest.

When he saw the trees, Éremón's boast turned into a glad cry. "There will be game in those woods. Fresh meat!"

The sons of Mílesios reached for their hunting spears and whistled to their dogs.

Afterward Mongan would wonder if he should have felt an intimation of the future then. Had any of the elders been with them, they might have recognized the portents. But the elders were not required for situations such as this; the Danann nobility were responsible for guarding the sacred island. And even the wisest of the nobles, as Mongan ruefully reflected later, had failed to observe the true nature of the invaders until it was too late.

Standing among the trees, one with the alder and ash, the holly and hornbeam, blending into the landscape so the strangers could not see them, the Dananns had been distracted by the arrival of the bard.

A tall dark-haired man had been the first stranger to set foot on Ierne. He leaped off one of the galleys and ran high-kneed through the foaming surf, carrying a leather case raised at arm's length to be clear of the water. The satchel was a work of art in its own right. Cut from the finest hides, it had been shaped to fit its contents, then embossed with curvilinear designs and brightly painted. As soon as the man reached dry land, he knelt to open the case. With reverent fingers he turned back a fold of white silk and lifted out his treasure.

The watching Dananns were transfixed.

There had never been such a beautiful harp. Even at a distance they could tell that the workmanship was exquisite. Bow-shaped and small enough to be cradled in the man's arms, the wooden frame was richly gilded. The neck and body formed sinuous curves that were perfectly balanced by the straight line of the forepillar. Every golden surface was elaborately ornamented. The nine strings were made of gleaming brass.

The man with the harp stood up in one lithe movement. He held the instrument high above his head and cried with all the power in his lungs, "Bard land!" Lowering the harp to the height of his heart, he ran his fingers lightly across the strings. They made a sound like spring wind rippling the willows. He smiled to himself. A lock of dark hair tumbled across his forehead as he bent his head and began to play. The music was totally different from that which he had played in the fog. Now the notes were fresh and joyous, golden and green. They danced on the air.

The high-arched feet of the Túatha Dé Danann could barely resist dancing with them.

More people were now splashing through the surf. A powerfully built man with ruddy hair paused to say something to the harper—who ignored him. The bard was lost in the moment. He and his harp might have been all alone, existing in a world outside time.

The Dananns found it difficult to look away from him. But they must. In spite of the impression he made, he was not alone; he was only the first of a veritable tidal wave of strangers hurrying to come ashore. In their eagerness, they abandoned all caution. They pushed and shoved and scrambled, the women as fiercely as the men. They were almost as tall as men and no less determined.

Torrian warned, "Someone is going to be hurt."

"That is not our responsibility," Greine remarked.

The spear carrier shrugged. "I was only saying."

"He was only saying," echoed Ladra.

Many of the foreigners carried swords in their belts. Swords with blades as long as a man's forearm for the men, and shorter weapons resembling a dagger for the women. The blades had been forged from a dull bluish metal instead of bronze.

Observing them, Fodla felt a twinge of unease. "It might be best not to reveal ourselves right away," she whispered to Greine. "Strangers in a strange land, they are bound to be nervous. We should allow them time to unload their ships and settle in."

"Settle in?" Greine gave her a sharp look. "Do you think they intend to stay?"

"Of course they intend to stay. Look at what they have brought with them. Cattle and sheep and goats and . . ."

"Armloads of children," Eriu interrupted. "I have never seen so many little ones all at one time." Her voice was very tender. "Those are colonists, beloved; the first colonists to come here since our ancestors Before the Before. Only good people could make such beautiful music. We must give them the warmest of welcomes, greet them with fruits and flowers and singing, offer them the best of everything we have."

Greine hesitated. Ierne had been theirs since the time of his grandfathers' grandfathers, and before. Feared and reviled because they were different—a difference that was their greatest blessing—the Túatha Dé Danann had found the one place in the world where they could be themselves. In gratitude, they had turned the island in the sunset into a paradise. They had been willing to share its bounty with the earlier inhabitants, but these were too primitive to comprehend what they were being offered. They hated the Dananns because they did not understand. And worshipped them too, because they did not understand.

Would it be the same with these strangers?

Or might they become comrades, learning and growing together? Was the long isolation of Danu's children about to be over?

❧

Greine watched with keen interest and some trepidation as the newcomers began to unload two of the galleys. Gaunt horses were led ashore on trembling legs; nervous, long-maned Asturian horses who carried the hot blood of the desert in their veins. They were to pull the chariots belonging to the sons of Mílesios: wickerwork chariots with timber wheels painted the color of blood, and round shields hanging from the sides. Battered shields with heavy metal bosses.

There was domestic livestock, too; a pair of half-grown bull calves and a small herd of pregnant heifers, plus some white-faced sheep. Every animal had been handpicked for its youth, strength, and quality. The calves would become seed bulls in time. While still young and amenable they would be trained to the yoke and used for ploughing the new land. Black Mílesian cattle provided milk and meat and fine, supple leather. The long-stapled wool that the Mílesian sheep produced was soft and durable.

As soon as the livestock was unloaded, the women began trying to herd the animals into groups. A pack of shaggy, long-legged hounds, happy to be on land again, raced along the sand and shingle, barking exuberantly and chasing anything that moved.

Cattle and sheep scattered.

Anxious women shouted at the hounds, irritable men kicked them aside, overtired children shrieked for no reason at all.

Meanwhile, the third and fourth galleys disgorged a similar cargo of people and equipment. The rest of the Gaelicians took their first tentative steps on what would be their new homeland. Weary but wide-eyed, they gazed around with the expressions of people just wakened from a dream.

When the unloading was complete, the chariots were

drawn into a line on the beach. Horse boys motioned to waiting charioteers, who stepped forward and took up the reins.

The ruddy man who had paused to speak to the harper strode to the center of the line. His charioteer greeted him with a salute. Éremón's chariot was the only one ornamented with rather bedraggled plumes. When he stepped up into the cart, the floor creaked under his weight.

He glanced first to one side and then the other, assessing the mood of his warrior brothers. Donn wore his usual grave expression, and Ír was staring down at his own knuckles, but Éber Finn grinned at Éremón. "At last, brother!"

Off to one side, Colptha was watching the chariot warriors with an expression that Éremón took for envy. Amergin was preoccupied with his harp. Bards had little interest in chariots.

Éremón settled his leather helmet with its bristling horsehair crest firmly on his head, then gave a terse nod. His charioteer cracked a whip in the air, and the pair of bay horses bolted forward as if the whip had slashed them. The other teams raced after them.

The warriors of the Gael screamed at the top of their lungs. They pounded their swords against their shields as they hurtled forward in an outpouring of explosive energy. The charioteers sawed on the reins; spumes of white foam streaked with blood poured from the mouths of the overexcited horses. Noise and clatter, rage and fury! They might have been a hundred, a thousand! They saw themselves as a conquering horde. So did the followers who ran after them. A seething mass of men and women and children, wild with joy at being on land again. Almost trampling one another in their eagerness. Shouting the traditional war cries of the Gael.

With a bellow of martial voices and the thunder of seventy-two hooves, the Mílesians invaded Ierne.

❧ SIX ❧

THE TÚATHA DÉ DANANN were shocked.

A warm welcome was out of the question and might prove fatal. With a hasty, all-inclusive gesture, Greine gathered his party and gave orders to withdraw before the strangers caught sight of them.

As far as the Mílesians could tell, Ierne was uninhabited.

Éremón undertook an initial reconnoiter of the surrounding area. Then he went back to the landing site. Before dismounting from his chariot, he raced his team in a wide circle, throwing up great showers of sand to impress the women—who were busy unpacking and setting up a camp for the night. They gave his display no more than a perfunctory glance before returning to matters of real importance. The children were tired and fretful, and there was cooking to be done. A night spent on the beach would not be so bad. At least the earth under their feet was not moving.

Taya, who had no children to tend as yet, went forward to greet Éremón. "Did you see anyone?" she asked anxiously.

"Not a tooth or a whisker of another person," he told her.

"This place is ours. It's everything I promised you and more."
Seeing Sakkar watching them, he called to the Phoenician,
"Amazing, is it not? This land is uninhabited."

"Amazing," Sakkar replied drily. He had not told the
Mílesians all of the stories repeated in the taverns of Tyre and
Sidon. If he had, they might have decided not to make the
voyage, and Sakkar was as eager as any of them for a new
beginning on the island in the sunset, the island on the rim
of the world.

Which he alone knew was populated by someone, something.

He recalled the mysterious inhabitants the sailors had
talked about in hushed voices. "Magic people" they had
called them. Were they gods? Demons? Incredibly powerful
sorcerers—or merely men more clever than those who sought
to rob them?

In his previous life, Sakkar had not indulged in abstract
musings. Rendered pragmatic by circumstance, he had relied
on the strength of his muscles for answers to problems. He
could hardly blame Age-Nor for abandoning him. What
good was a shipwright who could not repair ships any
longer?

Physical disability had forced the Phoenician to develop
a better tool: his brain. He was thinking very quickly now.

Sooner or later, the natives of Ierne were bound to make
their presence known. If they were more numerous or better
armed than the Mílesians, it would be prudent to befriend
them as soon as possible. The pretty speech Sakkar had made
to Éremón about honor and obligation was just that, a pretty
speech. His philosophy could be quickly adjusted. In the
crooked streets and dangerous alleyways of Tyre, he had
learned there was but one imperative: survive.

Always ally oneself to the strongest side.

Shielding his eyes against the sun with his left hand, the little man surveyed the tranquil face of Ierne. A fleeting vision of the coastal cities of the Levant slid across his memory, obscuring the verdant panorama before him. Tyre and Sidon, Biblos and Acre. Greatest of all was Carthage, built on a triangular peninsula covered with low hills and backed by the Lake of Tunis, the powerful capital of the Phoenician world. Towers, terraces, noisome crowds, and massive stonework hotly gleaming in the ubiquitous sunshine. Blowing sand and billowing dust, clouds of biting insects, shifty-eyed traders speaking incomprehensible dialects. Clever fingers briefly slipping into unguarded purses. Thousands of sweaty bodies trying to mask their stink with costly perfumed oils. And among rich and poor alike, the casual cruelty that had exemplified the only life Sakkar knew until fate delivered him to the Mílesians.

Now this. This luxuriously green island. This singular, solitary paradise. Whatever might be wrong with the place, it was better than anywhere else.

His eyes scanned the woodland beyond the beach. What sort of trees were those? Such dense leaves . . . were there any date palms among them? They surely must bear some kind of fruit. His mouth watered at the thought of fresh fruit. Figs and grapes and sweet purple plums. Perhaps . . .

When he squinted and tilted his head to one side, he glimpsed what might be a human form among the trees. Then it was gone.

Yet he knew someone was there. He felt the weight of their eyes.

If Sakkar had not possessed a powerful instinct for detecting danger, he would not have lived past childhood. Fortunately, there was no chill on the back of his neck now, no instinctive tensing of his leg muscles, so whoever watched

him was not inimical, at least not to him. There was danger, though. He knew it. Danger had come ashore with the warriors and their chariots.

It might be a good idea to do some exploring on his own, without waiting for Éremón and the others. The only person Sakkar trusted totally was himself.

Glancing around to make certain that none of the Mílesians were watching him, he set off for the trees.

❧

The Danann party drifted away from the coast like smoke blown by a gentle breeze. They were in no hurry. Sure of their own powers, they chose to remove themselves from the immediate vicinity of the strangers and await developments.

Only one of them hesitated.

As they observed the strangers, Lerys, wife of Mongan, had noticed a short, swarthy man who stood apart from the others. He held his right arm clamped against his side, and there was a curious asymmetry to his shoulders. The right one was higher than the other, with an odd, lumpy shape. Although it might be a congenital deformity, the shoulder looked as if it had been badly damaged through accident or violence.

She turned around and went back.

When the cold shade of the trees fell upon Sakkar, he drew a deep breath. The air smelled wonderful, yet strange. It made his nostrils tingle.

Perhaps he was making a mistake. The recent voyage had been hard from the beginning and terrifying at the end; perhaps his good common sense was . . .

A woman emerged from a stand of ash saplings. She was very small and slender, dressed in flowing draperies the color of water. Her heart-shaped face was as pale as the moon;

her violet-colored eyes were huge and brimming with sympathy.

What is wrong with your shoulder?

Although Sakkar was looking at her face, he did not see her lips move. Instead, words in a woman's soft voice sounded inside his head. They froze him where he stood.

Do not be afraid. We mean you no harm. We only want to know if we can help.

And then a different voice said, *Here you are, Lerys! I was wondering why you left us.*

Sakkar's teeth were chattering. In his mind he turned and ran back toward the beach faster than was humanly possible. In reality he remained paralyzed, watching slack-jawed as another woman appeared beside the first. On her unlined brow she wore a golden circlet set with glittering blue stones. Like a pouring of glossy cream, her pale hair cascaded over her shoulders and fell almost to her knees.

Sakkar had never seen a queen before, but he knew one when he saw one. She could not be anything else. To avoid embarrassing himself, he clamped his jaw shut to silence his chattering teeth. We never should have come here, he thought. Never, never.

The stately woman turned her glowing gray eyes full upon him. *That depends,* she responded, *on why you did it.*

Sakkar felt an inexplicable urge to kneel.

"He is very frightened, Eriu," Lerys said aloud in the language of her race. To Sakkar it sounded like birdsong and the tinkle of a stream running over pebbles.

Eriu replied, "That is not fear you see on his face, Lerys, or not entirely fear. He is suffering from complicated emotions in addition to his deformity. We can help his shoulder, but I am not so sure about his emotions. They are unlike our own."

Inside Sakkar's head, she asked, *Were you born with a misshapen shoulder?*

He understood these words perfectly—and was dismayed. It was unthinkable that a strange woman could enter a space that was his alone and start asking personal questions! A man should have privacy inside his own head.

But the habit of obedience was deeply ingrained in Sakkar, forcing him to reply. "I was in a shipwreck more than a year ago," he said aloud, "and the mast fell on me. The joint was crushed. It's never been right since."

Eriu rewarded Sakkar with a radiant smile. *You are fortunate. Your body will remember what it is like to be whole. Bodies never forget; we need only to remind them.*

She took her companion's hand in one of her own and reached toward Sakkar with the other. He shrank back.

The women did not appear offended. *What is your name?* Eriu asked politely.

His mouth was dry. "Sakkar."

Sakkar, she repeated. *It is a good name, firm but not hard. Where do you come from, Sakkar?*

His odyssey was too complicated to explain, even silently. "I came here with the Mílesians."

The gray-eyed woman looked quizzical. *And who are they?*

"The sons of Mílesios." This still explained nothing, yet she accepted it. *I am called Eriu, and my cousin beside me is Lerys. Please stand still for a moment, Sakkar. We will not hurt you.*

Her long, thin fingers closed on his ruined shoulder. He experienced nothing, neither pain nor comfort. And yet . . . and yet . . .

A peculiar feeling coursed through him like a flood of warm water. Starting at the base of his skull, his skeleton realigned itself. The sensation was one of incredible relief. When he felt the bones and tendons of his shoulder resume their normal position, Sakkar gasped. "How did you do that?"

You did it yourself, Sakkar.

"But you . . . I . . . it can't be . . ."

Yes it can, said Lerys. *Try and see.*

He gave his arm a tentative swing. The formerly crippled limb responded effortlessly.

Again, Eriu said. *This time use your arm just as you did before the injury.*

Sakkar followed her instructions—and discovered that he had regained the full range of motion in his shoulder. There was no pain at all. Impossible. Unbelievable. Yet when he made a fist his right hand was as strong as it had ever been.

"How can I ever repay you?"

Eriu laughed. *It was a small thing and you did most of the work yourself, Sakkar. No payment is needed.*

"But I must give you something! I am obliged."

Very well. Explain to me why the strangers are in this land. Do they think to establish trade here? If so, they are mistaken; we do not trade with foreigners.

When Eriu's gray eyes fixed on his, Sakkar could not lie. What good would it do to lie to someone who could hear his thoughts? "The strangers, as you call them, are Gaels, members of the tribe of Mílesios. They have come . . ." He bit his lip.

They have come, Eriu repeated, gently urging. *For what purpose?*

"Conquest," he admitted. "They've left their own land to start new lives here."

They cannot! Lerys cried inside Sakkar's head. *This is our sacred island. We will never permit colonization!*

Eriu turned toward her. *Be quiet, Lerys. Anything you say*

in haste might reveal more than he should know. We must tell the others about this at once.

Because their silent communication excluded him, Sakkar tried to read their expressions. But their perfect features might have been flowers; they gave nothing away.

Can you make him forget about meeting us? Lerys was asking Eriu.

If I take away the memory, Sakkar's body may forget the healing. Is that what you want?

Of course not. Ungifting causes a disharmony. I would not inflict that on him. Perhaps he will think it was a dream, Lerys added hopefully.

Perhaps, Eriu agreed. But storm clouds darkened in her eyes. *We must keep what we have learned about his language and share it with the others, Lerys. I fear we may need to communicate with these strangers again.*

A sudden wind whirled through the stand of ash saplings, propelling tiny grains of earth that stung Sakkar's skin. He threw up his hands to protect his face. The wind ceased at once. When he lowered his hands, the two women were gone.

Sakkar took a hesitant step forward, paused, turned around, started toward the beach, then stopped again. Looked in every direction. Nothing. No one—if there had ever been anyone there at all.

But he could not forget those gray eyes.

When he raised his right arm above his shoulder, it still worked perfectly. His body was not any younger or any stronger, but just as it would have been without the shipwreck.

Sakkar sank to his knees and pressed his forehead to the fragrant earth.

❧

Éber Finn saw the Phoenician returning and called a greeting to him. "Where've you been, Sakkar? The women are cooking some big blue fish, and it smells wonderful. If you didn't come back soon, I was going to eat your share myself."

Sakkar said nothing. He looked dazed. Walking past Éber Finn, he made his way to the campfire blazing on the beach, fed by a heap of driftwood. He held out his two hands toward the flames. He did not feel the heat. All he felt were Her fingers closing on his shoulder.

Éremón was having a similar but less sanguine experience. His wife Odba had managed to secrete herself among one of the Gaelician clans and make it safely to Ierne. She joined the other colonists on the beach and, to Éremón's alarm, tapped him unexpectedly on the back. He had never been so astonished. When he recovered himself, he accused her of stowing away as a deliberate ploy to ruin his future.

And Taya's.

The quarrel that followed was spectacular, even by their standards.

Éremón wanted to hit Odba. He wanted to hit somebody—anybody! It almost but not quite destroyed his appetite for the meal the women were preparing.

Sakkar remained remote from the busy scene around him. He was given tasks and he did them, he was given food and he ate it, yet all the time he was somewhere else.

As the sun set, the men dragged the galleys farther up the shore so the women and children could sleep on them. Amergin noticed that Sakkar was using both his hands to haul on the ropes. After the ships were in place and securely blocked, the bard sought out the Phoenician. "Your shoulder appears to be greatly improved," he said, indicating the limb in question. It now looked identical to its opposite number.

Sakkar ducked his head and scuffed his toe in the sand like a boy who had been caught in a lie. "Yes," he mumbled.

"How did that happen?"

"How?" Sakkar raised his head.

"Your shoulder. What happened to it, Sakkar?"

"My shoulder?"

Amergin was perplexed. The Phoenician had never been reticent; in fact, Sakkar was always willing to talk to the bard, delighted to find someone who took an interest in him as a person. The former shipwright had proved to be a treasure house of information about distant lands and exotic customs. Their conversations had enriched Amergin's mental store.

Now Sakkar seemed to be struck dumb.

Amergin tried to reestablish normal communication. "I thought your shoulder was permanently ruined, Sakkar."

"Yes." Sakkar stared into the distance.

The bard waited. Cleared his throat. Rearranged his worn tunic. His tranquil expression and relaxed body said he was not going anywhere until Sakkar talked to him.

With a visible effort, the Phoenician pulled himself into the here and now. "I met a woman."

Amergin raised an eyebrow. It was the first time Sakkar had ever spoken of a woman. "Which woman?"

"Not one of ours."

"Are you saying there are other people here?"

"Not . . . people. I don't know what they are."

Perhaps Sakkar had taken a blow to the head, Amergin thought, one that temporarily deprived him of his senses. Whatever had happened, it was serious. The bard stood up and looked around for help. "There's a man over here who's been hurt!" he shouted.

A druid healer labored over Sakkar for a long time, rolled back his eyelids and peered into his eyes, thoroughly examined his skull with fingertips as light as a moth's wings, smelled his breath and tasted his urine. Finally pronounced him uninjured—yet could not explain the dramatic change to Sakkar's shoulder.

Amergin was not satisfied. He resolved to keep an eye on his friend for a few days. Then he went to seek his own bed.

By the time Sakkar was left alone, the sky was a sea of stars.

Sleep eluded him. His brain had never been so active. He tossed and turned, remembered and imagined. At first light he took a disc of polished metal from the faded tapestry bag in which he kept his personal possessions. Peering into the mirror, Sakkar frowned at the face that looked back at him. It was entirely wrong for a man to whom something extraordinary had happened.

From a rolled leather case he selected a small knife and a set of razors with handles of polished horn. A soft pouch provided a well-worn whetstone. Chewing on his lower lip in concentration, Sakkar sharpened his neglected blades. Then he propped the mirror atop the tapestry bag and began trimming his beard. Since the injury that limited the use of his right hand, the beard had grown unchecked. Now it was an impenetrable tangle of thick black hair. After a few preliminary cuts, Sakkar's restored fingers began a patient search for the hidden man.

The Mílesians were waking up. Grunting, yawning, stretching, farting, scratching, calling to one another, talking about food. A horse whinnied. A baby cried. Odba and Éremón had an argument that roused the most determined sleepers. Donn organized a foraging party. Some went to seek game while others scoured water's edge for crabs and mussels and edible seaweeds. "Don't overlook anything that might be eaten. If in doubt, take it to the women and try it on them."

Sakkar worked on, oblivious. At last he scrutinized himself in the mirror again. What remained of his unruly beard was trimmed very tight and close, coming to a precise point on his chin. It gave a newfound distinction to what had been an ordinary face.

He might have been a desert nomad. He might even have been a Persian prince.

❧ SEVEN ❧

As the Mílesians made preparations for occupying their new homeland, Sakkar the Phoenician was given his choice of going on an expeditionary party with the warriors or staying in camp with the women—warriors' wives who would regard him as a coward for remaining behind.

So he reluctantly allowed Éremón's armorer to fit a sheet of hard-cured leather across his chest to protect his torso. The leather had been soaked in seawater and then moulded to shape with heated stones before it dried. A fitted helmet made of the same material was jammed onto Sakkar's head.

He had never worn body armor or a helmet before. The breastplate was stiff and chafed the tender flesh of his underarms. The helmet had been formed to a Gaelic skull shape and kept slipping down over his eyes.

When Éremón's attendant asked, "Are you a sword man or a spear man?" Sakkar had no answer, having never used either. From observation, he thought the sword seemed marginally less awkward, but both were alien to his hands.

"Must I carry weapons?"

The armorer, a grizzled veteran who had served the sons of Mílesios throughout their fighting lives, gave a snort of contempt. "Are you going to just stand there with one arm as long as the other while your enemy cuts you down?"

A memory of the woman with gray eyes flashed through Sakkar's mind. The enemy?

The armorer took advantage of his lapse in attention to press a weapon into his hand. "Here you are, shipbuilder. This will do for you; it's a short-shafted thrusting spear, easiest for a beginner. All you do is ram it into your opponent's belly, low down, give it a twist, then pull it out as fast as you can. If he doesn't die immediately, he will bleed to death soon enough. Think you can manage that?"

Without waiting for an answer, the man moved on to adjust someone else's breastplate.

Sakkar was left holding his spear and half-blinded by his helmet. The edge of his breastplate pressed painfully into his chest. Soon it would become an agony.

This did not augur well for his career as a warrior.

But here he was. Where fate had brought him. If there was one thing every child of the East learned early in life, it was that one's fate could not be avoided.

Sakkar had never taken part in a battle and did not know what to expect, but he was a quick learner. With the rest of the foot warriors, he would trot in the wake of the leaders in their chariots and copy the actions of his companions.

While he waited to get under way, he picked at his fingernails and stared at the sea.

Donn, the only one of the brothers with any organizational skills, appointed a band of scouts to precede the warriors. When they returned to report sighting a few natives bathing in a lake just beyond some hills, Éremón was elated. "What a perfect beginning! They'll be helpless and unprepared, and we can slaughter the lot of them. That will heat the blood of our warriors."

"Let one or two escape," counseled Donn, "so they can spread fear among the rest of their people. Their terror will be our best ally."

Éber Finn scoffed, "We don't need any allies; we are the sons of Mílesios."

They approached the lake as quietly as possible until the last moment. Then the chariots thundered toward the startled Dananns and the air was torn by raucous Gaelic war cries.

When it was over—the battle took no time at all—a dozen dead bodies lay in the bloody shallows. Young men and women, some with flowers in their hair, friends who had been celebrating the beauty of the day together.

Sakkar stood at the edge of the lake and watched the slender corpses bobbing gently in the rippling water. Water that seemed full of light. Brighter than any water he had ever seen before.

"I am afraid we have done a bad thing," he said under his breath.

Noticing Amergin on the opposite side of the lake, Sakkar made his way around to him. Amergin had taken no part in the attack because bards did not fight. They only observed and told of the battle afterward.

"We have done a bad thing," the Phoenician repeated to his friend.

Amergin cocked an eyebrow. "We? I see no blood on the head of your spear."

"Ah . . . no. I did enough fighting as a lad in the streets of Tyre. I have no taste for it now."

"Then why are you armed?"

"Sometimes it is easier to go with the tide. But when I saw

those people in the lake, hardly more than children, and with no way to defend themselves . . ." Sakkar stopped talking and looked toward the bodies in the shallows. Palely glimmering in the shallows.

Amergin recognized his discomfiture. "Finish what you started to say."

"Actually . . . they may not have been helpless."

"They were naked, Sakkar, frolicking in the water. What could they have done against us?"

"The day we arrived I met . . . at least I think I met . . . some of their race. They had no weapons either, but they were not helpless."

"I recall you mentioned a woman that night. Is that what you're talking about?"

"Yes, but I'm not sure it actually happened. Except . . ."

Amergin gave a sigh of exasperation. "Sometimes you try my patience, Phoenician. You can be as slippery as the rest of your race. Except for what?"

Sakkar dropped his chin so Amergin could barely hear him. "Except for my shoulder."

The bard stood very still. "That evening your shoulder was healed," he said thoughtfully.

"Yes."

"They healed it? The natives?"

"Yes. I mean, I think so. They have powers I can't explain, Amergin. You see, when I found them, or they found me, I was frightened at first because I was alone and . . ." He hesitated, then let the words come out at a rush. "They could talk to each other without speaking. Silently."

Amergin started to laugh, thinking it was a joke, but the Phoenician was not in the habit of making jokes. "If they didn't use words, Sakkar, how do you know what they were doing?"

Sakkar scuffled a toe in the dirt. "Because . . . they could put their thoughts into my head and understand my own." He turned his eyes back toward the bodies floating in the lake.

Amergin followed the direction of his gaze. "If you are telling the truth, Sakkar—and I don't know if I believe it—we may be making a mistake by attacking those people. Of course, we were all tired that day; perhaps you fell asleep and dreamed what you just told me." Narrowing his eyes, the bard tried to count the corpses floating in the water. Curiously, their numbers eluded him. Three? Five? More? Or less? Or were they there at all? Clouds had gathered overhead, and dark shadows played across the surface of the lake, obscuring the scene.

Amergin said, "Perhaps the natives here can work magic. I suppose it's possible. Remember the strange fog that prevented our landing?"

"I'll never forget it," Sakkar asserted, "but at least we survived. Not one of us was hurt."

"Are you saying the natives are harmless, magic or not?"

"I don't know," the little man replied honestly. "This is all new to me, and I'm . . . I'm confused, Amergin. Can we leave it at that?" Sakkar was beginning to wish he had told his hosts the more sinister stories about the island. In his own eagerness to find a paradise, had he led them to something very different?

But it was too late now.

❧ EIGHT ❧

THE ARRIVAL OF THE MÍLESIANS was disconcerting, but the Túatha Dé Danann did not foresee its being a catastrophe. I knew nothing about the invaders because my parents did not tell me. When I was supposed to be asleep, I occasionally heard Mongan and Lerys murmuring to one another in the night, but I made no effort to listen. People who share their space learn to give each other privacy. I understood that my parents' tender exchanges were not meant for me.

During the day our lives were unchanged—except my father began to be away more often and for longer periods. I assumed that his absences involved the tribes that Aengus had said were causing trouble.

Sunseason was also known as battle season, because that was when the soft, damp earth of Ierne dried up enough for fighting. Yet I never envisioned my father taking part in a battle. Mongan was the gentlest of men. My mother once told me that all Dananns were gentle unless a different quality was necessary.

"We have it in us to be whatever is required," she said. I did not understand. Then.

While Mongan was away, Melitt sometimes came down the valley to see if my mother and I needed anything. She never failed to bring a loaf of her fruit bread, still warm from the stone oven outside her house. Crisp at the crust but soft in the middle.

My father was usually home before moonrise, and if any of Melitt's bread was left, he ate it.

The remainder of sunseason passed slowly, sweetly, for me. A gift from my parents who tried to shield me from disturbance for as long as they could. One day can be half of a happy eternity if it is filled with expeditions and discoveries, with dreams and fantasies, with billowing white clouds and the smell of grass after rain.

Battle season traditionally ended with harvest time. My father stayed home then; there was a lot of work to be done in preparation for darkseason. Before the rains of autumn set in, I helped him to collect a large supply of fallen branches for firewood and to build a shelter to keep it dry. My mother showed me how to find and gather edible roots and other wild foods and store them in the earth. She had always done this by herself before; sharing it with me was an honor I appreciated. One more acknowledged step toward adulthood.

During that darkseason I learned many new things. My father taught me to shape flint into blades and to make footwear out of hides taken from the bodies of animals who had died in the forest. Mother showed me how to grind grain in a quern—which was hard work!—and make cheese from the milk of goats. She even let me use her precious bone needles to mend my own clothes.

The adult tasks gave me a heady sense of importance, although my own adulthood was still far away. Or so I thought.

Darkseason, which had seemed interminable when I was younger, passed quickly because I was kept busy. When my mother measured my increasing height against a line carved in our doorway, she said, "You will soon be taller than I am, Joss."

She sounded very surprised.

I arranged sticks at the edge of the clearing where our house stood, and every day that the sun shone I went out and measured the length of my shadow. I could feel my muscles swelling beneath my skin.

When the days began to lengthen, Mongan announced, "It is time you learned the use of weapons, Joss."

"Not yet, surely!" protested my mother.

"You yourself pointed out how much he has grown, Lerys. Our boy needs the sort of exercise that builds men."

My father took me to a distant meadow where my mother would not have to watch. He carved a serviceable sword for me out of an ash branch, with leaves curling around the hilt, and showed me how to place my feet . . . just so . . . and how to bend and weave with my body as I swung the weapon.

At first I was clumsy, but I soon became agile and enjoyed every moment as my father and I circled each other, feinting and attacking. I could see how much fun a real battle would be.

My father remarked, "You should have some brothers to practice with. I cannot bring myself to strike you, but obviously you need to take a few knocks. A few hard knocks," he stressed. "We must invite your male cousins to visit us. Perhaps they are big enough by now." He seemed preoccupied, however, and forgot to summon them.

When I boasted to the Dagda of my improving battle skills, he said, "Do not mistake warriors for heroes."

"But they are heroic!"

"Only if you consider killing to be heroic. Death is not the purpose of life, Joss. Life is the purpose of life."

"Then who are the heroes?"

"Those who master the mind." He tapped his skull with his knuckles. "Theirs is the victory. No sword lasts forever."

I could not resist arguing, and he knew it. "Minds die too," I countered. "When a person dies, his head dies and his brain and . . ."

"Thought does not die," the old man interrupted. "Thought has no body to be killed."

"I don't understand."

"Now you display the beginning of wisdom."

As the tiny new leaves began to spring out on the trees, we dug into the soft earth with our fingers and planted seeds. Once again I worked beside my parents. "This autumn you and I are going to make flour from the grain we've planted," my mother promised. "The bread we bake will be almost as good as Melitt's."

Then Mongan began going away again.

Goddess weather, my mother called it. The season of the sun. She never said battle season.

But that is what it was.

I have a very clear memory of the Day of Triumph. For a number of nights my father had not come home at all, and my mother could not hide her anxiety. At last Mongan returned to announce that the enemy had withdrawn without doing any harm to our people. He lifted Lerys into his arms and swung her around and around while she laughed with glee. She was a laughing woman, my mother. In their joy the two of them were like children themselves.

I danced about them, asking questions. "Which enemy? The Iverni? Or the Fír Bolga?"

"The invaders from the south," my father replied in an unguarded moment. Only then did I realize something important had been kept from me. "We tried a new defensive technique against the men with blue swords. They saw monsters form from shadows and giants take shape from trees. The illusions in their own minds frightened them so badly they will never bother us again."

Try as I might, I cannot remember my parents' faces at that happy moment. I only recall the glowing tapestries on the walls of our home. In Goddess weather my mother wove them from fresh flowers every morning.

Scenes from the long and joyful lives of the Túatha Dé Danann.

All of the Danann clans celebrated the Day of Triumph. We did not journey to the Gathering Place but traveled from one clan's territory to another, a colorful parade of men and women and children too. New songs were sung and new dances created to commemorate the event. People assured each other that the invaders would leave our shores before the next change of the moon, for who would face a repeat of such a terrifying experience?

They were mistaken in their optimism. Although the moon changed, the invaders remained. Stubbornly, the foreigners built shelters and hunted game and foraged for edibles and stayed on Ierne through another darkseason. Their children grew taller and their livestock grew fat on rich green grass that did not die in the cold.

Like a plague of hornets, the invaders emerged at the beginning of leaf-spring ready to fight again. Small skirmishes became major battles. The Dananns were pitted against a race that carried weapons made of a blue metal

harder than bronze and they approached war with ferocious glee.

We chose not to call the invaders by the name they gave
themselves. Because of their behavior, we did not allow them
the dignity of tribal identification. To us they were "the New
People." The name was meant as an insult, and bitter on the
tongue.

I asked the Dagda, "Does that mean we are the Old
People?"

"We were the new people here at one time," he replied.
"The incomers, the invaders. We meant no harm to Ierne; we
brought our music and medicines and ways of thinking and
intended to share them freely. But the earlier inhabitants
were afraid of us. Perhaps we were too different. They attacked us while our boats were still coming ashore and
made repeated efforts to slaughter our entire colony. When
we tried to negotiate, they swept our words aside like the
humming of bees. In the end, we were forced to defend ourselves. You know the rest."

"I know we used something called the Earthkillers. But
what were they?"

"A mistake," said the Dagda.

Time blurred. The faces of the adults blurred too; they
looked haggard. Men and women from far-flung clans came
to confer with my parents, sitting around our hearth and
drinking honey wine and barley beer, making suggestions,
planning strategies.

I recall a conference that included both the Dagda and
the Son of the Sun, as well as his wife, Eriu. My mother was
visibly delighted to have them under her roof; she glowed
that night. It was the last time I ever saw her glow.

I should have listened more closely, but as usual my mind
was wandering. Only one fragment of conversation caught

my attention and stayed with me. "We are coming to another fork in the road," Eriu said. "We must be strong. If we weaken now, we might as well be Unbodied."

I had never heard the word before. Afterward I asked the Dagda, "When she said Unbodied, was the great queen talking about dying?"

"Not exactly," he replied. Which told me nothing.

"Then what did she mean?"

"Being Unbodied is to stand outside oneself as an observer."

I felt an icy finger trace along my spine. "How do you get back in?"

"It is very difficult; the condition is not to be recommended."

"Then what is dying?"

"Dying is not the last thing but the least thing, Joss. Think of it as another way of traveling."

And that was all the answer I got.

❧

We had one more harvest before leaf-fall, although not the bounty of times past. The heads of grain were more brown than gold; they drooped upon their stalks like the heads of weary children. My mother said the energy that should have gone into stimulating the earth was being redirected elsewhere.

The men of our clan helped my father cut the grain we had planted. In spite of his age, even the Dagda helped. He looked almost as strong as a young man if you did not get too close. I swung a scythe myself until my entire body ached. As soon as our crop was gathered and stored, the men left to harvest someone else's field. Mongan went with them, of course.

Sometimes I heard Lerys crying softly in her bed.

Then the sun hid his face and the dark came back.

❧

Under the pressure of the invaders, battle had not been limited to sunseason but bled over into autumn and then into darkseason, so we had no festivals to celebrate the changes. That was the sort of enemy we fought. Foreigners who had no respect for anything.

Yet from snatches of adult conversation, I realized that not everyone wanted to fight them. I heard my mother say, "They are refugees just as our ancestors were, Mongan. We do not know what catastrophe drove them from their homeland, and they could not possibly have traveled as far as our own people. But they must feel just as lost and uncertain as we did Before the Before. We should show them mercy."

"It is so like you to say that," my father replied. "Do you suppose they would show us mercy if the situation were reversed?"

Lerys was not the only one who had misgivings about the war. The other Dananns continued to debate the rights and wrongs of aggression. Confusion clouded the atmosphere. During the short gray days and long cold nights of darkseason, a strange lassitude descended on the tribe, as if an invisible piper were playing the Sleepy Music.

More men came to confer with my father, and the tone of the conversations changed. There were words I had never heard used before: words like "pain" and "defeat" and "failure." The ugly, naked language of warfare.

The shadows in the corners of our house moved toward the center.

Meanwhile, the Dagda began to place more emphasis on the history he wanted me to learn. "The legends of our race are the proud inheritance of every Danann child," he said, "along with their chain of names. In the long-ago time when we challenged the Fomorians for the sovereignty of Ierne, we possessed weapons engraved with symbols of the arts we had brought with us from the land of our origin. Arts that must have seemed magical indeed to the primitive Fomorians."

Was he referring to the Sword of Light and the Invincible Spear? Were they the Earthkillers? Or was that something even worse?

When I asked the Dagda, he would not meet my eyes. "You would not understand yet, Joss; you are too young, and your mind is too vulnerable. We are not going to talk about those things because I do not want to put horrible images into your head. You would never be able to get them out."

Too young, although I had attended the Being Together. It was only a foretaste; I saw that now. Because of my size and the number of my seasons, I was still being excluded from knowledge. And I wanted to *know*. Curiosity is an itch that demands to be scratched.

The Dagda would not tell me about the terrible weapons, yet I could see that he was pleased by my eagerness to learn. So I kept asking questions, more and more questions. I skirted around the topic he was determined to avoid and nibbled at the outside edges of warfare, hoping I could trick him into giving something away.

That is how young I really was. I thought I could trick the Dagda.

He explained that over the generations highly stylized warfare had become a sport among our people, a way of releasing the excess energy we had in abundance. Both men and women relished the rigorous exercise. Those who did not care to compete gathered to watch, whistling and applauding and stamping their feet, throwing armloads of flowers and cheering wildly for their heroes. Poems of praise were composed for victor and vanquished alike, and the two sides feasted together afterward.

It sounded glorious. And perhaps it had been, once. When we were on the winning side.

But in addition to the lessons the Dagda taught me, I could not help hearing some of the things our visitors said when they came to talk with my father.

We did not appear to be on the winning side now.

The conflict was being fought in deadly earnest. There was no sport in it; no skill, no art. The New People were simply killing everyone who got in their way. Elders whose heads were silvered by the passage of time and youngsters with their unlived lives sparkling in their eyes were being cut down where they stood.

In response, even men and women with no taste for battle were taking up weapons and fighting back. We who hated nothing were learning to hate. Hate the strangers, the foreigners, the enemies who were alien from the shape of their heads to the style of their weapons. Some claimed they were not people at all, but they were.

People like us. People who wanted what was ours and hated us for a reason I could not understand.

✢❧ NINE ❧✣

ACCORDING TO THEIR OWN BARDS in succeeding generations, the Mílesian conquest of Ierne was a succession of epic battles against vastly superior forces.

Truth depends on who tells the story.

It was true that the warriors of the Gael had never encountered a foe as mysterious and enigmatic as the Túatha Dé Danann. With the passage of time, the Danann names would be added to the Gaelic pantheon of gods. The Children of Light were not the only opposition the conquerors faced, however. Their initial encounter with the Túatha Dé Danann at the lake had been only a skirmish; the first real battle had taken place a few days later, with different people entirely.

The sons of the Míl had been feasting on the bounty of the sea and preparing to move farther inland when Donn suggested fortifying an area near the coast. "We should have a secure base to leave the mothers and children in. Someplace we can return to if . . . just in case."

Ír grimaced in disgust. "You want to come back here and

eat fish and fish and more fish?" He bent over his pottery bowl and pretended to be vomiting.

Scotta said, "Pay no attention to him," in the voice of a patient mother whose child was still too young to behave himself.

The woman who had been Ír's wife for so many years she was no longer embarrassed by his antics continued chatting with Taya, who was friendly with everyone.

Odba sat alone on the other side of the fire and picked her teeth with a fish bone. Since her presence was made known, most of the other women had spoken to her—in a rather embarrassed fashion—but no one had befriended her. Hierarchy was important among the Gael, and on Ierne it appeared that Éremón held the highest rank. If Taya was his first choice, Odba must be relegated to a lower station.

She understood this, but she blamed Éremón long and bitterly in the dark watches of the night. She was learning that hatred could convey strength.

Éremón expressed reservations about building a fort on the headland. He thought it would be an unnecessary delay to the conquest of the island. In his mind the army of the Gael already had swept Ierne from one end to the other. "We should be on the move now," he declared, picking fragments of crab meat out of his beard. "Tomorrow at the latest."

Scotta had sided with her oldest son. "We would be fool-hardy to take the entire tribe into unknown territory," she said—ignoring the fact that they had just done that very thing. "Your father would never forgive us if we allowed harm to come to his grandchildren"—although Mílesios had never shown much affection to his grandchildren and hardly knew their names. It was the bard who remembered names.

"Our first step," Scotta continued, "should be to locate the most fertile soil and the best water . . . and any other natives. They will occupy the choice land and must be driven off."

"Don't worry about them," said Éber Finn. "Such frail people can never resist us. They would not even make useful servants, though if the women were pretty . . ."

Colptha hissed, "Don't you have enough women already?"

The others laughed.

Sitting in his personal space beyond the wide glow of the family's fire, Sakkar heard the laughter. He found himself in an awkward position on Ierne. He was not a Mílesian, nor did he belong to one of the lesser Gaelic clans that had accompanied them. He was not even a freeman. As a shipwright he had possessed a status beyond his dreams as a child. When he was supervising the building of the fleet, he had the Míl for a mentor and warmed himself at the old chieftain's hearth.

On the island at the rim of the world he was only . . . Sakkar the Phoenician. Which meant nothing here.

While Scotta and her sons filled their bellies, Sakkar had left his own tiny fire with a few crabs smouldering among the embers and retrieved the weapons he had been given. In the darkness beyond the campfires, no one would see him practice.

৯৩

Following Donn's instructions, the freemen began to dig a defensive bank and erect an earthwork wall while the sons of Mílesios led the expeditionary party farther inland. The participants consisted of seasoned warriors, both Mílesian and the best of the lesser clans, plus Colptha to represent the spirit world, Amergin to see and remember, and Scotta, who demanded to be included in her late husband's name. Heavily laden with her finest jewelery, her richest clothing, and a sword in her belt as befitted a warrior, she rode in the chariots of each of her sons in turn.

Éremón's chariot was so packed with his personal food supplies that there was barely room for him and his charioteer. He grumbled when things had to be rearranged to accommodate his mother.

Éber Finn had a little more room in his war cart, although his baggage included four tunics, a heavy cloak lined with fur, an extra pair of soft leather boots, and an inlaid box for his combs and razors and scented hair paste.

Colptha's supplies included bags filled with vile-smelling herbs and a collection of oddly shaped roots and branches. Scotta spent as little time as possible in his chariot. She confided to one of the other women that his roots and branches poked her in her private parts.

Amergin, who accompanied them on foot, wore his customary blue woolen cloak and unbleached tunic. His baggage consisted of a second tunic in the pack on his back and the harp in her case. Noble rank accorded him a chariot, which he rarely used. He preferred to feel the earth beneath his bare feet, the living earth. As a druid he was part of her and she of him.

As they traveled inland, they realized what a truly rich land they had discovered. Ierne was clothed with endless impenetrable forests of oak and elm and ash; enough timber to house and fuel countless thousands. There was pine and hazel, aspen, alder, holly, and elm.

An abundance of rivers and streams watered grasslands that were green both in summer and winter and could nourish more herds than the Mílesians had ever owned. Trees and bushes were laden with fruit and nuts; game of every description seemed eager to present itself to the spear.

They also caught glimpses of wickerwork huts among the hills, and once or twice they saw what looked like a ruined stone fort. "This is too easy," Éremón remarked to his charioteer. "Land can only be won through deeds of valor. Ask my brother the bard; he knows all the stories. If we don't have someone to fight, there will be no deeds of valor. Where are the people?" he called to his brother.

Éber Finn stood tall in his chariot with his mother beside him. "I see huts but no people. Perhaps they all starved to death."

"In a land like this?" Scotta retorted. "I don't think so. Be on your guard; we may have action yet."

Which is exactly what her husband would have said.

They had continued their journey unchallenged until they came to a range of purple mountains, jagged and dangerous as shark's teeth. When they reached the foothills, Donn suggested they encamp for the night, but Éremón and Éber Finn wanted to push on. "Before the sun sets there will be plenty of time to make ourselves comfortable."

This time Donn had capitulated.

The twilight did not last as long as they expected. The air turned cold and thin and blue and soon the ground was too stony for the chariots. When one of his wheels began to wobble on its axle, Éber Finn called out, "Let's stop now, brothers! Tomorrow we can either find a way through the mountains or choose a different direction entirely."

Éremón muttered in his beard. He did not like for anyone else to make decisions.

Donn led the way to a large stand of pines where they could tie their teams and wait for Amergin to catch up with them. Éremón went on by himself for a short distance, then reluctantly turned back.

The mountains ahead were grim and forbidding in the gathering twilight.

Éremón's charioteer had just wheeled the team to a halt beside Éber's war cart when a horde of demons burst upon them from the trees. Half-naked demons with tattooed skin and garishly painted faces; creatures who howled like wolves and carried stone axes and bronze-bladed weapons, which they wielded with savage intent.

The warriors of the Gael fought back as best they could, but the element of surprise almost defeated them. Step by step, they lost ground.

This was land the primitive natives knew well; they were able to take advantage of every tumbled boulder and fold of earth. They gave their opponents no chance to form a battle line. The threatening insults and grandiose boasts of Gaelic warriors, which were meant to intimidate their opponents, went unheard in the hysterical shrieking of the tattooed people.

&

From long habit, Amergin never allowed chariot warriors to get too far ahead of him; his long legs could trot tirelessly in pursuit of the horses. Where the warriors were was where the action would be, the raw material for bardic epic. Or there might be an opportunity to make peace between opposing sides, one of the prerogatives of a bard. When he heard the familiar sound of battle cries, he broke into a run. As he ran, he slipped Clarsah from her satchel so she would be ready if inspiration struck.

Amergin reached the dense stand of pine trees in time to see his mother draw her sword from her belt and slam it across the sword of a painted native, breaking his blade. "Take the blow of Mílesios!" Scotta cried as she brandished her weapon in triumph.

A man covered with tattoos darted under her guard and speared her in the ribs.

Before Scotta could feel the pain she was attacked again. She staggered sideways, determined not to fall. The enemy closed around her. She lunged toward one of the savages only to see him dance away, mocking the spectacle of an old woman trying to fight. Her anger was as hot as the blood flowing from her shoulder. Swords and spears and shouting; a stone club to the side of the head. Daylight became gray light, fading . . .

Scotta had thought she heard Amergin calling to her. She thought she heard the music of Clarsah. The besieged woman tried to shake off her attackers and go to her favorite son. The Gael always followed the harp.

A savage wrapped in otter skins tore her head from her shoulders with a bronze blade.

Amergin's shout of horror rang through the pines.

When the painted savages saw a man holding a harp in numb fingers, they stepped aside for him.

Ír killed the person who had killed Scotta. But it was too late. His mother's head lay on the ground in a spreading lake of blood, with her blue eyes open. When Ír crouched down to close them, he lost what was left of his mind.

The other sons of the Míl were beyond shock. Beyond pain and grief and even rage. While they stood beside Scotta's dead body, every man made a silent vow in his heart.

When they looked up, the Ivernians had melted away. It was a victory, of sorts.

At Donn's direction they buried Scotta where she fell, an honor accorded to warriors killed in battle. Her other sons thought she should be carried back to the rest of the tribe, but in the end Donn was given his way. He was the oldest.

On the following day, a tomb of stones and sod was raised over Scotta. Colptha conducted the funeral rites. This displeased Éber Finn, who complained to his charioteer. "Colptha talks as if our mother was a sacrifice to the land. That's not the way it was."

Scotta was interred with all the property she had brought with her, which made Éremón unhappy. He wanted to keep her velvet cloak and the best of her jewelery to give to Taya, to make up for the unexpected inconvenience of having his first wife along. But the others were watching and he did not dare.

Ír alternately blubbered like a baby and tried to demonstrate how he slew Scotta's murderer. He almost injured several of the mourners before Amergin succeeded in taking his sword away from him.

At the end of the ceremony, the bard sang a eulogy for his mother. Then he removed a glittering brass wire from his harp and laid it atop the tomb.

In spite of his grief, one recurrent thought kept coming back to Amergin: the painted, tattooed natives had recognized a bard and stood aside for him.

Only Celtic tribes did that.

৯৯

After Scotta's burial there was no stopping her sons. As soon as a fort was ready to protect the noncombatants, the Mílesians declared war on all the inhabitants of Ierne, on any and every one. Day after day, season after season.

No mercy.

৯৯

My mother would be fatally wounded on the Day of Catastrophe, near the end of the Great War. "Catastrophe" is another word for change.

My sister, Drithla, was born that same day. "Drithla" is another word for sparkle.

❧ TEN ❧

As the war with the invaders continued, the Danann elders and the children too young to fight were sent into hiding. There was no longer any pretence of normalcy. Our land had become a dangerous place for young and old alike, and survival was imperative.

My parents asked the Dagda and his wife to take me and five small cousins to sanctuary. I resented being classed with the little ones and insisted my place was with the adults. Yet I knew I was not quite one or the other.

In the presence of the Dagda I still felt like a child.

Fortunately for us, his wife, Melitt, whose name was the word for honey in the old language, had talents aside from the baking of fruit bread. When it was raining, she anticipated sunshine; in darkseason, she prepared for the light. No matter how bad things were, she could summon a mouthful of chuckles. She was exactly the right person to accompany us.

By now a presentiment of what was to come was darkening the horizon. We needed someone cheerful to blow the clouds away.

I did not yet realize they would never blow away.

Our nearest clanfolk brought their children to our house before sundown: my cousins Rimba, Sinnadar, Demirci, Trialet, and Piriome—three small boys and two little girls. There was not much sleeping that night. The whispering went on and on until Mongan told the children, rather irritably, to be quiet. Before dawn we were given packs containing food and blankets and filled water skins to tie around our waists. When the Dagda and his wife arrived, they were carrying supplies too. Among the four adults there was a brief but determinedly cheerful conversation; then we were hugged good-bye as if it were an ordinary day.

But we knew; even the smallest of us knew. Not the face of the thing that hovered over us but its dark shadow, its malign intent.

Our journey from the river valley began with the sunrise. As we set out, the Dagda told us about our destination, but my imagination kept galloping off in other directions. Thinking about Mongan and Lerys; what would they do today?

How soon would they come to bring me home again?

The Dagda said we were going to a place he knew well, which had been constructed long ago. That was the point at which I stopped listening. "Long ago" was as meaningless to me as Before the Before. I couldn't imagine a time without me in it. As far as I was concerned, my vividly alive self had sprung into being full-blown and brought the world with it. How could there have been anything before that?

When the Dagda realized he had lost his audience, he fell

silent, except for an occasional remark to his wife. We walked. We drank from a clear spring, ate a few mouthfuls of food from the packs on our backs, and walked again. My cousins chattered among themselves, but I was occupied with my own thoughts.

By observing the position of the sun, I realized we were not traveling in a straight line but in a very large circle. Two, three, then more, alternating with long zigzags. When I remarked on this to the Dagda, he said, "Well done, Joss. You are correct; we are not going a great distance but leaving a long trail that will be impossible to follow."

The pack on my back grew heavier as the day progressed. My feet were heavier too, and harder to lift. I began to regret that I had slept so little the night before. The second time I stumbled the Dagda picked me up and sat me on his shoulders with my long legs dangling down.

I was astonished that such an old person could lift me, much less carry me. Yet when we wearied he carried each of us in turn. His shoulders were broad and more sinewy than they looked, and his snowy hair smelled of wood smoke.

He was a man.

And I was not.

Yet.

Shortly after sunset we came to a wide river. Swift-flowing brown water, hissing, hurrying water. The Dagda was eager too, picking up the pace. We struggled to keep up as he led us along a reed-lined riverbank. Where the rushing water was diverted by a ridge, he turned his back on the river and began climbing. By this time I was so tired I did not think I could follow him, but I did; we all did. Melitt came at the end of our little procession, shooing us through the gathering twilight like a mother bird with her chicks.

At the top of the ridge the Dagda took some flints from

his pack and struck them together, making sparks to ignite the torches. Their sudden flare drove the darkness back. Melitt held both torches high while the Dagda edged past a large boulder, then placed his hands on a heavy stone door and slid it aside as if it weighed nothing.

He came back to take a torch from his wife. "Follow me, all of you," he commanded. We did—and were swallowed by the earth.

୧୫

After several anxious heartbeats, I realized we had entered a cavern. Or perhaps a tunnel. The sweet smell of the soil was hauntingly combined with the dry scent of stone dust.

Ancient stone dust.

How could I know that?

Following the Dagda, and with Melitt bringing up the rear, we walked single file along a narrow passageway between upright boulders taller than a man. The passage had been constructed with a gentle upward incline and a slight angle at midpoint. At the end of the passageway we came to a circular chamber built of more massive stones. When we entered, we were enfolded in a muffled silence.

The hair lifted on my arms.

The Dagda and his wife wedged their torches into niches in the stones, filling the chamber with a warm, honey-colored light. "Now," Melitt told us, "you can rest. We will be safe here."

At those words my bones failed to support me any longer. I sat down abruptly on the floor of the chamber.

Melitt collected all the packs and emptied out the contents. She handed out blankets to make beds while her husband poured a small measure of honey wine for each of the children.

And for me. Who was glad to be counted as a child.

A small part of me wanted to stay awake and ask questions, but most of me had other ideas. After a few sips of wine, I fell fast asleep. A dizzying slide down into darkness.

When I awoke, the torches were still burning. Their dark smoke hung on air that was just as warm—or as cool—as it had been when I went to sleep. It might have been midday or midnight; both were the same in the womb of the earth.

When we had finished yawning and rubbing our eyes, the Dagda led us back down the passageway to relieve ourselves, but he would not let us go all the way outside. "It would be dangerous now," he said.

Adults often made remarks like that to keep children from doing what they wanted to do, but in this unfamiliar place, at this worrying time, we were willing to accept his warning.

After we devoured a meal of bread and soft cheese, the Dagda took up the explanation he had abandoned the day before. We sat around him in a little circle, listening obediently. "We are inside an immense earthen mound on top of a ridge above the river," he said. "The mound is not a natural formation but was constructed long ago by layering turves and stones."

"Long ago" was taking on new meaning for me. "Ancient time!" I blurted out. "That's what I smelled last night when we came in. Ancient time."

"You are perceptive," observed the Dagda. "I suppose that is how it appears to you."

"But . . ." Something teased at the edge of my mind. "But you said time is an illusion with a purpose."

He nodded.

"Then how do you explain . . ."

"There are things you must learn for yourself," the Dagda said. "The most important lessons are always learned alone."

I was more baffled than before.

Next the Dagda called our attention to the huge stones that formed the walls of the chamber. They had been painstakingly fitted together with pebbles forced into every gap. "What you see is no accident; this is the work of highly skilled craftsmen. Look at this." He raised a torch while we tilted our heads back and gazed up. Up and up, into dancing shadows and quiet mystery.

"The vault of stone above our heads is over four spear lengths from the floor," said the Dagda. "The huge capstone at the top seals the dome so the interior of the mound remains perfectly dry, even when rain is plummeting down outside. A network of stone channels carries the water away."

My cousin Rimba, a sturdy little boy with an outthrust jaw, asserted, "You're making that up."

The Dagda's smile was almost lost in the forest of his beard. "I assure you it is true. On rainy days I used to come here to listen to the water gurgling in the walls. The builders cut drainage channels into the tops of the roof stones and sealed any gaps with sand and burnt soil, so the chambers and passageway would stay absolutely dry. It seemed magical to me when I was a boy, and it still does—not the concept of drainage, which I understand, but the breadth of mind that envisioned this structure.

"I grew up here, you see. Here and around here, in the valley of the cow goddess. When I was a boy my parents tilled the rich soil along the banks of the river. In one season we could grow more than enough to feed ourselves and our animals for the next three, so we had ample time to lie on our backs and gaze at the stars."

"I do that too!" I burst out.

"Do you really? What do you think they are, Joss? Better still, what do you want them to be?"

I caught my bottom lip between my teeth and wished I had kept my mouth shut.

Unperturbed, the Dagda went on. "Among the stars we found constellations like tribes and felt kinship with them. The wonders in the sky had inspired the building of temples and . . ."

My voice cut across his again. "What is a temple?"

The Dagda blinked; came back to us. My interruption had summoned him from a distant place.

"Temples and their purposes are a subject for another discussion, Joss," he said sharply. "There are two others nearby that you will visit someday, but this one is the most important. I explored it when I was no older than you; I even cut into the earth far enough to learn the secret of the channels. Only later did I realize I had committed a desecration. It is unfortunate that you are so young; you may never live to benefit from . . ."

"Hush, husband," said Melitt. "Do not frighten them; *teach* them."

"What was I saying? Ah, yes. This temple is the work of people who practiced powerful magic. Their control of the sun is still demonstrated in this very chamber."

"Control of the sun!" exclaimed my cousin Sinnadar, he of the pointed ears. He was deeply impressed. So was I, but I was reluctant to interrupt the Dagda again.

"If we stay here for much longer—and I hope we will not have to—you can observe this for yourselves," the old man said. "It is only one of the secrets of this temple. The mound that covers us is very large, yet the chambers within it are small. They and the passageway were built first. Then the mound was raised over them. A score of fully grown adults—do you remember how many that would be, Joss?—would overflow the central chamber."

I lowered my eyes in embarrassment. As the Dagda knew full well, I had made no effort to learn about numbers.

He continued. "Three small chambers, mere recesses, open onto this one. Each is furnished with a stone basin; the largest has two. Now"—he moved the torch again—"look closely at the ceilings and walls of the recesses. They are carved with symbols from the language of the builders. The room with two basins is the most elaborate. More carvings can be seen in the central chamber and on the standing stones in the passageway. Amuse yourselves by looking for them, but you will not understand what you find. They take a lifetime to read."

He sat back and allowed us to explore for ourselves. His wife busied herself with the tasks women always find to do. Melitt had not given us any of her fruit bread yet, but I had faith that some was in her pack.

Our sanctuary was indeed a place of wonder. But as the Dagda told us, its secrets were not ours to discover.

We examined the mysterious carvings and made fanciful guesses about their meanings. I was the first to notice a figure by itself just inside the recess at the rear of the main chamber. Three rounded shapes flowed together into a single design. In the flickering torchlight it might have been a pattern of stars.

I returned to it again and again. Tracing the fluid curves with my fingers and my eyes.

"Does the triple spiral speak to you, Joss?" asked the Dagda, stepping up behind me. It was an interesting choice of words.

Was that another adult thought?

I turned to face him. "You mentioned the people who built this. Were they like us?"

For some reason my question amused him. "Life comes in many forms, Joss. The invaders from the south are not quite like you and me, and the same is true of the Fír Bolga and the Iverni and many other tribes. Tall or short, dark or fair, clever or primitive, they are branches from one tree, though each is different."

"And the temple builders—were they another branch?"

The Dagda pretended not to hear me. Instead, he said, "There is another triple spiral carved on the great stone that shields the entrance. You may not have noticed it in the dark last night, although it partially blocks the passage. The triple spiral in here and the one on the Guardian Stone are the only examples of their kind on Ierne. Do you suppose they are symbols from a language that existed Before the Before?"

He knew the answer before he asked me the question. He always did.

That morning, that evening, whichever it was, the Dagda presented me with a riddle I resolved to solve if it took a lifetime to do it.

A more immediate problem was that of keeping five active children occupied while we remained inside the mound.

Five children. Not six. Five children and me.

Without being asked to, I undertook to entertain the little ones. I suggested they pretend the stone basins were boats and imagine fishing from them or going on a voyage. The game was fun for a while, but the strongest imagination could not overcome awareness of the stone walls that surrounded us. Or make me forget that word the Dagda had used: "desecration."

I kept saying "be careful with that" until my small charges rebelled.

Piriome demanded to know when we were going home. The little girl repeated the question again and again in her high, silvery voice, until her male cousins exchanged superior glances. Boys do not whine, their expressions said.

When they grew more tired and bored, even the largest whined.

We ate, we slept, another day dragged past and then another night. At least I think it was night. Then another day. Melitt and the Dagda discussed practical matters—such as how long the food would last. Once or twice I saw her reach out and press her hand on one of his. A tender gesture that touched me, although it was not about me.

Nothing here was about me. In the shadows beyond the torchlight lurked the unguessable.

Of my own volition I restricted my meals to only half of what I had eaten in the beginning. I was aware that our food stores were running out.

The stones began to press in on us. The walls around us drew closer, with all the weight of the earth behind them. The dome above us sank lower. "It drops down in the night when we're asleep," fearful little Piriome confided to me.

The air became chokingly thick with torch smoke. The stench from the passageway where we relieved ourselves was dreadful. When the Dagda went to try to clean it up, I followed him. "What do you think you're doing, Joss?"

"I want to help you."

"This is no task for a child."

"I'm not a child," I insisted. Without waiting for him to offer, I took some of the bundled sticks and dead leaves he carried. We crouched side by side, scrubbing away the filth and parceling out a little of our water for rinsing. It was an unpleasant task. To distract myself, I said, "Can you tell me any more about the people who built this?"

For once the Dagda gave me a straight answer, but it was not enlightening. "Only the stones survive," he said. He dropped his few remaining sticks and straightened up to massage the small of his back. "Now—shall we see if my wife has any fruit bread left?"

As I followed him up the passageway, my attention was caught by a sound from outside. A distant roar, like the voice of an angry sea. I caught hold of the Dagda's elbow. "Do you hear that?"

He turned to face me. Cocked his head for a moment. "The question is, Do you hear something, Joss?"

"Of course I do. It's . . ." I struggled for words. "It's coming from far away and it's terrible, like hundreds of voices all screaming at once. What is it?"

He did not answer. But his shoulders slumped as if receiving a blow.

When we entered the chamber, I could still hear the roaring, even through the embrace of the earth. No one else appeared to hear anything unusual. Neither the Dagda nor I mentioned it again. Gradually the sound faded away.

That night everyone was restless. To lull the little ones to sleep, Melitt sang the songs of a gentler time. Listening to them, I tried to hear my mother's voice.

The Dagda made several trips down the passageway and returned without saying anything. At last, he lay down and took his wife in his arms. I presume they slept.

A cry of alarm roused me from a troubled sleep. I pulled my blanket around me and ran into the passage. In the dark I collided with one of the standing stones and bumped my forehead very hard but felt no pain until days later.

The entrance to the passageway was shielded by the boulder the Dagda had referred to as the Guardian Stone. For all its size and bulk, it was not sufficient to protect my bare legs from a chill wind blowing up from the river.

I stepped outside with no idea what to expect.

The stars were dimming with the promise of dawn. The Dagda was holding a torch aloft. By its light I saw my father coming up the slope toward us, carrying a large bundle in his arms. Mongan staggered as he walked; his unsteady feet slipped on the grass. The old man hurried to help him, but Mongan warned him away. "Mine," said my father in a shredded voice. At first I thought he was carrying a bundle of robes with the sleeves hanging down. Then I saw her white hands. And a familiar bracelet on one slim wrist. The middle of the bundle was soaked with blood.

Mongan stopped in front of me, breathing like an ox that had been ploughing stony ground. His reddened eyes burned into mine. With a trembling hand, he uncovered her face long enough for me to see it. "Remember," he commanded.

The word sank into my flesh and crystallized in my bones like an early frost.

❂ ELEVEN ❃

"ONLY THE STONES SURVIVE" was one of the many sayings the Túatha Dé Danann passed on to their children. The words hid a deeper truth. Staring down at my mother's dead face that morning, I learned the world was not what I had thought it was. And survival was conditional.

"Remember," Mongan reiterated.

And I did.

At his command, my spirit opened like the petals of a flower. Half-naked and trembling with emotion, I began to absorb. No effort was required; I could not have stopped myself. Every detail of my surroundings burned itself irrevocably into my mind.

The lake of the sky was fading from bottomless blue to icy rose, the herald of approaching winter. From where I stood, the breast of the hill hid the river from me, but I could hear the song of dark water. I could smell the mud in which the reeds grew. Brittle reeds chattered in a rising wind.

My skin reported the advance spears of icy rain striking my cheek.

We would have an early frost.

Behind me—the back of my neck was aware of its size and weight—rose another hill, smaller and steeper: the mound built by those who were here Before the Before. I turned around to look at it. And caught my breath.

The front of the mound was covered with white quartz pebbles that reflected points of fire from the Dagda's torch. Seen from below by travelers in boats on the river, the structure would have glimmered like the moon.

Temple.

Carrying my mother in his arms, Mongan edged around the Guardian Stone and entered the passageway. I followed at his heels. The Dagda and his torch were close behind me. By its wavering light I saw my father gather his dead wife closer, trying to keep her dangling feet from being bruised by the stones lining the passage.

To this day my legs recall the slight angle of the slope. My nose can recapture the scent of sweet earth and stone dust. My ears still hear the hiss and crackle of the torch and the first gurgle of rainwater in the drainage channels buried in the walls.

I remember.

Where the passageway took a slight bend, Mongan paused. I almost bumped into him; I do not think he was aware of me. He carefully adjusted the weight he was carrying before we entered the main chamber.

Melitt gave a little moan when she saw him with his burden. The old woman's body folded in upon itself, assuming the shape of grief.

Mongan carried Lerys to the recess at the back of the central chamber and laid her down, oh so gently, in the stone basin. Then he briefly fumbled amid her bloody clothing.

He lifted up a tiny pink creature.

Before coming to us my father had delivered his daughter himself, cutting her free from the dying womb of his wife. I can only imagine the pain it had cost him to rescue their child.

My first glimpse of my sister was as baffling as anything else that happened that night. Mistaking her for a small animal that had gnawed my mother's breast, I darted forward to punish her with my fists.

With the next heartbeat I saw her clearly. As clearly as I shall always see her in my mind. A wizened, bowlegged scrap of a thing with blood drying on her skin; the long head and large eyes and a wisp of pale hair atop her skull; the miniature fingers opening and closing on the air. The unformed features already resembling my mother's.

"Remember," my father said a third time.

From that moment and forever, I could not forget. My dead mother's face and my living sister's tiny fists and the capstone above us and the mass of earth and stone containing us. One of my cousins beginning to sob. A tiny spider weaving its web to bridge the space between two rocks. The blood ringing in my ears and my mother's blood drying on her daughter. I shall carry those memories to my grave.

Yet time passes, and passes. And still I live.

Before you ask, I do not know how old I am. My people had such long lives they did not bother to measure them. They lived as long as they wanted and then moved on.

Except for me.

❧

My cousins and I were herded into a different recess, and Melitt tried to arrange a blanket across the opening. "The youngsters do not need to see this," she said over her shoulder.

"No," the Dagda agreed.

I protested. "But she's my mother!"

In a voice I hardly recognized, Mongan said, "Come to me then, Joss."

Melitt raised the edge of the blanket, and I went out.

My father stood beside my mother's body, gazing down at her. His back was rigid with the effort to control himself. When I joined him, he turned to me and rested his hand on my shoulder. Only a few days before, he would have put his hand atop my head.

My eyes were now on a level with his chin.

For the first time I *saw* Mongan of the Túatha Dé Danann, really saw him rather than just recognizing him as my father. I had never seen any of them in that way before; they were simply the furniture of my life.

When I was a child.

Mongan had silver-gilt hair and large gray eyes that sloped downward at the outer edge. The planes of his face were finely modeled, with a noble brow and tapering chin. His ears were only slightly pointed and fitted close against his skull.

Until I saw the invaders up close, I would not appreciate how slender my father was. We all were. By comparison with the sturdily built foreigners, the Children of Light looked as ephemeral as frost and fire. A puff of wind might blow any of us away.

Looks can be deceiving.

I watched my new sister being cleaned and wrapped in a blanket and saw the beginning of the process by which Melitt and Mongan tended my mother. The Dagda stood off to one side, his lips moving silently. I was reminded of the distant roaring I heard the evening before. The roaring that was over now.

Sound without words; words without sound.

Mongan and Melitt gently removed my mother's bloody clothing and bathed her ruined body with our drinking water. The final steps of preparing her were too intimate to see. Melitt asked her husband to take the rest of us outside.

The thin cry of the baby followed us as far as the Guardian Stone.

The fresh, cold air was welcome after the noisome atmosphere in the chamber. I drew a deep breath and filled my chest all the way to the bottom. The rain had passed; the rising sun was celebrated by myriads of songbirds. Placid sheep were grazing on the hillside.

Children with little experience of life are unprepared for the event of a death. My cousin Demirci suddenly burst into tears. His younger brother Trialet gave a nervous giggle, and little Piriome caught my hand and pressed anxiously against my side. As for me, I just stood there. Letting the day fill me up.

⁂

I had once asked the Dagda, "What was I before I was born?"

"You were you. A rather different version, but you."

"What will I be after I die?"

"You can still be you," the old man replied reassuringly. "A different version, but you. Minds forget, but spirit remembers."

⁂

Without Lerys, there was no milk to feed Drithla. Fortunately, Melitt could do more than bake bread. She carefully selected various items of food and chewed them to a soft paste that she blended with water, then fed to the baby on the tip of her finger. Drithla tasted it, suckled at the proffered finger as if it were a nipple, then refused the remainder by spluttering and crying. Melitt altered the mixture slightly and tried again. And again. A drop of honey; the squeezing from a berry. Try again.

The baby consumed enough to stay alive. Then all at once she began eating with enthusiasm. Soon she was thriving on her diet; the spark of life in my little sister was very strong. Life has a way of enduring.

So does death. The opposite ends of the same experience, the Dagda said.

My mother's death introduced me to the uncertain border-land that lies between the dead and the living. Mongan insisted that Lerys was always near him, close enough to summon if he chose. She might be singing songs beside the lake, he said, or dancing in a beam of sunlight in the meadow.

I wanted to believe him; I did believe him. The expression on his face assured me she was visible to him. He cocked his head as if listening to her voice. My eyes could not see her and my ears could not hear her, but that was my fault and not hers. Lerys was *there*; a permanent yet intangible presence.

Faith was my father's greatest gift to me.

Mongan na Manannan Mac Lir was a prince of the highest rank. Nobility confers obligation. Mongan's share of the fighting was over, but the real struggle had only begun.

As his son and heir, most of it would fall to me.

The New People gave us no time to mourn.

While the blood was still drying on the battlefield where my mother died, they began sending out warriors to locate the remainder of the Túatha Dé Danann. It would be a mistake to leave any members of such a troublesome race alive.

❧

Cynos, son of Greine and the great queen Eriu, summoned an urgent meeting of what remained of the Danann army, to be joined by the surviving elders. Not at the Gathering Place, which now was behind enemy lines, but in a glade hidden deep in the woods. Cynos was the ranking warrior of his generation, the courageous men and women who had borne the brunt of the war so far and been almost destroyed. A brilliant crop full of promise for the future, brutally harvested by blades of cold iron.

Cynos himself had been badly injured. There were not enough of the tribe left to perform the healing ritual, but some of the wounded would survive anyway. Until they died, they would bear, on their beautiful, perfect bodies, the battle scars, like constellations of cruel stars.

Cynos was carried to the glade in the woods on a litter.

My father took me with him. He walked to the meeting on his own feet but kept one hand firmly on my shoulder. Only he and I knew how much he needed my support.

The Dagda was accorded the place of honor as chief elder. Melitt sat next to him with little Drithla in her arms. The sadness in the old woman's eyes was mirrored in my father's, and surely in mine too.

Cynos was barely able to talk. He only managed to gasp, "We have to plan our next step," before doubling up with a violent fit of coughing. A second try was no better. At last he gestured to Mongan, as the next in rank, to conduct the meeting. My father began with a tight-lipped speech of welcome while Cynos lay crumpled beside him like a pile of discarded blankets.

When it was the turn of those in attendance to speak if they wished, Dos, whose throat was swathed in cobwebs held in place with linen, croaked like a frog. But at least we could hear him. "We made a grave error by demonstrating any of our powers," said the Prince of the Lakes. "The invaders will enslave us in order to gain control of . . ."

Dos was interrupted by Torrian, the youngest of the surviving princes. There were only five of them, counting my father. One of Torrian's ears was torn, and a jagged wound on his forehead was seeping fluid. The heat of battle was still in him, though; I sensed it quivering in the air. One of his grandfather's grandfathers had been Nuada of the Silver Hand. "On the contrary, Dos," he said. "We should have hit them with everything we had."

"Everything but the Earthkillers," amended the daughter of Fodla the Wise.

"*Especially* the Earthkillers!" cried the younger brother of Samoll the spear carrier. "We should have used them on the foreigners as soon as they set foot on our shores!"

One of the elders was shocked. "Remember what Eriu said? We cannot employ horrors without becoming horrible too."

Like a river that burst its banks, unvoiced mutterings poured into my defenseless head. The sudden pain left me reeling. When I looked around for help, I saw the Dagda watching me with a quizzical expression.

Can you hear me, Joss? No, do not try to answer yet. Let your gift grow until it is stronger.

"I don't want it!" I cried.

You have no choice. You must have inherited the gift from your mother; it only comes to a few of us. And never before to a child.

I looked away from him and closed my eyes as tight as I could, willing myself to shut everything out.

The argument continued on two levels, and I was the unwilling recipient of both. If the full complement of the tribe had been alive and present, their silent voices would have destroyed my mind.

Never to a child, the Dagda had said.

"We could survive here for the darkseason," one of the elders suggested. I could barely hear him through the cacophony in my head, but I struggled to concentrate. "Maybe the invaders won't come this far. If they do, perhaps we can avoid them for a while as we did before. Then by leaf-spring, we can . . ."

In a voice clotted with pain, a woman grimly predicted, "By leaf-spring we'll all be in chains."

"We came here by sea," said someone else. "We could build boats and . . ."

"And go where? Back to the last place we came from? By now another race will have been there for generations. It was good land, and they won't give it up; why should they? They would rightly see us as invaders."

"Persuade them that we come in peace!" exclaimed Melitt. Warm, soft, old Melitt who never raised her voice.

Torrian scoffed. "Would that make any difference to long-settled people who must consider themselves natives by now? I seriously doubt it. We would have to fight them, and what weapons would we use? Should we dig up the Earth-killers and try to carry them back across the sea? They would probably disintegrate on the voyage. We would arrive with only our battered bronze and have to face iron again, I suspect. I can tell you how that would turn out."

"More and more war," rasped Dos. "Killing and more killing. No end to it. No end at all." With a groan like a death cry, he pulled his cloak over his head.

The Dananns turned toward my father then, seeking answers. Mongan looked old. Older than the Dagda, older than the hills. "As a people, we outgrew our enthusiasm for killing long ago," he said wearily. "We brought upon ourselves the original catastrophe that left us homeless. Before the Before our ancestors thought they finally had found a new home here. This island fit us like our own skin. If we leave it, we may be homeless forever. If we stay, we will be slaughtered or enslaved; probably both. There are no other choices."

"Use the Earthkillers!" someone screamed.

Another shouted, "Let's die fighting!"

The noise in my head was building again. I clapped my hands over my ears, but it did no good, no good at all.

The group divided into factions. One segment argued for rearming and making one more effort to expel the invaders, even if it meant using the Earthkillers. Another said we should leave the island altogether and take our chances on the open sea. A few thought it might be better to surrender and plead for mercy, but they were shouted down: "We are a free people! We must always be a free people!"

The Dagda caught and held my eyes. *This is not the best place for you, Joss. Go to the temple, where you can think clearly.*

I stared at him.

Go now, he commanded. *Seek the silence and what you may discover. Stay there and do not return until I summon you.*

Before the buzzing in my head completely overwhelmed me, I stood up and slipped away. To the timeless silence of the temple on the ridge.

Where the Guardian Stone was waiting.

❧ TWELVE ❧

AMERGIN HAD LONG PONDERED the mystery of the tattooed savages who had stood aside for a bard. They must be Celtic people, he concluded. Not unlike us in spite of their garish appearance. But how did they come to be here? And for how many generations have they occupied Ierne?

Should we slaughter our own?

There were other mysteries on his mind as well. Time was one. Ever since the fleet was lost in the fog, he had been aware that time was different in this place. The duration of day and night were undefined, and their passage uncertain. How long had the Mílesians been here? Sometimes it seemed as if they had marched across the island already and won a score of battles; the memory of them resonated at the edges of his mind. On other days, everything looked new, seen for the first time, and the future was still ahead.

Was it possible that the past and the future were interchangeable on Ierne? Was he remembering the future? Did he have yet to experience the past?

Could either of them be changed?

When Amergin mentioned this curious notion to the tribe's diviner, the druid Corisios, the other man confirmed his impression. "I've been trying to read the omens and portents ever since we got here," he told Amergin, "but every time I throw the bones or examine the droppings of birds, the answers come up different."

"Doesn't that worry you?"

"I don't know what to think," the diviner admitted. "I've reported my findings to Donn and Éremón, and they don't seem too concerned. Éber Finn even laughed. 'It will sort itself out when we get used to the place,' he assured me. But then, Éber's no druid."

"How about Colptha?"

"Ah." Corisios tugged at his lower lip. "He offers his sacrifices and comes to his conclusions, but he doesn't share them with me."

The diviner's revelation worried Amergin. Until they came to Ierne, the druids had worked in unison as representatives of the spirit world. If Colptha was using it as an opportunity to satisfy a selfish need of his own, there could be serious repercussions.

The spirits were always watching.

When the weather was dry, Amergin took Clarsah from her case and cradled her against his chest so she could observe the land through which they passed. The harp was a being of remarkable sensitivity, deeply affected by the kiss of the wind and the caress of the light. In spite of her mysteries—or perhaps because of them—Ierne's beauty was inspiring.

Amergin was not so arrogant as to believe Clarsah's music sprang from him.

The Mílesians and their followers might appear to be a co-hesive army, but in reality they were riven by dissension. In the vacuum left by Donn's emotional withdrawal, Éremón and Éber Finn increasingly contested for the leadership. At first their rivalry had been limited to making sarcastic remarks about each other, but it had degenerated into criti-cism severe enough to drive a wedge between their respective admirers. Heroes always had admirers.

Colptha observed with keen interest the heated argu-ments between his brothers. The sacrificer overheard many things not intended for him; he had a habit of insinuating himself into the surroundings without drawing attention.

Their most recent encampment was on the edge of an ex-tensive bogland. The chief advantage of the bog was that it provided an unobstructed view in all directions; the chief disadvantage was that it might swallow any person reckless enough to venture across it. In many areas the surface looked deceptively stable. Luring unwitting sacrifices.

Colptha liked bog. There was none in the homeland of the Mílesians, but from the first he had appreciated its qual-ities. Bog was indomitable. Bogs in low-lying areas overcame oak, pine, yew, and hazel to create a rich mix of slowly rotting vegetation that supported a stunning variety of life. Moun-tain bogs clothed hills and even mountaintops, waging war on the ubiquitous heather and often moving of their own volition.

Armies of bog. Bog that kept its secrets.

Colptha liked bog.

He had been gathering bog moss and deer's-hair grass for a druidical concoction when he observed Éremón and Éber Finn mired in a furious quarrel. Fists were shaken, spittle flew. The sacrificer drifted in a wide arc that took him downwind until he could hear their every word clearly.

When they finally noticed him, Éremón gave a start. This made Colptha smile his fanged smile. "Ierne is in the grip of a strange sorcery," he informed his brothers with unshakeable certainty. "I've been aware of it ever since we were lost in that evil mist before we landed. The light shifts continually; the patterns of the clouds are abnormal; the wind comes from every direction and none. Nothing here is *natural* or *ordinary*. Had you not noticed?"

Both men shook their heads. Their response elicited another fanged smile from the sacrificer. "Of course you hadn't; such things are beyond the understanding of warriors. That's why you will need the help of a great sorcerer if you are going to conquer Ierne. If *one* of you is going to conquer," he added almost under his breath. Just loud enough for them both to hear. Just loud enough to sow a seed.

Éremón said, "I suppose you refer to yourself, Colptha. Are you offering to be on my side, or Éber's?"

"Now wait here . . ." Éber Finn began, but the sacrificer interrupted.

"I'm offering to give you both the benefit of my talents," Colptha blandly replied. "Let me call your attention to the proliferation of stone structures in this land; cairns, tombs, call them what you will. The natives don't live in them; their huts are made of more perishable material. Sticks and leaves and suchlike. Druids' intuition tells me that a more powerful race once inhabited this land. Their magic lingers here, but I can fight it for you."

"We can do our own fighting," Éremón said through tight lips. "We are warriors."

"And Amergin is a gifted druid," added Éber Finn, "so if we require one we have him."

Colptha was well aware that his brothers did not like him. None of the Mílesians liked him, which was as it should be. Respect, he believed, was engendered by fear and not fondness. "Amergin spends his days fingering a harp and staring off into space. You need a more substantial ally."

"I need an armorer who can put a better edge on my sword," growled Éremón.

❧

Like a tidal wave, the invading army was sweeping across the hills, through the forests and along the watercourses, searching for any of the Túatha Dé Danann who might have eluded them so far and intent on killing every person they met.

The battle trumpets screamed for slaughter, and the Gaels obeyed.

It was easiest to swing the sword and thrust the spear and think about nothing else at all. Let the red rage bubble through you and think about nothing else at all. Keep going until you were so exhausted you fell asleep on your feet; eat what was put in front of you; collapse into a roiling cauldron of senseless images and monstrous noise; awake and start over.

If you were lucky, you got killed before you had to think about any of it.

Some warriors had other reactions. Donn was almost indifferent to warfare, although he acquitted himself well enough in battle. He had been trained for it since childhood. He could fight with one part of his mind while another part swore at the gravel in his boot or tried to remember a phrase from one of the bard's songs.

Sakkar's childhood had prepared him for a different sort of struggle, giving him the cunning of a rat in an alley. The Gaelic combination of manic bravado and agile artistry baffled him. Besides, he could not help thinking about the woman with gray eyes.

Sakkar had yet to blood his sword. He knew he could never strike Her.

≈❧

Armed with belligerence and bronze, the warriors of the Fír Bolga ambushed the Gaels whenever the foreigners came close enough. In retaliation, Éremón attacked a Fír Bolga settlement while they were asleep, which was not considered honorable. The suggestion came from Colptha. Startled awake, the natives fought with tooth and toenail but were overcome. To crown his triumph, Éremón took the elderly chief of the Fír Bolga as his prisoner. Colptha wanted him for a sacrifice to ensure future successes, but Éremón refused, claiming he was going to keep the old man as a pet.

During the night someone had cut the chieftain's ropes and let him go.

Éremón accused his brother. Éber Finn angrily denied it. The split between the two of them was widening.

When Amergin urged Éremón to a reconciliation, he was told, "Éber's jealous of my authority. He's always trying to get back at me, one way or another."

"Are you sure he was to blame? I've never known Éber to be petty."

"Then you don't know him at all," Éremón retorted. "He's been that way for years. Colptha can tell you."

It was Colptha who had freed the Fír Bolga chieftain; Colptha who had planted suspicion of Éber Finn in Éremón's head. Power for its own sake was a highly addictive drug, and the campaign in Ierne was providing the sacrificer with a number of opportunities to feed his addiction.

❧

On a morning of rainbows and uncertain weather, the army of conquest approached a rolling meadow below a hill draped with clouds. The mist obscured the top of the hill, but the warriors following the chariots were not curious. Scenery was just scenery. A few men were dreaming of their next meal. The rest were watching the back of the person in front of them and trying not to tread on his heels.

Amergin and Clarsah stopped to observe a rainbow. They saw at least one rainbow every day on Ierne, and the bard was captivated every time. When the last band of color faded from view, he wiped the harp with a square of white silk before tucking her into her case. The air was damp, and Clarsah needed protection.

Yet Amergin's mind was elsewhere, distracted by the strange thoughts of a druid. Rainbows. A promise of beauty too lovely to last. On Ierne, the dreams of his childhood and the desires of his manhood were assuming fresh vitality. The blood was pounding more hotly in his veins. Why? Could rainbows be captured here? Were the tales about everlasting life true?

He felt more at home on Ierne than he ever did in the land where he was born. Was it because his mother was entombed here now? Was he feeling the influence of her spirit, perhaps?

He was about to sling the harp case over his shoulder and trot after the others when he was engulfed by an overwhelming sense of Scotta's presence.

Here. Now.

"Mother," he whispered, closing his eyes.

Light ran through him like blood.

When he opened his eyes again, he was not alone.

❧ THIRTEEN ❧

THE GUARDIAN STONE had been waiting for me in front
of the temple.

A long oval in shape, the rough gray boulder lay on its
side. Both ends were rounded; the surface facing outward
was covered with bold carvings. A deeply incised vertical
line ran partway down the middle of the design. To one side
of the line was an immense triple spiral, twin to the smaller
one in the temple.

The figure held my gaze. Demanding that I come closer.
Look and see.

The flowing curves of the three connected spirals em-
bodied the essence of motion. Movement forever captured,
never stilled. Like rivers flowing beneath ice. Like stars in
their ceaseless courses.

A shock of recognition took my breath away.

I had no name for what they represented, but those spirals were part of me. I was part of them. If I watched for one
heartbeat longer, they might begin to swirl, draw me into
themselves, into their center, into . . .

My entire body tingled painfully, the way your foot does when it goes to sleep. The scene around me grew blurry; the air had the metallic scent common before a storm.

I could not move. Yet I felt more incredibly alive than I ever had.

Time was not.

But I was.

Always had been. Always would be.

Here. Now.

Unable to do anything else, I stared at the stone until the tingling faded.

It seemed to take an immeasurable time.

At last my vision widened to include the gleaming bulk of the temple, the grassy slope down toward the river. The earth solid beneath my feet and white clouds scudding overhead. Nothing had changed.

Yet I had changed.

Something in my flesh and bone had . . . been altered, ever so slightly.

I did not know when or how, but I could feel the difference. In this place, I could feel the difference.

I looked at the Guardian Stone again. An inert boulder ornamented in the distant past by hands long dead, conveying images whose meaning was forgotten.

But it was not that simple. The stone remembered the meaning.

Recalling the triple spiral in the recess at the rear of the central chamber, I wondered if it was meant to be an echo of the larger figure.

Or a link?

I painstakingly examined the rest of the carvings on the Guardian Stone. Smaller spirals on the other side of the vertical line were supported by wavy shapes that curved along the bottom of the design to flow into the base of the triple spiral. This arrangement reinforced the impression of constant movement.

Near both ends of the stone were irregular squares. Straight lines and sharp angles suggested solidity and permanence.

My nostrils detected the unmistakable scent of ancient stone dust.

To my surprise, I discovered remnants of brilliant blue pigment in the carvings. Although aged and weathered, the color was still vivid. At one time the designs would have stood out in sharp relief, describing a dynamic pattern in rigid rock.

Except for the symbols they carved, the artists had left no trace of their identity. There were no discernible marks of the chisel. The figures had been picked out, patiently, meticulously, with an unknown tool in hands dissolved by time.

Raising my eyes from the great stone, I made another discovery: above the entrance to the passageway was a large rectangular opening plugged with blocks of quartz. There was no clue as to the purpose this roof box might serve, but obviously it was a carefully planned feature of the temple.

Behind the Guardian Stone was the heavy stone door that the Dagda had moved aside so we could enter. Too heavy for a man alone to shift, it was closed now. I did not recall anyone closing it when we left. While one person might edge his way around the Guardian Stone, a band of invaders would have to clamber over the monolith to shift the door.

So many questions and no answers.

The ever-present wind blew across the ridge. Birds sang in trees at the foot of the slope. Forever flowed on, like the curves of the spiral.

Here, I thought. *If I ask the right questions, the answers are here.*

Tranquility encircled me like a gentle hand cupping a frightened bird. Somewhere out there my people were arguing and trouble roiled, but I was insulated from it. Where I stood was elsewhen and otherwise.

Was this reality, and the rest just passing noise?

Does noise matter if we refuse to listen to it?

More huge stones were embedded in the base of the mound. I walked all the way around, counting them as I went. Recalling numbers as the Dagda had taught them to me, information I had thought forgotten.

The most elaborately inscribed stones were the Guardian Stone at the entrance and one directly opposite at the rear of the mound. Some of the others were carved and some were not—or if they were, the carving must be on the side facing the earth.

Communicating with the earth?

The temple was not alone on its hill. The surrounding area was studded with smaller mounds, variously shaped stone circles, and standing stones. There was even a cobbled pathway that might have been a ritual processional. When I looked closely, I could see the remnants of postholes in the soil. Timber structures as well as stone had once been part of this . . . whatever this was.

I returned to the Guardian Stone. Perhaps it was a map. The large triple spiral might be this very temple, and the small spirals other temples. The squares could indicate houses and the wavy lines the river. Or rivers. Or even the sea.

That much made sense, or could be forced to make sense, but what of the vertical line in the center? Was it directing the viewer into the temple?

Was it a pathway pointing down to the river?

Or up to the sky?

I stepped back and refocused my eyes on the great stone,

seeking stars. Before I could find what I was looking for, the surface of the boulder lost definition. The sun was dropping toward the hills on the other side of the river. Its gilded rays touched the white quartz pebbles on the mound and set them ablaze.

Sacred fire, sacred ground.

Time spiraled back on itself, past and future flowing together.

In this place.

❧ FOURTEEN ❧

WHEN I LEFT the Guardian Stone, I made my way down the long slope to the river, eager to return to the forest beyond. Night would fall soon, and I did not want to be alone in the dark. After the storm of war, no Danann wanted to be alone.

I found my people encamped in an oak grove. They had already eaten their sunset meal, but my father had saved something for me. I hardly tasted the food, so absorbed was I in my own thoughts. Eventually, I began to listen to what the Dagda was saying. "After endless discussion and with not a little rancor, we have determined on a strategy to use against the enemy, Joss. But it will be a gamble. So many of the brave and bold, the kind and clever, are gone; even if we agreed to unearth the Earthkillers, we do not have enough collective strength left to use them. We must try something else."

"A different kind of weapon?" I was still hoping he would explain about the Sword of Light and the Invincible Spear, but he did not take the bait.

"Not a weapon at all," said the Dagda. "We shall call upon the resources of our sacred island in the heart of the sea and the fear that lurks in the hearts of men. The preparations will take time, though. Producing the Green Wave will require everything we have to give. Meanwhile, the Great Queen plans a final meeting with the New People. It is being arranged through their bard. Eriu hopes they will agree to a truce that makes desperate measures unnecessary."

I heard Prince Torrian grind his teeth. "They won't agree to a truce, the filthy murderers, and even if they did, they wouldn't abide by it. They just want to kill and kill and . . ." His voice broke.

My father said sadly, "We must not believe that, Torrian. If it is true, we are all doomed."

His words echoed in my ears again and again during the days that followed. The Dananns were so determined that it did not seem possible, at least to me, that we could fail. Every member of the tribe had a part to play. There were long, earnest conversations about location, and intense discussions about timing—the most elusive aspect of Ierne. Energy was wrung out of my people like water from a wet blanket. Children gathered small sacrifices to offer to the land and the sea, while men and women combined their skills to arrange a terrifying trap. On another level, they simultaneously were planning for a cessation of hostilities and a peaceful future.

Hope is the cruelest trap of all.

We discovered that in the final battle.

At least my people did. Once again, and over my furious protestations, I was relegated to the status of child and sent into sanctuary to await the outcome of the conflict that would determine all our futures.

While time, amorphous time, its tentacles wrapped

around past and future alike, brooded over the island of
Ierne.

∞

The Mílesians assumed their traditional battle formation,
with the chariot warriors in the lead, riding in their carts and
bedecked in full battle gear. Éremón issued orders that foot-
warriors below noble rank were to be naked and in a self-
induced state of sexual arousal. This often was the practice
among Celtic tribes when going into battle, a proven way to
intimidate the enemy.

Sakkar, humble foot warrior and former shipbuilder, was
unable to achieve the startling effect Éremón wanted. He
could not imagine having an erection under the circumstances, so he held his shield in front of his disappointingly
flaccid penis and hoped no one would knock his protection
aside.

For the foot warriors, the battle would degenerate into a
pandemonium of screaming insults and fists beating on
shields. They would be choking in a cloud of dust if they
were in the front rank behind the chariots or slogging
through a sea of churned-up mud and horse dung if they
were farther back. Either way, they must blindly plunge into
a press of warm bodies and strike out in every direction,
killing to avoid being killed.

The Mílesian nobility who rode to battle in their chariots
before dismounting to fight on foot had a different experience. They too yelled and screamed and beat on their
shields, but in the beginning they would be above the fray.
They would be able to see individual faces and bodies.

According to their custom, the noble Mílesians would
challenge and engage the leaders of the opposing side first.
The surviving nobility of the Túatha Dé Danann, the kings

and queens in their royal splendor, the princes who waited for the onrushing chariots with beautiful, fearless faces.

≥✸

Sakkar tried to remain close to the chariots because Amergin stayed close to the chariots. To the bard's remaining brothers, this battle would be retribution for their mother's killing.

Amergin was not seeking vengeance. He carried no implement but his harp, had no objective but to prevent the destruction of a singular race.

He did not know what the Túatha Dé Danann were, but he knew what they were not. They were as different from the Mílesians as Egyptian hunting dogs were from a pack of wolves.

Seamen and merchants from a number of lands and backgrounds frequented the trade routes along the Iberian coast. Amergin had met many of them over the years and observed them with interest. They possessed different complexions and customs and spoke different languages, but all had one thing in common. They were men in the same way the Mílesians were men.

The intuition of a druid informed Amergin that the Túatha Dé Danann were human, but they were not men.

They were what men might aspire to be.

To kill them would be an abomination.

He knew them; knew them to the depths of his spirit.

≥✸

They had stood around the bard in a circle, the delicate little men and women with their large eyes and gentle fingers, and they had touched his mind. Not with their fingers.

A spark within him had responded to memories lost in

time, recognized the same folk as beloved companions still. When as a boy he sat dreaming beside his father's hearth, they had been part of his dreams. When as a man he gazed at the sea and wondered what lay beyond, they had been waiting for him.

On Ierne.

And among them had been the young woman called Shinann. Shinann of the Túatha Dé Danann, a riverrun of a girl, filled with light and laughter. She who was meant to be the other half of the bard.

They had known each other the moment their eyes met. The moment he realized he would never be alone again.

As the Mílesians approached the battlefield, Amergin turned to face his oncoming brothers. He strummed Clarsah with enough passion to break the strings. He cried out to Éremón and Éber Finn, "Stop where you are! There is no need for bloodshed! This land asks no sacrifice of blood; her gifts are gifts of the heart and the mind, and she offers them freely. Here we can acquire knowledge even druids do not have. The Túatha Dé Danann can *help* us if we . . ."

Éremón and Éber Finn were not listening. They only heard the trumpets of war and the fists beating on shields and the roar of the crowd at their backs.

By now the Dananns knew they stood no chance. If the invaders ever had been inclined toward showing them mercy, that impulse was well and truly lost.

The Dananns came to battle equipped with bronze weapons, long outdated, and the subtle arts of the mind, but there was no place for subtlety in what was about to happen, no place for bronze either.

Heartsick, Greine raised his arm to signal to his people.

They drew the weapons they had concealed among their swirling rainbow-colored clothing and prepared for the inevitable.

⁊❦

After it was over, Éber Finn recalled in disbelief, "They came to battle dancing, with flowers in their hair!"

"Obviously, they didn't expect us to butcher them," said Éremón.

"We did more than butcher them; we betrayed them."

"I don't see how you worked that out."

"We—you yourself, Éremón—had agreed to a truce. Or have you forgotten?"

"Oh. That." Éremón gave a negligible wave of his hand. "You surely didn't think I would honor that. It wasn't even a truce. It was only an arrangement the bard accepted. He had met some of the Túatha Dé Danann before the rest of us did and formed a favorable opinion of them. Amergin has a favorable opinion of everyone until he finds a knife in his back." Éremón curled his lip in contempt. "Bards can negotiate for peace, but I refuse to accept their right to tie the hands of a warrior.

"Look what happened as a result of Amergin's misplaced faith. The supposedly safe route the Dananns suggested we use to reach this place marched us straight into an armed camp of the Fír Bolga—who were more than ready for us. We were lucky to get away with so few losses. I consider every dead Gael a charge on the bard."

Éber Finn was shaking his head. "You're saying he betrayed us? You know Amergin better than that, Éremón. I think he fell under the spell of one of their women. He truly thought the Dananns had no interest in war; that's why he urged a formal meeting with their leaders."

"That's ridiculous. They may not look much like us, but they're men, aren't they? And all men are interested in war, for how else can people acquire more land? For that matter, how else can we prove we really are men? I tell you, the Túatha Dé Danann were determined from the beginning to destroy us, and they came very close to doing it. Colptha warned us they were creatures of tricks and treachery, and he was right. Any friendship they offered was a lie."

"It was not a lie!" Éber Finn insisted passionately. "When we met their royal family, the one called Eriu held out her hands and said in the sweetest voice I ever heard—the sweetest voice, Éremón!—'May your descendants live here forevermore.' And she *meant* it. I could tell. There was no malice or deceit in that woman. Her nature was one of incredible generosity. She was offering us a homeland with them. With those amazing people. As a *gift!*"

Éremón shot his brother a look of contempt. "Colptha called you a gullible puppy that day, and you still are."

"Colptha's dead," Éber Finn retorted. "Why do you keep mentioning him? Is he haunting you, Éremón?"

"I didn't kill him. Amergin hit him in the head with his harp."

Éber Finn looked disgusted. "With you someone else is always to blame, aren't they? Blame Colptha for everything, then; thanks to his advice, you refused the best offer we'll ever have! Instead of accepting her kindness with the gratitude it deserved, you shouted the most outrageous insults at Eriu, just as you did to the tattooed savages. You didn't seem to realize there was any difference between them.

"And do you remember how the Danann queen responded? She said, 'I tell you this: neither you nor your children will have joy of this island.' No angry threat could be more chilling than those bitter words, spoken in the same sweet voice. At that moment, the marrow turned cold in my bones, Éremón."

"The woman was only trying to scare us," the other asserted. "You know what women are: a lot of smoke with little fire."

"Those who can command the sea don't need fire," Éber Finn said bitterly. "You saw the Green Wave."

At the mention of the Green Wave, Éremón shuddered in spite of himself. No Gael who had survived that day would ever forget the wave.

Terror transcended time.

Following Éremón's inflammatory response to the Danann queen, there had been no avoiding conflict between the two races.

But thanks to urging from members of both sides, they had reached an accommodation of sorts, one based on their respective concepts of honor in warfare. Invader and native had met one final time atop a long green ridge the Dananns called their Gathering Place. There it had been decided—with Amergin's help and over the strenuous objection of Colptha—that the Túatha Dé Danann would be allowed adequate time to prepare for battle.

Greine, speaking for the Túatha Dé Danann, had agreed. At the suggestion of his royal half-brothers, Cuill and Cet, he had requested nine days to make his people ready.

On behalf of the Mílesians, the bard had accepted the terms. "We will return to our settlement on the southern coast, where our ships await us, and retire beyond the ninth wave," he said. "When we come ashore again, we will bring all our people with us, and the battle will be joined. Where shall we meet?"

Seemingly unconcerned by the mention of "all our people," Greine had suggested a plain beyond the mouth of a large river. "Your fleet can be harbored in the river mouth. The plain itself is level and well-drained, with no surface stones to damage the wheels of your war carts."

Éremón had put his own stamp on the proposal by declaiming, "Let this honorable agreement become part of the history of our people, remembered in the name of Éremón, son of the Míl." What fools these Dananns were! he thought silently. Now the Mílesians would have the rest of the Gaelicians with them, a number sufficient to overwhelm any Danann force.

"In the histories of both our tribes," Greine had murmured, "let your name be so remembered." On your heads be it, he thought to himself.

No truce, then. No peace.

Instead, there would be the rivermouth, and the plain, and the Green Wave.

After that meeting, there had been little rest in the Mílesian camp. Colptha was angrier than anyone had ever seen him. The sacrificer had excoriated everyone involved in the negotiation and predicted a dire outcome, but for once Éremón had ignored him. He was pleased with his cleverness in claiming credit for the decision. Honor was paramount to the Gael, and Éremón's had sometimes been in question. No longer, though. Whether Amergin liked it or not, the wording of the pact would be part of bardic history now.

Éber Finn had not been happy with the plan in spite of the numerical advantages it would provide. He was convinced that he would be a better leader in the battle to come than his brother. After all, Colptha had said so, and he was a druid. Colptha knew things.

It was time for Éber to rally his supporters. While Éremón

was devoting himself to his customary enormous meal, his brother had quietly approached one warrior after another, collecting them in twos and threes and groups. "I would have handled this situation much differently," he assured them.

They required little convincing. Éremón's pomposity was not universally admired.

In the shadows beyond the campfire, someone else was busy too. Colptha had trailed after Éber Finn, eavesdropping on the recruiting. When he considered the balance of power had sufficiently shifted, he took his brother aside. "Attack the Dananns in their camp this very night, Éber," he hissed in a penetrating whisper. "Kill them as they sleep. By doing this, you will prove your leadership with one swift stroke, and Éremón's remaining followers will flock to your side."

Amergin had been sitting not far away with his back against an oak tree, tuning Clarsah. An idle breeze brought the sound of a serpent's hiss. One of the harp's brass strings responded with a discordant twang. Amergin tensed, strained all his faculties to hear what proved to be the voice of his own brother.

The bard quickly put the harp back into her case and went to accuse Colptha of fomenting rebellion.

Colptha shrieked his denial.

Druid faced druid with unshielded fury.

The warriors of the Gael had gathered around them: men whose fighting skills had been honed since childhood, men who defined themselves by their ability to inflict physical injuries and destroy life.

To them, a battle between druids was as thrilling as it was rare. Druids possessed weapons of the mind. The wounds they could inflict would be invisible; the results in the afterlife could be horrendous.

In the excitement of the moment, the warriors forgot who supported Éremón and who was aligned with Éber Finn. They even forgot what had precipitated the quarrel. Ír did not understand at all; he thought it was some kind of game and cheered them both on. But Donn understood well enough. For years he had observed the tensions growing between his brothers. Hot blood, hot tempers, hot ambitions—Donn had held himself apart, forcing himself to remain cool. Privately wondering if madness was Ír's way of escaping from a closely woven family destined to tear itself apart.

On that ill-starred night, Donn had watched with grave concern as his druid brothers dueled, each pitting the strength of his mind and his will against the other. In the end, Colptha had backed down. To Donn's relief, the bard's anger burned too hot for him to challenge.

But later, as Colptha lay wrapped in his blanket, he had promised himself, "Amergin will be sacrificed. On Ierne, I will silence the voice of the bard forever. Then only my voice will be heard."

🌿 FIFTEEN 🌿

THE FOLLOWING MORNING, the Mílesians had set off to collect the rest of the colonists. They had moved swiftly, hoping to avoid the primitive tribes and save their energies for the ultimate adversary.

They did have a few skirmishes on the way south, but a larger problem was the division within their own ranks. Every night, more men were sleeping around Éber Finn's campfire, and fewer around Éremón's. Éremón missed the sense of brotherhood that had distinguished the Gaels until now and looked forward to a heroic battle with the Dananns that would unite them against a common enemy.

Amergin hoped to discourage that battle entirely, but whenever the bard had tried to speak to Éremón about it, Colptha had thrust himself between them. The sacrificer only had one song to sing, but he repeated it every chance he got. "Fight the Dananns and kill them—kill them all! They are our mortal enemies. Feed the Mother their blood so we will prosper in this new land."

Éremón did not want to listen, but the words slid into his ears anyway.

Persuading the rest of the colonists had not been as easy as Éremón envisioned in the high tide of self-congratulation. Odba argued with him on general principle. Even Taya did not take his side. Most of the women wanted nothing more to do with perpetually damp wooden galleys and leather coracles reeking of mildew. "Why not stay here?" they asked. "This is a pleasant place; the weather is warm and the head-land protects us from the wind. We've already set out our salt pans, and they're almost half full."

Éremón had tried to override their objections, and to his surprise Donn backed him up. "You don't need to gather salt when all you have to eat is fish from the sea. The soil here is very stony; your children can't eat stones, and they will soon tire of fish. We have always been cattle people, and there is rich pasture land waiting for us. If we go overland, it will take many days, during which you and your children will be in danger of attack by savages. But if we travel by sea, it is only a short journey."

Donn's argument was indisputable.

With many a wistful backward glance, the Gaels had once again loaded their livestock and belongings and the pack of reluctant hounds and entrusted themselves to the sea.

The fleet had sailed north along the sunrise coast. The journey was uneventful until they came to the specified river mouth, which was just as Greine had promised. Éremón had felt a sense of vindication. Things were going to turn out well in spite of Colptha's ravings. Beyond a fine natural harbor, he could see grassy hills and fertile meadows.

Aboard Donn's galley, the bard had removed Clarsah from her case and prepared to commemorate the landing.

They were exactly nine waves from shore when the sunlight disappeared. A storm of incredible proportions roared toward them.

From Éremón's ship, Colptha's scream had soared above the wail of the wind. "Amergin has betrayed us all to sorcery!"

The bard had tied Clarsah to his belt and joined the crew struggling to turn the galley into the gale. He looked up just in time to see a dark green wall hanging over him: a mighty, onrushing wall of water high enough and heavy enough to smash an entire people. There was no time to compose a death song for Clarsah to sing. Time had run out.

The Green Wave crashed down.

No seaman, no matter how experienced, could have resisted the spawn of that storm. The enormous force of the green sea had battered everything in its path, tearing planks from galleys and hurling men and women into the sea. In moments, the little coracles had been swamped. Terrified would-be colonists had died with the vision of rolling pastureland still in their eyes.

Amergin had struggled to keep his footing on the slippery deck of the galley while he looked for a rope to throw to the nearest survivors in the water. When the ship rolled, he was swept overboard.

Donn shook his fist at the storm. The apathy that had plagued him since the death of Scotta was washed away now. "The land denies us! I myself will put this island under sword and spear!"

The wind had slammed with all its force against the side of the galley. The sea heaved; the vessel heeled over still farther, partially righted itself, then went under, catapulting terrified humans and panicked livestock into the water.

Amergin had come spluttering to the surface in time to

see the ship go down. Éremón's galley was not far away, but swimming had never been a part of bardic studies. But he could feel the harp against his body, depending on him for survival.

If he drowned, Clarsah would die too, taking generations of music and history with her.

Clenching his teeth, Amergin began to fight the waves.

A section of timber with Colptha sprawled atop it struck him, and he caught hold of the broken end. "Get away!" shouted the sacrificer. "This raft is mine!"

"It will hold both of us."

"It will never hold you, bard. You'll die in the sea as you deserve, a sacrifice I gladly offer!" Putting both hands on Amergin's head, Colptha had pushed him under.

The bard had fought his way back to the surface and lifted Clarsah clear of the water. Colptha promptly seized Amergin by the hair and tried to thrust him down again.

Clarsah struck the sacrificer's head with a force that made her brass strings roar.

Aboard Éremón's galley, Ír had seen Donn's ship go down. Donn, who was the bedrock in his life. Without his oldest brother, he knew the madness would consume him, the madness the two of them had tried to hold at bay like a rabid animal for so many years.

The madness that Ír suspected was the truth of the world.

Long-legged, golden-haired Ír, the most beautiful of the sons of Mílesios, had leaped onto the ship's rail and dived into the sea without hesitation, determined to save Donn. But the water was dark and the sky was dark, and he could not find his brother.

Nor would he let the madness win. For Donn's sake, Ír had grabbed the first body he came to and propelled the limp little form toward hands reaching down for it. Loving hands and calling voices. He had rescued several children before the dark sea finally claimed him.

Sakkar the Phoenician was also a survivor. When he caught sight of Amergin's dark head among the waves, he had shouted for a rope to be thrown to the bard.

They had waded out of the sea together.

Éremón's wrecked galley had washed ashore in the river mouth. So had many of the bodies, including Éber Finn's senior wife and two of his children. And Ír. And Colptha. And Donn.

When Donn's body was recovered, his wife, wailing and tearing out her hair, ran headlong into the sea that had killed her husband. She had misjudged her footing and drowned without calling for help. When her sodden body washed ashore, what remained of her hair had resembled a straggle of seaweed.

"Yes," Éremón responded to Éber Finn's question. "Yes, I remember the Green Wave." He spoke in a whisper, as if afraid that any word he said might be the one that summoned the monster sea. Memories were the cruelest of enemies. The only way he knew to put an end to the terror they engendered was to destroy an entire race.

At his command, the remaining Gaelicians had assembled their battle force. The surviving chieftains had gathered their men around them. The trumpets of war had outscreamed the song of the harp.

Amergin the bard had been a reluctant witness to that final battle. Unwilling yet unable to stay away, by the nature of his gift he was compelled to observe and commemorate events of importance to his tribe.

As they neared the designated battlefield, the Mílesians had observed only a small number of Dananns gathered on the plain. Éber Finn shouted to his brother, "I thought there would be thousands of them!"

"There are thousands," Éremón called back from his chariot. "The rest are in hiding, waiting to ambush us."

Éber Finn had mentally added this remark to a long list of mistakes he was holding against his brother. The field was a vast meadow uninterrupted by woodlands or rock formations. The pallid winter light was too dim to create dark shadows. There was no place where anyone could hide. No ambush, then, and only a small army facing them. Victory was a certainty.

"Let's get it over with," Éber Finn said briskly to his charioteer. The sooner the battle was concluded, the sooner the real business of establishing leadership in Ierne would begin.

The snorting of horses, the creaking of chariots, the insistent tramping of feet; so many feet pounding the earth. Warriors checking their weapons. Making crude jokes and grinning at one another. Relishing the excitement to come.

When Amergin had tried to persuade Éremón and Éber Finn to turn aside, his brothers, deaf to reason, thought he was exhorting them to deeds of valor. They had not listened to his actual words. Words meant nothing on a battlefield.

And it was a battlefield now; the opposing sides were near enough to see each other clearly.

Once Éremón left his chariot, he did not look at faces. He liked to think of the enemy as a shoal of fish, a sea of anonymous bodies. It was easier to kill them that way. He stepped down from his cart with his sword drawn, watching for the regal apparel of Danann nobility.

He was disconcerted to find himself confronted by a small child.

For a critical heartbeat, Éremón hesitated.

No, not a child. She was a young girl, a slim girl with a glowing face and sparkling eyes that were transformed even as he watched, until they became the features of a beautiful woman.

Beyond her, Éremón glimpsed other Dananns similarly changing. Children were turning into adults; old men, into young.

Colptha had warned, "Nothing here is *natural* or *ordinary.*"

Éremón hefted his iron sword.

The lovely young woman looked into his face and laughed.

In an agonized voice, Amergin cried, "Shinann!" as the two armies came together in the center of the plain.

Éber Finn, determined to be first to kill a Danann chieftain, had ordered his charioteer to drive across the front of the Gaelic line in an attempt to cut off Éremón. When he saw him, Éremón roared in fury, "You won't get my place!" He turned away from the woman and ran to drag his brother from his war cart.

The enemy was temporarily forgotten as two brothers struggled for supremacy.

Amergin tried to dodge around them to get to . . . but there was no avoiding the explosion of battle that now convulsed the meadow. The Túatha Dé Danann, men and women alike, were throwing back the rainbow-colored cloaks they wore to reveal the weapons hidden beneath them. Bronze-bladed swords, bronze-headed axes, obsidian knives sharpened to a deadly edge.

Delighted to see that their festive and beflowered opponents had come to fight after all, the howling warriors of the Gael engulfed them.

But the Dananns did not wait to be killed. They flowed away like quicksilver, leaving iron swords slashing through the air at . . . empty air.

The Dananns' agility was astonishing. They shifted from place to place more swiftly than the eye could follow. With a sideways blow here and a clever maneuver there, they parried the weapons of the Gaels, then danced out of reach.

Without killing anyone.

Sakkar put his own sword back in his belt.

He caught a fleeting glimpse of Amergin's blue cloak as the bard elbowed his way across the field of battle. Bards did not take part in combat, so why was he risking his life? Sakkar made a spur-of-the-moment decision to become bodyguard to his friend rather than trying to kill strangers. For what must be the tenth time already, Sakkar pushed his helmet up so he could see better and ran after the blue cloak.

The battle that should have been swiftly concluded turned into a contest unlike any the Mílesians had experienced. Brute strength was useless against an enemy you could not catch. But the Dananns did not run away. They concentrated on wearing the invaders down and exhausting them, and for a while they succeeded.

To Éremón it was like fighting shadows. His temper, barely under control at the best of times, exploded. He ran at one band of Dananns after another, hacking at them as if he were trying to cut down trees. Sometimes he felt the resistance of a body. More often not.

The experience was common that day.

At last the warriors of the Gael were able to surround and close on their quarry, pinning them down through sheer weight of numbers. When iron met bronze, there was no contest. The roar of bloodlust mingled with cries of pain. First Cuill, then Cet, were cut down in the front lines.

In spite of the death of his royal brothers, the Son of the Sun had refused to give ground. Greine stood to meet the invaders head-on. The only concession he made to their superior force was to hold his shield in front of his body.

Desperate to intercept Shinann, Amergin ran in that direction.

Greine was unaware of the approaching bard. The Danann king had just caught a glimpse of his wife amid the confusion, and his attention was focused on her. There was a smear of blood on her cheek, yet Eriu still wore the serene expression he loved so well.

When she felt the warmth of Greine's eyes upon her, Eriu turned toward him. And smiled. As if the two of them were all alone on a morning that would forever be sunseason.

A few paces away, Éremón had just hacked another Danann prince to death. When he recognized the Danann queen, he started toward her.

Greine sprang forward to lift his sword above the Mílesian's naked back.

With instinct wiser than thought, Amergin seized an abandoned sword from the bloodstained grass, knocked aside Greine's shield, and drove the sword through the Danann's belly.

The warm flesh of the Son of the Sun folded around cold iron.

Reason returned to the bard in a horrific flood.

This is worse than killing Colptha! he thought with horror. He stepped back and let the weight of the dying king's body pull it from the blade.

Blithely unaware that Amergin had just saved his life, Éremón moved on, looking for a more worthy opponent than a mere woman. A good battle had a rhythm, and this was turning out to be a good battle, in spite of a slow start. He wanted to attack another warrior and leave the mark of Mílesios on him.

Eriu flung herself onto the ground beside her husband and lifted his head and shoulders onto her lap. When she bent to press her lips against his cheek, he opened his eyes.

The twilight was falling too early; he could not make out her face. "Eriu?" he said.

"I am here."

Following the bard, Sakkar emerged from the melee. He stared down at them; at Her.

Greine said again, "Eriu?"

"Do not try to talk; save your strength."

"There is nothing left to save. How goes the battle?"

Her lips formed no words, but Greine knew. "We have come to the fork in the road, then," he said. "And we go your way, my brave queen. I did not give the order. The Sword and the . . ." He fought to capture the last breath. "Eriu? When the morning comes, this will only be a dream."

She felt him slipping away. She gripped his shoulders and called out with all her strength, "In the morning, Greine!"

Slipping away. Going out. Gone.

Sakkar looked from Eriu to Amergin and back again. Identical anguish was etched on both their faces.

Gently, gently Eriu laid her husband down and straightened the body that agony had contorted. With trembling fingers, she smoothed his sweat-soaked hair back from his brow. Her gray eyes paused on his terrible wound; absorbed the whole of it, the hurt and destruction; turned away. She spread her cloak over him and got to her feet like an old, old woman.

Then she who must nurture any living creature in pain walked toward Amergin. She laid the palm of her hand flat on his chest. "I exonerate you of this, bard."

He flung the fatal sword as far away as he could. He hated it as he had never hated anything before.

Eriu left the dead king on the trampled grass and went into the heart of the battle. Glided with her back straight and her head high, looking to neither right nor left, until one of her enemies mercifully struck her down.

Sakkar did not see Her die. In his head he heard one sweet, pure note rise above the tumult of the battlefield like the song of a lark, then stop abruptly.

When the tide of battle moved farther down the field, Sakkar helped Amergin search among the bodies left behind for a young woman the bard described as "small and beautiful and perfect." It was not much of a description.

Amergin had seen Shinann with his heart rather than with his eyes.

As Sakkar observed while they went from one slain Danann to another, the same description fitted all of them. "She's not here," he said to Amergin to give him hope. "So she's not dead."

Yet it was hard to believe anyone could have survived the slaughter. After the last battle of all, the blood-soaked Children of Light lay amid their tattered banners. One or two moaned or stirred slightly, but their wounds were too terrible for hope.

Amergin was sickened. He returned several times to the

body of Greine and gazed down at the noble face. "I would have been proud to call him brother," he told Sakkar. "There was no need for this, not for any of it. I killed him to save my brother, but for all I know, this was the better man."

Sakkar asked, "What do you suppose he meant when he said he did not give the order? What order? After that, he said something about a sword, but he had his sword with him. I don't understand, Amergin."

"Neither do I."

When they came upon a Danann who was only slightly wounded, the man refused their help but told them, "We did not use the right weapons; that was our mistake."

The battle lasted until there were too few living Dananns left on the field to fight. At that point, the combatants on both sides simply put their weapons down. It was not a triumphant occasion. No member of the Túatha Dé Danann knelt in surrender before the Mílesians. None of them knelt at all.

Éremón and Éber Finn ordered that their wounded warriors be cared for and their dead taken to their waiting kinfolk for burial. There were surprisingly few Gaelic casualties. In the long twilight, they were gathered and carried off the field.

When the Mílesians finally made camp for the night—at a distance beyond the pervasive smell of blood—Éber Finn sat with his two surviving brothers beside a smoky fire. No matter how close he held his hands to the flame, he could not get them warm. "I don't think we behaved very well today," he commented.

"We won," snapped Éremón.

"They didn't fight back."

"Of course they fought back. I have bruises all over my body and a deep hole in my shoulder . . . here, look at this!"

Éber squinted at the wound. "That's not so deep. If a man was really trying to kill you, he would have . . ."

"It wasn't a man; it was a woman. With a spear."

"A woman!" Amergin leaned forward. The firelight revealed his tired, drawn face. "A small woman about as high as my heart?"

Éremón told him, "I killed a number of those today."

"The one I'm asking about is . . ."

"Is out there somewhere, as cold as a frog in a puddle by now." Éremón gave a dismissive wave of his hand. He was very tired. His back ached, and his arms were weary from the weight of his weapons. Not to mention the yawning cavity in his belly that should be filled with a hot meal. "Where are my women?" he shouted into the darkness beyond the fire. "Is no one roasting meat for me? A battle won and two wives to my name, and yet I'm being allowed to starve to death!"

✤✧ SIXTEEN ✧✤

WHILE THE BATTLE was at its height, many friends had
come to our aid. The Children of Light held all life to be sacred, and the life of Ierne had responded in full measure. The
birds whom we fed when the frost and ice of darkseason
depleted their food had flown to the farthest reaches of the
land, summoning the few Túatha Dé Danann who did not
already know about our peril so they might hurry to help us.

Allies nearer to the battlefield had joined in the struggle
too. The swift and clever deer had come out of hiding and
appeared at the edge of the fighting in order to distract the
foreigners, the hunters. Some of our enemies had left the
battle in order to pursue and murder them. Calling it sport.

On the battleground, brave badgers and ferocious stoats
had emerged from setts and tunnels in the earth to bite the
trampling feet of the Mílesians. Hares and foxes and even
graceful little pine martens, who were among the shyest animals on the island, had scampered across the field long
enough to draw the attention of the foreigners, then raced
away again with a baying crowd in pursuit.

Meanwhile, clouds had gathered themselves into mountain peaks, turned dark, turned black, conspired with sunbeams to create shifting patterns of uncertain light to confuse the New People. Mist had risen from the ground and swirled and roiled with a life of its own. Howling wind had constantly changed direction in order to disconcert the invaders still more.

But there had been too many of them. And in spite of our loyal allies, too few of us.

As the battle abated, the Dananns who had not been slain sought hiding places. The forests beyond the battleground had welcomed them. Sheltered them. Enfolded them. A fortunate few of the Túatha Dé Danann became one with the trees, and their enemies never recognized them.

I should have fought in that final battle. But I was not allowed. For reasons I could not understand—or forgive—I was saved. Perhaps at my father's command, though more likely it was the Dagda who had made the decision, exiling me to the temple on the ridge while all our futures were being decided.

The shapeless time of Ierne was stretched to the breaking point while I communed with the Guardian Stone.

When the summons of the Dagda rang through my head, I could not tell if he sounded triumphant or grief-stricken. I ran with all the speed I possessed until I neared the oak forest where I had seen him last. Suddenly aware of the length of my strides, I stopped in my tracks. Felt again that peculiar sense of being *changed*. Extended one arm and gazed down at it. My forearm looked longer than it should. The muscles were strong and well-developed, and the hand at the end was larger than I remembered. A man's hand with veins and sinews. It could be a trick of the light, but I did not think so.

When I closed my fingers and made a fist, it was a man's fist.

I took a deep breath and started to run again.

The Dagda was waiting for me in the glade. His face glistened with sweat, and he was breathing hard, as if he had been running too, although I never knew the Dagda to run. "You were gone a long time," he panted as I came up to him.

"You once told me that time is an illusion with a purpose."

"So I did, Joss. Do you understand what that means?"

"Not yet, but I'm beginning to."

He peered at me in the gathering dusk. "You will. And soon, I think, from the looks of you. You are no longer a child."

His words were an affirmation. "I am no longer a child," I agreed.

I hoped he would say something further about the change in me, but he did not. The Dagda preferred to dispense information in pebbles rather than boulders.

Sadly, there were facts that required no words at all. His face told me everything I did not want to hear.

"Where are the others?" I asked, fighting to keep my voice under control. "Surely some have survived."

"They are caring for our dead," the Dagda replied. "We could not leave them on the battlefield for the enemy to find. If I had realized that you were . . ."

"That I was what?"

He would not be drawn, the old fox. "That you are so strong," he said. "You could have been a big help."

"I still can."

"Yes, but not in that work. Come with me now; you will have other opportunities."

≈❧

Éremón had decided to be magnanimous in victory, to make certain everyone knew it was a victory. After collecting the Gaelic casualties, he had instructed his warriors to gather the dead Dananns, claim battle trophies if they chose, and present the bodies with full honors to the remaining representatives of their tribe.

The warriors had returned to report that there were no dead Dananns on the battlefield. The Mílesians were shocked. "The entire whole tribe fought and died there!" Éber Finn protested. "There were not enough left alive to carry off any bodies! So where are they?"

No one knew.

Red-faced and sputtering with frustration, Éremón ordered his men to search every meadow and woodland, every beach and bogland, and bring back enough of the living Túatha Dé Danann to offer a formal surrender to him.

Without that, no conquest would be recognized under Gaelic law.

The searchers found only the deserted timber halls of the Gathering Place and the silent scrutiny of the Stone of Destiny.

≈❧

But we were still here. A few of us.

Within a single change of the moon, our sacred island was transformed. Leaves still clung to trees and grass remained green in the meadows; sometimes the fading sun shone, but shadows gathered in dark pools where no shadows had been before. The night wind sobbed like a woman. The land we loved was tainted with sorrow.

The customary funeral rituals were not performed for my mother, nor for any Dananns slain in the final battle. We gave them monuments that refuted mortality. Stone cairns appeared at dawn on the mountaintops and songs of grief were sung in the glens. Melancholy paeans blended into one voice composed of wind and sea, leaves dancing and grasses rustling, rivers running and streams laughing and raindrops kissing the earth. The unique voice of the Túatha Dé Danann who could not, would not die.

The haunting beauty of the music imparted comfort, but I could not join in the singing. My head seemed to fill with the clamor of minds in battle.

When held to the ear, some shells give back the remembered roar of the sea.

Our diminished tribe became one body, one clan, constantly moving from place to place to avoid detection. We knew the island as the foreigners never could. Knew the secret places of Ierne's body and hid ourselves there.

But the New People were relentless. Thwarted of the formal surrender they wanted, they hunted us as if we were game animals, using spears and dogs. The baying of their great shaggy hounds terrified our children.

Children and old people now comprised the majority of the Túatha Dé Danann. There were few living men of fighting age aside from my father, and fewer women.

Prince Cynos died in spite of all we could do. Died bravely, with clenched teeth but a smile on his lips. The Dagda worked over him tirelessly yet could not heal his wounds. I was disappointed in the old man who once had seemed to epitomize all knowledge. He must have heard it in my thoughts.

"No one person has all the answers, Joss," he said to me. "Imagine a pottery bowl that has been smashed. If you gather up the pieces, you may be able to reconstruct the bowl, but if even one piece is missing, it will no longer hold water."

"You're referring to the Being Together?"

"Just so."

"And some of the pieces are missing?"

"Just so. Too many essential abilities—gifts, if you like— are not available for the healing ritual. The ones we still have are . . ." He paused, seeking a word he did not want to use. "Insufficient. Insufficient for the purpose at hand." He forced a smile. "But the tribe is not impoverished, Joss. Gifts are passed on in the blood, and we know that at least one of your mother's has come to you."

"What about my father? What is his . . ."

The Dagda raised a hand to silence me. "Discover the answer for yourself; that is the only way to learn. I have taught you to ask questions. You must teach yourself to find answers."

Silently, I vowed that if I ever became a teacher, I would answer every question put to me.

I tried to identify the special gifts in people I knew, but only a few were obvious. Most were too subtle; my father's eluded me altogether. I could not ask him outright because it was too personal. He kept his pain hidden, yet anything might touch on an open wound.

The sweet song of a blackbird could make Mongan flinch as if he had been struck by a fist.

My mother's death had affected him in a number of ways. Even when he was physically present, he could be inwardly absent. To lure him back, I called attention to myself as often as I could. Once, when we were drawing water from a well in the forest, I claimed—with a shameless lack of honesty—"I'm not afraid of the New People, you know."

"Mmmm." Mongan hefted the heavy wooden bucket over the lip of the well and poured its contents into two pottery jars, which I would carry. Then he lowered the bucket for more water.

"Do you think the New People hate us?"

He flicked a disinterested glance in my direction. "Does it make any difference?"

"If anyone hates me enough to try to kill me, I'd like to know why."

He made an effort to rouse himself. "Hate is a festering illness of the spirit born of fear, Joss. Those who hate are so consumed by fear that they may kill for the sake of killing— as if by taking another creature's life they could add the stolen span to their own. This is an element of character that we do not possess, I am glad to say."

I had to ask: "Don't you hate the man who killed my mother?"

Mongan fixed his eyes on me. Looked at me, then through me and beyond me to some distant point. Without another word, he finished drawing the water and beckoned me to help carry it back to the others.

I understood there were questions I must never ask my father for fear of . . .

For fear of what? Hurting him more than he was hurt already?

With each day that passed, my father spoke less and less. I began to wonder if he even saw me. He never commented on how much I had grown, although I was now taller than he was. There was stubble on my jaw and hair in my groin; in another season I would be a man, while my cousins were still small children.

My father never noticed.

In order to avoid the New People, we shunned the light of day. When I recalled how much my mother had loved to dance in the sun, I was almost glad she was not with us.

Mongan said she could see us, though. He was barely talking to anyone else, but I heard him in the night, endlessly talking to her.

In spite of his personal pain, my father fulfilled his responsibilities as a leader. Because growing and harvesting grain required staying in one place—and therefore being vulnerable—we could no longer make bread, so Mongan directed us to collect the acorns that lay in abundance under the oak trees. Pounded into a paste, they could be baked and eaten like bread. Melitt sweetened them with wild fruits and honey and cooked them on hot rocks in the sun. I thought they tasted better than ever.

Or perhaps it was because I was very hungry.

In our new situation, there was no allotting one task to men and another to women. Obtaining food was important to us all. We scoured the countryside at night, looking for things we could eat. Knowing which leaves and roots and nuts and mushrooms were safe and then collecting enough to fill hungry bellies required a group effort.

Ierne produced more than enough to feed her children lavishly—if we made the most of the bounty she provided.

Unlike the New People with their long-shafted spears and their baying hounds, we did not hunt the stag and the boar. The Túatha Dé Danann did not eat fellow animals. We fished, but were careful to put back the gravid females. Piriome's mother had the gift of recognizing them and taught the rest of us.

We had much to learn.

Something we did not know, but feared we would learn

the hard way, concerned the Fír Bolga. When they discovered we had been defeated by the Mílesians, would they take the opportunity to attack us themselves? How could we possibly resist them with our depleted numbers?

To protect ourselves, Mongan insisted we must all remain together. A young woman called Shinann was a particular worry to him; I could see that from the anxiety in his eyes whenever he looked at her. Once or twice, I heard her referred to as "the first born of a new generation." Knowing what I now knew about gifts and abilities, I concluded she must be exceptional.

Shinann was exceptionally reckless, that much was certain. Ignoring my father's injunction, she wandered wherever she liked and returned whenever she chose.

She had been born to one of the clans in the west, at the edge of the Cold Sea, and was the only member of her immediate family to have survived the Day of Catastrophe. It is hard to know how she survived. People had seen her on the battlefield; she would have been an easy target for the invaders. Yet alive and unharmed, Shinann wandered through the forests and along the valleys in broad daylight while other Dananns stayed captive to their fears.

Mongan did not ask me to keep watch over her. I did that of my own accord, keeping her within my sight but not letting her see me. It was like a game children might play. I followed her at a distance, scurrying into hiding if I thought she might turn my way. But Shinann was always turning. Forever changing her direction, dancing and flowing and hurrying from one spot to another as if nothing could hold her longer than the blink of an eye.

She was one of those who ignored the bonds of time.

Every day, she went somewhere different. A dark pine forest softly carpeted with needles, a brilliant lake where sky and water were twins, a high mountain valley hoarding a pocket full of snow, a fetid marsh brilliant with butterflies.

A road trampled into the innocent earth, scored with the marks of horses' hooves and chariot wheels.

SEVENTEEN

EVERY MORNING, Éremón dressed in full battle regalia, including leather body armor and crested helmet and a sword in his belt with traces of blood rusting the iron blade, like a badge of honor. The failure to gain a formal surrender rankled him, but he was not about to let it spoil his enjoyment.

In their encampment, the Gaels were preparing for a festival to mark the change of the seasons. Éremón wanted to include a special feast to celebrate his victory over the Túatha Dé Danann. He would hold it near the river mouth, where they had come ashore, where so many had drowned.

His way of defying fate.

Meanwhile, he accompanied some of the freemen to the edge of the battlefield with instructions to mark the outline for a project he had in mind. Éremón planned to construct a stronghold for himself in keeping with his new status. His fortress would consist of a huge earthen embankment, roughly circular, with a deep trench outside it, the whole enclosing an area large enough to contain the structures and domestic livestock required for a victorious chieftain's household.

A massive, solid structure, firmly planted in the earth, announcing to all that Éremón ruled here!

There was to be a richly appointed dwelling for Éremón and Taya, including a great stone hearth where they could roast an entire wild boar. The house would be built of timber with broad oak beams to support the thatched roof. Nearby would be an area for not one but several stone ovens, living quarters for Éremón's personal guards and attendants, pens for his horses and a shed for his chariots, outbuildings for storing grain and making beer—and a modest hut for Odba. Éremón's first wife would have had a fine big house for herself if she had not refused him.

Let her sit outside her door and see how well the more compliant Taya was treated!

In the mind of Éremón, the project grew faster than grain sprouted. He also decided to build strongholds for his sons on land of their own, beginning with Moomneh. And even better houses for the boys Taya was going to bear him; boys who would be as strong as their father and as handsome as their mother. The heirs of Éremón would be able to claim the most desirable women for their wives. His grandchildren and their grandchildren would be born on fertile earth he had claimed through his own efforts. His loyal followers would receive . . .

"And what's all this in aid of?" inquired a surly voice. Éremón turned to find Éber Finn pointing toward the men who were measuring the site.

"My family, of course. I'm going to build a fort and give the surrounding territory to my sons."

Éber Finn's eyebrows wriggled toward his hairline like a pair of ginger-colored caterpillars. "You intend to claim all that land for yourself? I don't think so."

Éremón dropped one hand to the hilt of his sword. "I won it on the battlefield," he said through clenched teeth.

"*We* won it on the battlefield," Éber Finn corrected, raising his voice to an angry bellow. "Myself and the rest of the Gael fought just as hard as you did, and we deserve our share of the spoils!"

Immediately, several clan chiefs rushed forward to make demands on behalf of their kin.

Éremón was genuinely surprised. From his point of view, he not only had led the expedition and commanded the warriors, he had taken all the risks. The battle was his to win, as other battles had been for his father before him, and therefore the richest prizes should be his and go to his sons after him.

When he tried to make this point to Éber Finn, his brother had the temerity to laugh out loud. "You're the last-born, Éremón, your claim of inheritance comes last, not first."

Soorgeh, one of the Gaelician chieftains, added, "You're also the man who let the enemy escape. Why are you entitled to anything?"

"I didn't let them escape! They were all dead, don't you remember? But when we came back . . ."

"They were gone," Éber Finn interrupted. "I remember that well enough. They tricked you, brother. Colptha warned you they were sorcerers, but you wouldn't listen. Why didn't you post a guard on the battlefield?"

"They were *dead*," Éremón reiterated. "There was no reason to guard the dead."

"Obviously, we needed to guard those. You go on making mistake after mistake, don't you? Why our father put you in charge I'll never understand, but you're not in charge anymore."

Burly warriors, their aggression still unappeased, crowded around Éremón and began to castigate him. His own followers hotly defended him. If he lost, they would lose, and they had seen how rich and fertile the land was. Their women and children had seen it too.

Fighting strangers was one thing; fighting for land already won was something else entirely. Quarrels long suppressed and grievances held in abeyance burst out like fires in dry grass. The dissension the sacrificer had cultivated in the tribe for his own amusement found voice in a furious roar that could be heard over a long distance.

Sakkar wanted to stay well out of it. Years spent in the Levant had taught him that once property was concerned, friendships, old alliances, and even family ties could be obliterated. If he took sides now, he could be excluded from part of the tribe, and that was the last thing he wanted.

Sakkar knew they would never think of him as one of their own, but that was how he had begun to think of himself. Neither a shipbuilder nor a Persian prince but a man of the Gael. He saw no need to limit the size of a dream that would always be his secret.

He remained a silent observer of the uproar until Amergin arrived.

When the commotion of the quarrel reached his ears, Amergin and Clarsah had been in a clump of willows, attempting to capture the sibilant song of the little trees. At first, the bard tried to ignore the irritating racket. As the noise gained heat and volume, he sighed, put the harp back into her case, and went to see what he could do about the latest problem.

"Here you, bard!" Éremón shouted as he approached.

"We need an arbitration; my brother's trying to deprive me of what is rightfully mine!"

Amergin could see that the quarrel was already out of control. The brehon judges who should have been consulted, and whose judgments would have been binding, had been among those drowned by the Green Wave.

Amergin did his best to placate his brothers. "There is more than enough land to give to everyone," he assured them. "It may take time to determine the various holdings to the satisfaction of the recipients, but we have plenty of time. The Túatha Dé Danann will not challenge us again, and neither will the other tribes. As soon as they learn what happened here, they will leave us alone."

Éber Finn folded his arms. "And how long will that take? Just at a casual estimate?"

Amergin noticed Sakkar standing at the edge of the fracas. "Sakkar over there has assured us this is an island. We haven't explored its limits yet, but anything as large as this battle can't remain secret on an island."

"Is that right?" Éremón called to Sakkar.

He responded with a noncommittal grunt.

"Stop mumbling in your beard and come over here!" Éremón demanded.

Sakkar, whose tightly trimmed beard was no longer thick enough to mumble into, shot a pleading look at Amergin as he joined them. "Yes, this really is an island," he affirmed.

To be certain, Éber Finn said, "So nothing stays secret for long?"

Sakkar was floundering. "I couldn't promise that. Secrets are hard to control . . . I mean . . . things happen here which can't be explained . . ."

Éber Finn asked the bard, "What in the name of all the

gods is this man talking about? Is he going as mad as poor Ír was?"

"There's nothing wrong with his mind," said Amergin. "He's a Phoenician, and they don't think the same way we do, but he's an asset to us." Seeing the stricken expression on Sakkar's face, he put an arm around the smaller man's shoulders. "Come with me, Sakkar. I think I have half a pot of beer among my things."

After further grumbling and several scuffles that solved nothing, the dispute faded away. Not over, still at the back of the mind, but temporarily superseded by more immediate considerations such as food and sleep.

Shinann of the Túatha Dé Danann was curious about the shouting that came to her on the wind. The friendly wind that so often brought important information. She waited until the angry sounds subsided and then drifted in their general direction, using the folds and hollows of the land for concealment. But not too much concealment. She did not want to make it impossible for her busy shadow to follow her; that would take the fun out of the game.

Awful things had happened and great pain had been inflicted, but Shinann had not surrendered to it. Life went on. She knew where the bright-eyed mother hedgehog burrowed under the leaves, where silken sacks were hanging as they incubated butterflies, where patient seeds waited in the cold dark earth to become flowers. Waited like wood mouse and mountain hare; gray seal and spotted fawn and tiny pipistrelle; the multifarious children of Ierne who endured death and life as they came, two halves of one whole.

That particular image kept recurring in Shinann's mind: two halves of one whole.

Tragically, she had recognized her other half only to discover that he was the enemy.

It was Shinann's nature to mourn until the flood of grief threatened to engulf her, then fight her way back to light and life. On this day and for her own amusement, she was leading Mongan's son on a merry chase. Their route lay through part of the territory overrun by the New People.

Shinann intended to avoid the invaders herself, but it might be interesting to see how Joss reacted to them.

She made a wide circle around the plain on which the final battle had been fought; she could never set foot on that earth again. Beyond the battleground, she discovered a swarm of noisy New People polluting a pleasant valley fringed by streams. Urinating in the water. Throwing stones at the birds in the trees.

A cold knot formed around Shinann's heart.

Picking her ground carefully, she led Mongan's son to a location from which he would be able to see the encamped invaders without being seen. Then she waited for him to recognize the enemy.

It is important to know your enemy.

When Shinann was satisfied that Mongan's son had observed enough, she made a sudden movement to catch his attention. Then she broke into a run, and he ran after her.

He could not catch her. No one could ever catch Shinann.

She followed a stream into a damp woodland thinly populated by leafless ash trees and a stand of alders. Seen from a distance, the many-stemmed alders were unprepossessing, more nearly shrubs than trees. Viewed up close, their crimson twigs and catkins glowed in the late winter sun. Shinann paused to appreciate their gift of beauty. Everything that contained the spark of life was beautiful to her.

Out of the corner of her eye, she watched as Joss came

closer. The stand of trees was too scant to provide him with enough cover.

He hesitated, unsure if he should follow her.

Smiling, she stepped out into a ray of pale sunlight.

Following Shinann meant pushing myself to the limits. Sometimes she moved so fast I had to run at top speed to avoid losing sight of her. She would halt when I least expected it and be as still as a stone. I had to do as she did. The slightest movement on my part might catch her attention.

One time when she halted abruptly, I understood why. Ahead of us, in a little valley partially screened by a stand of willows along a streambed, was a large encampment of foreigners. Men were unharnessing horses from chariots or cleaning hunting implements; women were skinning deer and building cooking fires; children chased one another while they shrieked with laughter.

Even at a distance, I knew who they were.

The New People. The enemy.

Shading my eyes with one hand, I strained to make out the details. By a sheer act of will, I narrowed the visual distance between us until I had a good look at them. The invaders resembled the Túatha Dé Danann in that each had two arms, two legs, and one head, but they were much taller and heavier than we were. Their hair displayed every shade of brown from near black to copper to ruddy gold. The women shaped theirs into curls and waves and twisted plaits. Most of the men had beards.

Only our elders grew beards.

Another difference between us was in the way they moved. The Túatha Dé Danann glide as light as feathers; where we have passed, there are no footprints. Clumsy and heavy footed, the invaders stomped across the earth as if unaware they were treading on a living being.

Their clothing was nothing like ours, either. I did not recognize the drab material from which it was made, though I supposed it was coarsely woven brown or black wool. The men wore layers of thick clothing that must have hampered their movements. Voluminous mantles were awkwardly draped across their shoulders and held in place with massive ornaments. Peeping from under the mantles were short coats, while their lower limbs were encased in leggings and low boots.

Women and children alike were dressed in robes that hung to their ankles and were dyed in muddy colours like goose-turd green and the yolk of an underdeveloped egg.

Everyone, even the children, displayed masses of jewelery. The daylight played on stacked arm rings and broad neck rings and elaborate clothing fasteners. Gold and silver and copper and electrum.

The invaders must be incredibly wealthy, I thought. It was apparent from what they wore that they thought our land was very cold. And they talked continually.

Into my head seeped the metallic clamor of alien tongues.

Suddenly, Shinann began to run. I ran after her. Away from the New People.

At some distance downstream from the encampment, we came to a damp, low-lying woodland. Shinann slowed to a walk and began to wander among the trees. She might have been a hunter looking for small game. Many animals make their homes in such places: hares and hedgehogs and red squirrels, foxes and stoats and badgers and shy pine martens, swift clever otters and elegant red deer. But the Túatha Dé Danann do not eat meat. Shinann's only interest in the local wildlife must be curiosity.

I understood about curiosity, having more than my fair share, but this was no place to satisfy it. We were still too close to the camp of the invaders for my taste. They might send out a hunting party at any time and come upon us.

I had to find a way to lure her away from danger without revealing myself. Crouching low to the ground, I started to creep forward. Just as she came out into the open.

To my surprise, she looked straight at me as if she knew I had been there all along.

EIGHTEEN

SHINANN LAUGHED. I straightened up, feeling foolish.

She held out her hand toward me. "Come on, Joss, it's all right. If you are so determined to know what I do, you might as well do it with me."

"I was afraid you were in danger."

"And you thought I was unaware? What a kind boy you are. Except"—she narrowed her eyes sharply—"you are not a boy anymore, are you? I thought you were much smaller."

I was both pleased and embarrassed.

"Did Mongan ask you to be my bodyguard?"

"He . . . ah . . . this is a duty I gave myself."

Her eyes sparkled with an inner amusement. "I see," she said in a serious voice. "A man's duty to his kindred, no doubt. Did you know we are relatives, Joss? Your father and mine are, or were, cousins."

"The Day of Catastrophe?" I guessed. "That's when my mother was killed too."

"I know."

Her voice was soft but not damp with sympathy; I could

not bear sympathy. To move away from the pain of my mother, I said, "I suppose most of the Dananns are related."

"Most of them," she confirmed, "though some more closely than others. We have never been a very large race. Are you tired? Would you like to sit down for a while? That log over there looks dry."

Following her gesture, I saw a large log lying only a few paces from us. I would have been willing to swear it was not there before. But all my attention had been focused on her, of course.

As we sat down side by side, I noticed that Shinann's body gave off a delicate perfume. If scents had color, hers would have been pale blue and green.

"Is this not better, Joss?"

"It is, but I'm really not tired."

"Of course not, a strong young man like yourself. Mongan must be very proud of you. Do you know what his name means in the old language?"

It had never occurred to me to ask what my father's name meant in the old language. There were so many questions I had not yet asked.

"Changer of Shapes," said Shinann. "Your father can assume other forms if he wishes. There are tales told about when he was a young man . . . Do you have the gift as well?"

She was studying my face. Any words I might have spoken dried in my mouth.

"Life is a school," she went on casually, as if her previous statement was unimportant, "and we are always learning. If you plan to follow someone by pretending to be one of the trees, you probably should learn how to *be* a tree. Take my hand."

Speechless, I accepted the hand she extended to me.

Shinann led me to a tall ash tree with an unkempt, ragged

crown. I was absolutely certain the tree was not there earlier. She greeted the ash as if it were an old friend, then took her hand from mine and put her two palms flat on the trunk of the tree.

"Do as I do, Joss. That's right, both hands. Now empty your mind."

"How do I do that?"

"Think of nothing."

It was impossible to think of nothing. Shinann must have known it because she laughed again. "Try and capture the moment just before you fall asleep, when you stop being aware of yourself. Be aware of the tree instead."

I tried. I really did.

"Totally aware, Joss, with your whole being. Aware of the texture of ash bark, so smooth and gray. Aware of the hungry grasping of the roots deep in the earth. The stirring of sap as it flows through the trunk, keeping the tree alive. Feel it moving through you. Feel what the tree feels. Do not try to imagine anything, just let it happen to you. In you. Accept the tree. Become the tree."

I stood with both my hands on the tree and . . .

. . . and . . .

The magic came to me then.

On the following morning, Éremón took Taya for a tour of the battlefield. He drove his chariot himself, cracking the whip ostentatiously over the backs of his team until Taya remarked, "Every time you do that, the horses lay their ears back. Perhaps you're upsetting them."

"Of course not! I'm an excellent driver. They just need to be reminded that I'm in charge. Watch this!" He tried to snake the whip alongside one of the horses to force the pair to turn in the opposite direction, a maneuver he had watched his charioteer perform many times.

The horses veered in their tracks and bolted.

The chariot rocked up on its side with one wheel digging deep into the soft sod. Taya gave a shriek and grabbed Éremón—who was struggling to keep his own balance. Moments later, the couple were tumbled onto muddy and broken ground.

Taya got to her feet with all the dignity of a princess. Without saying anything more to Éremón, she brushed off her clothes with her hands, gathered her disarranged hair into a knot at the back of her neck, and walked away.

A deeply embarrassed Éremón was left to run after the horses as they careened around the battlefield, dragging the overturned chariot behind them.

A couple of days passed before Éremón could persuade Taya to go for another ride with him. She expressed no desire to see a battlefield where so many had died, so he took her as far as a long green ridge crowned by timber columns.

"The view from here is spectacular," he explained as they approached.

Yet the closer they came to the hill, the more uncomfortable Éremón felt. He had the profound conviction that he was being watched. He was about to turn the horses and drive away when Taya tugged at his arm. "Is that where we're going, Éremón? Look; isn't someone up there?"

They had discovered Amergin, wandering alone where he had first seen Shinann.

He did not know if she was still alive, but he would feel it if she died. A great hollow would open in the center of him. Since it had not, he kept looking for her, watching for her. The ridge was important to her people, so maybe she visited it from time to time. Amergin visited it from time to time;

almost every day. He had not expected to find Taya here, though; Taya whom he had once thought of marrying.

She was delighted to see the bard. Éremón was less so, but Taya was not attuned to the nuances of his personality. She took it for granted that Éremón and his brother were on good terms. After Éremón tied up the horses, she placed herself between the two men, taking each by an elbow while she steered them around the hilltop.

At first there was little to observe but mist and fog. When a breeze sprang up, the clouds were swept away to reveal the heart of Ierne spread out below them as far as the southern mountains.

Taya was enraptured. She wandered along the ridge, admiring the carvings on the wooden columns. "This is the most beautiful place in the world," she pronounced as she stooped to pluck a tiny flower blooming far out of its season. Having no interest in flowers, Éremón walked on without her. And found himself facing the Stone of Destiny.

It hummed.

Éremón was unable to move.

Taya came running up, filled with the joy of discovery. "What an unusual stone, is it a monument?" she asked. Before Éremón could answer or warn her back, she touched the pillar stone with her fingertips. Then she trustingly rested her cheek against its grainy surface.

With an effort, Éremón regained the use of his limbs. He reached out to pull her away. One of his arms inadvertently brushed the stone.

He sprang back as if he had been burned.

Taya did not notice. She snuggled against him and looked up into his face. "I have never asked you for a bride gift," she said sweetly, "or anything at all for myself. Give me this hill, Éremón. For my own, my own place. Let it be known henceforth as Tara, the Hill of Taya, and when I am dead, build my tomb here."

Glancing over her head, Éremón saw Amergin watching them. The bard who had wanted Taya for himself. The bard who had thought he could challenge a warrior!

The division of Ierne was sealed beside the Stone of Destiny.

No one realized it at the time.

Éremón lifted Taya above his head and held her there, pinned against the sky like a trophy brandished aloft.

❧ NINETEEN ❧

AFTERWARD, WHEN I THOUGHT about that day with Shinann—and I thought about it often—I was not sure if I actually became a tree, but I was certain she had opened a door for me. Where it might lead I could not guess and did not care. I was still young enough to mistake change for growth.

If my father had been more receptive I could have talked to him about it. I did not think he would scold me, but I found it impossible to begin the conversation.

I had other things to keep me occupied. Being frequently on the move was exhilarating; I could feel myself growing stronger through a succession of challenges. Find new hidden places where we could live for a while, make certain there was fresh water nearby and an adequate food supply, determine if there were any primitive tribes in the area, help transport our ever-decreasing belongings . . .

The most recent refuge we had discovered was a string of limestone caves that honeycombed the cliffs overlooking a bountiful fishing river. Ierne in her bounty possessed many such caves, but I liked these because they were near the former territory of my own clan. Besides, it was a refreshing change to leave the forests for a while. The living trees were our friends, but it felt good to have a roof over our heads when the rain threw its shining spears.

A few of the limestone caves were big enough to house an entire clan. Since the Day of Catastrophe, the largest surviving family of the Túatha Dé Danann, a group from the south, numbered twenty-seven.

Mongan's clan had ten. In addition to my father, Drithla, and me, there were Rimba, Sinnadar, Demirci, Trialet, and Piriome, whose parents were dead, and the Dagda and Melitt. The task of caring for the little ones increasingly fell upon myself and the elders. My father was with us and yet not with us. Sometimes I watched his shadow on the wall to be certain he was real.

Because Shinann had told me she was related to Mongan, I hoped she would join us in our cave, but she stayed with Dananns from the west. I understood; there were substantial differences in the clans. Each had been uniquely influenced by the region they occupied, and in any situation they preferred to be with their own.

I wondered if the New People would have the same experience.

That was a very adult thought.

When we found the limestone caves, they already were inhabited by bats, a large population of little creatures with pointed faces, leathery wings, and a pungent dung whose eye-watering odor came out to meet us. We made no effort to displace them; this had been their home first. During the day, they clung to the ceilings of the caves like densely packed leaves, peacefully asleep. At sundown, they awakened to go hunting, sweeping out of the caves in great clouds, emitting a high-pitched music that only a few of us could hear. They did not return until the dawn.

Making accommodation with them should not have been difficult: they were children of the night; we were children of the light. There was room enough for us all above the river. But the bats frightened some of the children. Little Piriome cried whenever they stirred. Rimba called them "monsters" although they were smaller than one of his feet, and several times I had to stop him from throwing stones at them.

Only my sister, Drithla, snugly nestled in Melitt's arms, loved them. She laughed when the bats swooped overhead and reached her dimpled baby hands toward them. I was so proud of her then.

Our real problem was one of timing and could not be re-solved. We needed to stay hidden during daylight and go out at night, like the bats, in order to forage. This meant bats and Dananns were crowded into the caves together during the day. The bats were wonderfully clean; they bathed each other with their tongues and used a communal dung heap. But that smell!

Perhaps they thought we smelled bad too.

Living at such close quarters in the caves could not be a long-term solution, although it did give me an opportunity for frequent conversations with the Dagda. How strange that I had once resented his trying to teach me. Now I soaked up everything he said. I was grateful to my father for giving me the gift of remembering.

But did I ever thank Mongan for it? Sadly, that is one thing I do not remember.

Sadness was in the eyes of the Dagda too, when I once surprised him gazing at me. "Is something wrong?"

"Everything," he replied. "You are missing out on so much, Joss."

"Like what?"

"Your first Being Together should have been the first of a series of rites of passage as you gradually matured. When you were ready, it would have been my privilege to introduce you to the temple on the hill and the two that stand near it. You would have learned their rituals and prepared to take part in them. But we cannot do that now.

"Our ancestors left their original home because it became uninhabitable, and they were determined not to allow that to happen here. The temples were part of their effort. Everything must be kept in balance, Joss; balance is one law that can never be broken."

"I don't quite understand."

"I know you don't. Children are supposed to learn gradually, as they are able to absorb knowledge. Maturity is coming upon you too quickly, and neither you nor I are ready."

I tried to persuade the Dagda that I could learn whatever he wanted to teach me, but he would not be hurried. In his mind, there was a natural progression he refused to disrupt. "It has been difficult enough to adapt ourselves," he kept saying.

But we kept talking together in the gloom of the caves.

When I told the Dagda about my experience with Shinann, he was pleased. "She is a remarkable individual; you are fortunate that she likes you. Her generation was a great leap forward for us. Until they came along, talents were dispersed unevenly among us, and almost at random, but the few children who were born in Shinann's season were extraordinarily gifted. The elders recognized it first. We speculated among ourselves as to what the future might hold, what wonders would be performed when these young people matured."

"Tell me!" I urged.

A light faded from the old man's eyes. "They never had the chance to show us, Joss. Even for members of the Túatha Dé Danann, they aged slowly, ripening like the sweetest fruit on the vines, and we did not rush them. We knew they would be worth waiting for. But"—the Dagda's lower lip trembled, reminding me how old he really was—"the New People arrived," he said flatly. "The brightest flames of Shinann's generation were extinguished on the battlefield. They are gone now, except for her."

There were so many things I had not been told! My childhood had passed like a pleasant dream while titanic forces were destroying my future, and I should have *known*.

I did not say those words aloud, but the Dagda heard me. He put one withered hand atop my own. "When you have children of your own, Joss, you too will want to protect them."

"Why would I want to have children to raise in a dark cave filled with bats while savages outside hunt them with spears!" I did not realize I was shouting until I heard Piriome start to cry.

Melitt came bustling forward from the rear of the cave to scoop the little girl into her arms and rock back and forth with her, murmuring shapeless sounds of comfort. Over Piriome's blond head she chided, "Now see what you've done, Joss. Do you want to be the last of the Túatha Dé Danann?"

"No! I mean of course not, but there are plenty of other youngsters who . . ."

"There were never plenty of youngsters," said the Dagda, "but we always thought there were enough. Until now." He shook his head.

In the dark of the cave, I felt the weight of the future we might not have.

It was too heavy; I went outside to walk along the river-bank. The sun had not yet set, but I did not care. Let the New People, the Mílesians or whatever they called themselves, try to attack me! I would tear them limb from limb; I was stronger than they would expect, stronger than even I knew—seething inside with the fury of one who has been robbed of riches he did not appreciate until it was too late.

Something shivered the reeds on the far side of the river.

Busily gathering material for weaving baskets, two Ivernian women, mother and daughter, had been unaware of the passage of time. Usually they would have returned home before the sun sank so low, but on this day they were too engrossed in their conversation to notice.

The daughter had just learned that she was carrying her first child. She was little more than a child herself. She was proud and fearful and needed the sort of reassurance her husband could not possibly give. Birth was a natural act she had seen many times before, but when it was happening to her, everything was different. She was bombarding her mother with questions. How much longer would she have to wait for her baby? What foods should she be eating? Should she still accept her man into her body? And perhaps the most important of all to such a young woman, what changes would take place in her body?

Her mother had borne a number of children; the Iverni were a fertile race. But this was her eldest surviving daughter and had a special place in her heart. She took time to answer every question at length until the girl was satisfied.

The reed gathering took longer than usual.

When they noticed that the light was failing, they hurried to collect one last armful of material, wading into the shallows with their scythes ready.

The mother gave a shout of alarm.

Her daughter looked up to see a strange man staring at them from the opposite bank.

The river was old and winding and deeply cut through the hills, but shallow in this season. The man could easily cross over to them. It was too late to run. The mother stepped in front of her daughter and extended her arms to both sides like a wall of protection.

I had been brimming with courage until I found myself actually facing strangers. My mind hurried to catch up with what my eyes were reporting. They were only two women, not Dananns, and not dressed like Mílesians. Each held a small bronze scythe in her hand.

They looked as horrified to see me as I was to see them.

Hate begins with fear, said a remembered voice in my head.

"Don't be frightened. I won't hurt you," I called out to them. Even to my ears, my voice sounded tentative. It was not strong enough to carry across the sounds of the water. I drew a deep breath and tried again. Louder.

One of the women gave a shriek and dropped her scythe. Seizing the arm of the other, she pulled her up the riverbank, and they ran for their lives.

When I told the head of my clan about my unfortunate encounter with the two women, Mongan was unconcerned. "We are sure to be seen from time to time, Joss, but those two don't sound menacing. Did they threaten you?"

"They had scythes for cutting reeds, but they were too busy running away to use them."

"Two frightened women are no danger. Forget about them."

"What if they tell others about us?"

"They do not know anything about us, do they? All they

saw was you alone on the riverbank. And what others would they tell? You said they were not of the New People."

"Their clothes were different; they belonged to one of the primitive tribes, I think."

"There is nothing to fear from them, then," Mongan said dismissively. "Go and play with the other children and let me be."

His words shocked me, confirming my worst suspicions. My own father was not aware that I had become a man.

The Dagda was asleep—he was beginning to sleep a lot— and did not hear our conversation. When he awoke, I did not tell him about it. To do so would betray a weakness on Mongan's part. Circumstances had made him chief of the Túatha Dé Danann, and my loyalty must be to him, even if he did not recognize an important change in his own son.

TWENTY

THE MÍLESIANS had won the battle with the Túatha Dé Danann, but there was no peace. Éremón's fort was not built, and the outline was not even delineated on the earth with stones. To the surviving sons of the Míl, it represented a war yet to be fought.

"Don't take sides," Amergin warned Sakkar unnecessarily. "I know my brothers, neither Éremón nor Éber Finn will give the width of a hair in this matter, and you don't want to get caught between them. Ever since they were knee-high, those two have fought about everything: who was the strongest, who was the bravest, who was the favorite—and our father encouraged them. He was raising them to be warriors like himself, and he wanted to make sure they would be fiercely competitive."

"What about your other brothers?" Sakkar wanted to know. "Donn was a warrior too."

"Yes, but Donn had more than one side to him," said Amergin. "Fighting was something he did only if he had to—and then he usually won because he used his mind as well as his body. He never went looking for a battle, though. He filled his life with other interests."

"As you and Colptha did."

"Druidry isn't an interest, Sakkar. It is born in a person like the color of their eyes. Druids come in different sizes and shapes, male and female, with a variety of abilities. What sets us apart is that druids are in touch with the unseen world."

An old superstition fluttered awake in Sakkar's belly. "What unseen world?" he asked warily.

"The one that lies behind what you believe is the real world. Every drop of water and grain of sand here casts a shadow there. What appears solid here is not solid there. Druids recognize this; we acknowledge no hard edges and permanent boundaries. All things are one, and occasionally we can glimpse the connections."

Sakkar's forehead folded into deep ridges. "I don't understand that at all."

"If you did, you would be a druid."

"What about Ír, then? He had no boundaries."

"My beautiful brother?" Amergin's smile was nostalgic. "Ír stood up and walked sooner than the rest of us did; he talked sooner too, and he could do anything the first time he tried. If Donn had not been the firstborn, I think the clan would have made Ír chief by acclaim when Mílesios died.

"But about the time his beard started to grow, our mother had noticed that Ír was having trouble. He did not always think clearly and was easily confused. His mind was like a grasshopper; he did not seem able to control the direction it took. Ír was not a druid, all agreed on that, yet he sometimes saw things which were not there and talked to invisible beings. Mílesios shouted at him, but that only made it worse.

"When people outside our family began to comment on Ír's behavior, Scotta consulted the druid healers. A whole string of them examined my poor brother and employed treatments they swore would cure him. They didn't. The sacrificers demanded calves to use in exhorting the spirits to correct his infirmity. We gave up some of our best animals, and still Ír did not improve.

"At a loss for any other answer, Scotta finally decided that Ír had an excess of potency which he had inherited from his father. Sexual heat was scrambling the young man's brains, she declared. Mílesios agreed; the diagnosis flattered him. To ease the problem, he asked a Gaelician clan chief for any woman of marriageable age who would accept his son. For Ír's sake, the Míl would even settle for a token dowry.

"When the bride was brought to us, we were pleasantly surprised. She had all of her teeth and seemed willing to overlook Ír's nonsense; I suppose she thought it was a small price to pay for marrying into the dominant clan of the Gael. The children she bore to my brother in swift succession were as handsome as he was. But bedding a woman was not the cure; as time passed, Ír's thoughts and actions became ever more bizarre. Then, as you saw for yourself, after Scotta was killed he never made sense again."

"Perhaps he was born mad."

Amergin considered Sakkar's suggestion. "Perhaps," he said thoughtfully, "we are all born mad. Only some of us grow out of it."

❧

Neither Éremón nor Éber Finn thought himself mad, yet their moods were increasingly unpredictable. They quarreled for the slightest reason or none at all, and their irritability infected their followers. The Mílesian camp split into two distinct communities around separate campfires. Unfounded accusations were made, heartily denied, and passionately defended. Men who had been lifelong friends stopped speaking to one another, and their wives became bitter enemies.

More than once, Amergin was summoned to separate two women who were rolling on the ground, pulling hair, and trying to claw out each other's eyes.

Frequently, Clarsah's music sounded discordant, as if her strings were tarnished.

Amergin tried talking to his brothers separately in an attempt to root out the poison. It was about land, of course; quarrels were always about land or cattle or women, but this was more vehement than most.

Of the surviving Mílesians, the bard was the only one who had enough authority to resolve it.

When Amergin was a child, he had tried to separate fighting puppies and been bitten not only by the puppies but by their mother. Her fangs had inflicted a much more painful wound than the youngsters' milk teeth.

It was one of the many lessons from which a druid could learn.

Scotta, who would have had strong opinions and perhaps been willing to fight for one son over the other, was gone now. It remained for Amergin to do all he could to restore amity to the clan.

He waited with druidic patience until a balmy evening when the air smelled like leaf-spring. He had spent the day on the hill, which he now thought of as Taya's, although to him it seemed that Shinann was everywhere there. He never saw the Danann girl and was unable to find out anything about her, but there were places where he felt her presence strongly. On the Hill of Tara it was the most intense—which did not surprise him.

Silent except for the omnipresent voice of the wind, invisible except for whatever occupied the standing stone, Tara was occupied by an elemental force. Amergin could feel it. Time, which had little importance on Ierne anyway, was suspended on the hill. An afternoon could pass in the blink of an eye. Or take half a lifetime.

Tara.

Before he climbed the hill, Amergin had removed his soft leather boots. Gazing out from the crown of the ridge, he had tried to envision the whole island. None of his people had explored its limits yet or even knew its shape. Ierne was a mystery shrouded in mist. Yet as he stood on Tara, Amergin *knew*.

He returned to the Mílesian encampment—now split into two parts—and waited until the day's principle meal was over. When men's bellies were too full for fighting and their eyelids began to droop, he summoned his brothers to a quiet meeting between the three of them.

"This island will be shared," Amergin declared with a traditional authority that even his brothers could not question. The official pronouncements of bards were sacrosanct. Their capacious memories contained the complete genealogies of the tribes; without them, there could be no inheritance.

"Ierne will be occupied in equal portions," Amergin continued, "by the followers of Éremón and those of Éber Finn. Éremón will take the north and east, since he has already claimed the Danann hill as a gift for his wife. Éber Finn will have the south and west, with a gentler climate for his wives."

The two brothers exchanged glances. At first, each thought he had received the better deal and felt triumphant.

But Éremón was thinking faster. "I claim the bard to come with me as ranking druid," he said before his brother could have the same idea. Amergin was not Éremón's favorite person at the moment, but it was a way of adding more prestige to his holdings.

Although Amergin would have preferred to go with Éber Finn, he agreed. Éremón was the more difficult of the two, and it was necessary to pacify him if possible.

Besides, Tara was the last place where Amergin had seen Shinann.

On the following day, the Mílesians began to make permanent plans. There was great excitement throughout the entire tribe of the Gael at the prospect of having land allotted and acquiring individual clan holdings.

Éber Finn's followers would have the most distance to travel, so they asked for a larger share of the communal food supply to take with them. They also wanted the few cattle and sheep who had survived the Green Wave. "In my territory, we'll have better grazing for livestock," Éber Finn stressed.

Éremón refused outright. "My people need those animals more than yours do. It may be colder in the north; we will need adequate hides and plenty of warm wool and . . ."

For once, Sakkar could not help himself. "This is only an island," he interrupted. "Surely you can trade with each other for whatever you need."

The two brothers responded with a single voice. "I won't do any trade with him!"

Under his breath, Amergin said, "I warned you, Sakkar."

The negotiations took an unconscionable time. From the beginning, every single detail, no matter how trivial, was dragged out and argued over. When Amergin could bear it no longer, he took Clarsah and went off by himself for a while.

Sakkar soon followed him. He found the bard sitting under a tree, frowning down at the strings of the harp. "Will Éremón and Éber Finn be able to work things out between them?" Sakkar asked.

Amergin sighed and put Clarsah back into her case. "You said it yourself, Sakkar; this is an island. My brothers know they both have to live on it. I only hope they are intelligent enough to realize they must cooperate sooner or later."

Sakkar sat down beside the bard, stood up to remove a troublesome pebble from the ground, and sat down again. Stretched out his legs. Scratched his itchy jaw. He had decided to let his beard grow out again—or shave it off. He was not certain which.

"Your brothers may be intelligent," he said, "but there is no doubt about their being obstinate. In the land I come from, obstinate men hold onto their views until war breaks out or their children's grandchildren die of old age. This island may not be big enough for Éremón and Éber Finn, but at least there is plenty of timber here. We could build more boats, Amergin."

"And sail where? We were exceedingly fortunate to arrive here alive and make landfall. Besides, who would build the boats? I don't like to say this, but you are not a young man, and time is not on your side."

Sakkar shrugged both of his shoulders. "Time is different here."

Amergin raised an eyebrow. "You've noticed that too? Sometimes you surprise me, Sakkar. You may be right about time being different here, but I don't know how we can use it to our advantage. The best thing for you and me, my friend, is to shape the lives we have left so they are worth the effort we made to come here."

My friend. Sakkar felt a quiet glow inside. The bard calls me his friend. Whatever happens, my life will have been worth the effort.

The two men continued to sit beneath the tree with Clarsah in her case propped between them. There was no more

conversation, only a companionable silence, until the petu-
lant tug of necessity dragged them to their feet and back to
the Gaelic encampment.

The shape that future lives would take was very much
in question. The division of the island would prove to be less
troublesome than dealing with divided loyalties. Hard
choices had to be made not only by the Mílesians but also
by the Gaelician clan chiefs, because neither Éremón nor Éber
Finn possessed their total loyalty. Every chieftain had to
weigh the potential advantages—or disadvantages—of going with one brother or the other. A man must peer into the
murky future and try to guess what it held for him and his
clan.

In the privacy of their blankets on the damp ground,
intense discussions took place between husbands and wives.
The women of the Gael did not always agree with their
menfolk. Under brehon law, they had rights of their own.
More than one chieftain set out in the morning to assure
Éremón that he stood with him, only to return later to report
a change of mind. Éber Finn had the women's vote.

Within the family of Mílesios it was agreed—after a lot
of arguing—that the widow and children of Ír would go with
Éremón. The remainder of Donn's family would accompany
Éber Finn. But that was only the beginning.

Over a period of several days, the entire tribe of the
Gael—including children, grandchildren, cousins, adherents
of nominal kinship and freemen—had to be similarly appor-
tioned. Amergin's presence was required again and again to
persuade someone of the necessity of agreement.

Sometimes he succeeded. Sometimes not.

Inevitably, the perceived self interest of every individual
was involved. Those who accepted Éremón as leader of
the tribe were determined to stay with him because they

believed he would be more prosperous and his wealth would benefit them.

Those who doubted Éremón's self-proclaimed right to rule wanted to follow Éber Finn not only because they preferred him personally but also because they wanted to protest his brother's usurpation of power.

In some families, there were quarrels that would not be forgiven for generations. If ever. The Gael knew how to carry a grudge.

Éremón and Éber Finn also had to agree on the distribution of communal property and of the livestock, except for their own horses. The brothers quarreled over each individual cow and sheep. Every cracked water jar and sickly hound puppy became an item of inestimable value whose acquisition was imperative for both sides. Insults were hurled and fists were shaken, but there was no actual fighting between them.

The most important question already had been decided.

While irrevocable choices were being made, Sakkar considered his own fate. *My friend.* That relationship must be weighed against all the others.

At the end of a long, fraught day, when the livestock finally had been separated, Sakkar sought out the bard. He found him sitting on the wrong side of a cooking fire, oblivious to the smoke blowing into his eyes. Sakkar startled Amergin out of his reverie by saying, "You're downwind here, why don't we go around to the other side?"

"A friend who looks after me," the bard said. "I'm a lucky man."

As they waited for the deer roasting on the spit, Sakkar remarked, "Everything seems different now, doesn't it? Even the people. I miss the way Éremón used to laugh at himself; he doesn't do that anymore."

"He doesn't laugh at much of anything now," Amergin agreed. "Éber Finn has become the sunnier man. It happens that way sometimes; the gentlest calf in a herd can develop into a nasty-tempered bull."

Sakkar said, "I've been giving a lot of thought to what you said about shaping our lives. If I only had myself to consider, I think I would rather follow Éber Finn. But you and Soorgeh will be with Éremón, and Soorgeh has a red-haired daughter called Sive . . ."

Amergin smiled. "You have come a long way, little ship-wright."

"I have; a very long way. From Tyre on the Middle Sea to Ierne on the edge of the world. Now I want to build a family. My own family!" Sakkar abruptly flung his two arms wide.

Amergin had never liked Sakkar as much as he did in that moment, when the essence of the Celtic spirit shone from a swarthy little man born on a very different shore.

"You have my blessing," the bard told him. "Build yourself a stronghold and sire a lot of children on that handsome big daughter of Soorgeh's."

"I intend to," Sakkar replied, deciding in that moment to let his beard grow. "We will need many children if we want to people this island with Gaels."

The riddle of time as experienced on Ierne continued to intrigue Amergin. The Gael, whose tribal ancestors were Celts from the cold forests of the north, had always been an energetic people. Eager and naturally impatient, they ran more than they walked. Their every movement was brisk, and their voices were often strident.

Yet something was happening to the Gaelic branch on Ierne. Perhaps only a druid would have noticed that Éremón's people—Éremón's new tribe—were almost languid as they went about their daily tasks, frequently stopping to talk to one another at great length about trivial matters. Éber Finn's people—Éber Finn's new tribe—slowed the rhythm of their speech and lowered their voices to a musical lilt. They too engaged in rambling conversations, as if the day would never end and they had nothing else to do.

Yet not so long ago these same men and women would have been bustling with energy as they contemplated their next adventure.

Not so long ago? *How long* ago?

When Taya strolled by, carrying a basket half filled with nuts she had gathered for Éremón, Amergin called out to her. She turned toward him with the brightest of smiles. "So the great bard remembers my name," she teased. "I am flattered."

He did not feel playful. "How long have we been here, Taya?"

"Since before the great battle. Why?"

"That isn't what I meant. How long have we been on Ierne?"

She set the basket down on one of the wooden benches that Éremón had constructed so he could sit and watch his fort going up. Surreptitiously smoothing her gown, she said, "I don't understand what you're asking, Amergin. Is this another of your druid riddles?"

"I just want to know how long: how many days, how many changes of the moon?"

"I don't count them. I don't count anything but strands on a loom or eggs in a nest. Why should I? That's all I need to know. The seasons here are very mild, and one is much like another, so I cannot tell how many have passed."

"We need to be more precise than that, Taya. We shall be ploughing and planting grain, lambs and calves will be born, fruit will ripen and must be found and picked at the right time . . . We have to tend to everything in its own season."

Exasperated, she said, "Is that what you want? To be in charge of the seasons? I never did understand you, Amergin."

"No," he replied sadly. "You never did."

⁊⁊

The day of Éber Finn's departure arrived. His followers said good-bye to family and friends on Éremón's side as if they never expected to see them again. They knew they would be separated by more than distance. A shadow that only a druid could see was standing in their way. Like splitting a mighty oak log, a wedge had been driven into the heart of the tribe and was pushing the two halves apart.

Colptha, Amergin thought bitterly. I should have stopped him sooner. But he was my brother.

The justification gave the bard no comfort. The solidity of time might be uncertain, but as far as he knew it only ran one way; there was no going back.

Events had their own momentum now.

TWENTY-ONE

ONE MORNING Mongan awoke with a smile on his face. Even in the permanent dusk of the bats' cave, I could see it. My father had not smiled since the Day of Catastrophe, not even when little Drithla's first tooth appeared. But when he spoke today, his voice was bright and cheerful. "I am going to the cairn today," he announced, "and I'm not going to wait for sundown to do it. Would you like to accompany me, Joss?"

I need not ask which cairn; there was only one for my father. Yet since it was completed, he had never visited the burial mound of our clan. Neither of us did. Lerys was not there; she was dancing in the meadow with the butterflies.

When we told the Dagda where we were going, he urged us to change our minds. "Let her peace be undisturbed, Mongan, it was hard won."

"Peace?!" my father burst out. "Do you think she is at peace now, when I need her so much—do you think my Lerys is lying in the dark with her eyes closed and her hands folded and a dimple in her chin? Then you know nothing about her, old man!"

His irreverence startled me. My father had never showed the Dagda anything but respect. Deeply embarrassed, I snatched up my cloak and followed my father as he left the cave. I could not imagine what I would say when we next faced the Dagda.

Mongan set out quickly, gathering speed with every stride. My legs had grown long enough to allow me to keep up with him, which was just as well, since he never looked around to see if I was there. The pace cannot have been easy for him; he had never fully recovered from the injuries he suffered on that fateful day. Yet he ran with the gliding gait that only the Túatha Dé Danann know . . . and I ran with him. Ran until distance ceased to matter. Ran until the cairn rose before us, looming through a silver mist.

Mongan stood still.

I halted beside him. He reached up and put his hand on my head just for a moment, ruffling my hair. "Remember, Joss?"

"I always do."

"That's good." The lines and wrinkles that grief had carved in his face were fading away. My father looked young, almost boyish. "Stay here and watch," he said, "so you will know."

"Know what?"

Instead of answering, he began to climb up the jagged surface of the cairn. The stones had been skillfully placed to discourage anyone from attempting them, and I feared the effort was beyond his current capabilities. The slightest misstep would result in a nasty fall.

I prepared myself to go to his rescue.

The mist swirled around me. Touched my cheek. Bathed my eyes, blurred my vision. I could taste it on my lips; the taste of an ancient sea.

When my eyes cleared, I saw that Mongan had made it to the top unaided. The mound must have been higher than I thought; he looked very far away. He was standing as straight as a blade of grass in leaf-spring, fresh and young and new. Slowly, one step at a time, he began to turn, sweeping the land with his gaze.

When his eyes reached me, he lifted one hand in a cheerful wave, and . . .

. . . was not there anymore.

I thought he had fallen down the other side. I ran all the way around the great cairn looking for him. Calling his name. Trying to calm the fierce pounding of my heart.

I never saw Mongan again.

Yet sometimes I still feel his hand resting on my head. Just for a moment. Ruffling my hair.

&❧

It was nightfall by the time I returned to the cave. Going in, I met the bats coming out and had to duck low to allow their passage. Exhaustive searching had failed to find my father or any trace of him, nor had I seen anyone else who might know what happened to him. I reported this to the Dagda and Melitt in a low voice; the children did not need to be alarmed just yet. I would leave it to the Dagda to explain to them in his own way and his own time, as teachers do.

He listened to me without comment, then turned to his wife. "So here we are," he said.

Melitt took his gnarled old hand and pressed it against her cheek. "You expected . . ."

"Of course, though I doubt if Joss did. No child can be ready to see a parent go, and Mongan did not prepare him adequately. It's understandable. His heart and mind were still with Lerys and . . ."

"To see a parent go *where*?" I interrupted. "Where has my father gone, and when will he come back? If you know, you must tell me!"

I thought my earnest pleading would force an answer, a straight answer. Now, so very much later, I can see that it did.

"Mongan won't be coming back," the Dagda told me. "They almost never do. And who can blame them?"

He went to stand in the entrance of the cave and gazed down at the river. The shape of his back and shoulders silhouetted against the light told me I would get no further answers from the Dagda.

Melitt pitied me, I think, but she knew this was something I had to face alone. She busied herself with a woman's tasks, and I envied her their protection.

Thinking about myself again, at first I did not appreciate the difference Mongan's loss would make to anyone else. When the Dananns learned he had gone and was not coming back, they were stunned.

Without a leader—a chieftain, a king, a trusted person whose authority all agreed upon—what remained of the tribe was cast adrift.

Their shock was followed by anger and a sense of betrayal. "How could he do this to us?" people asked one another. "How could Mongan leave the Túatha Dé Danann with no chieftain?" "What are we going to do now?"

I understood their feelings; they were the same as my own.

The obvious answer was for the Dagda to assume leadership again. He was a fixed star in our sky, a light that had never failed. The Dananns clamored for him to take up the fallen staff of authority. The survivors of disaster were eager for the words that would give them hope again.

The Dagda had no answer for them.

Or rather, he had an answer that no one recognized. Doing nothing can be an answer in itself.

Lacking any guidance, the Dananns fell back on the routine they had established. The food collected during the night was distributed, and the clans retired to their caves to eat and rest during the day. And to worry; people who had been strangers to worry. There was a lot of discussion about the future. If we had a future, which was questionable now. We had women and children and old people but very few men—how could that sustain a tribe?

And where would new leadership come from? A tribe without a head was no tribe at all.

Since Before the Before the chieftains of the Túatha Dé Danann had been strong, wise, and experienced. Men mostly, although the Dagda had told me of several royal women in the ancient days who had accepted the mantle of leadership and acquitted themselves nobly.

Now our royal line was extinguished like a torch in the wind. Mongan had been the last surviving prince. Among the refugees in the bat caves, there was no one able or willing to lead us.

The Dananns continued to press the Dagda to be our chieftain. While he was asleep one morning, a group of women made an urgent pilgrimage to our cave to insist that he comply. Melitt tried to stop them, but they pushed past her.

"Cornering an old man in his lair," she complained to me out of the side of her mouth, "is like attacking a wolf with no teeth."

Slowly, painfully, the Dagda got to his feet to face them.

"It is your duty to lead your tribe," they insisted.

"It is my duty to keep you from making a mistake," he replied. "You need someone young and strong; I am old and weary."

They shouted him down: "Not old, never old!"

An emotion akin to anger flashed in his eyes. "There is nothing wrong with being old. Reaching a great age is the reward for a life well lived, and you will not take it from me. I have my thoughts and memories and the sweet temptation of sleep waits in my bones. Someone else must supply what you need."

"But there is no one else!"

"Then lie down and die," the Dagda advised.

That was more than they wanted to do.

The Túatha Dé Danann formed into tiny clusters of conspiracy, buzzing with importance while they tried to force into being a person who did not exist. Tradition demanded that a chieftain be of royal blood. The few children of royal rank who were still alive were too young.

The only alternative was a chieftain who had not been bred to lead. No one liked that idea. "You might as well suggest that a man give birth," one woman said scornfully.

As for me, I wandered from cave to cave, sat and listened and thought, shared food and water and worry, but did not contribute to the conversations. I felt as lost and abandoned as the rest of them. On my fingers I counted off the names being mentioned as possible leaders: Droma, who could no longer stand upright, thanks to the point of an iron spear lodged in his spine; Agnonis, blinded by a blow to the head; Saball, who had only one arm, and that without a hand at the end; and Tamal, once the most courageous of warriors, who now flinched at shadows and wet his blanket like an infant.

This wreckage was what remained of the Children of Light.

However, it was not all that remained. In almost every clan there were children. One, three, seven little Dananns with spun silk hair and sapphire eyes that would see a world yet unborn. Mongan was gone and the Dagda wanted to sleep, but when I met those trusting eyes, I could not look away.

With renewed purpose I sought to engage the Dagda in meaningful conversation. "Is it possible the tribe might continue satisfactorily without a leader?"

"Even ants," he intoned in his best teaching voice, "have a queen whose existence gives their lives purpose and a single direction."

"We are not ants. We can think for ourselves."

Stroking his beard, he looked down his nose at me. "How do you know ants can't think, Joss?"

I had no answer to that. Shortly before dusk, I went outside and searched until I found a nest of ants. After scraping away the surrounding detritus of dead leaves and dry twigs, I stretched myself full length on the ground with my head close to the entrance and listened to the sounds coming from within the nest. Dry chitinous sounds, rough scraping sounds, hissing and rustling and . . .

"What do you think you're doing, Joss?" Shinann's voice inquired above me.

Embarrassed to be discovered in such a childish position, I jumped to my feet. "I was trying to hear the thoughts of the ants."

Her unique laugh sounded like water rippling over stones. "Do you understand the language they think in? It must be very different from ours."

"You believe they do think?"

"Whatever lives thinks in its own way," said Shinann. "Remember when you put your hands on the ash tree? You felt what the tree felt. If you had stayed there for long enough, you might have thought what the tree was thinking."

When I returned to the cave, I repeated her words to the Dagda. "I told you Shinann's generation was remarkable," he commented. "Between them, they brought an exceptional amount of knowledge into thislife."

"Into this life? They brought it from somewhere else? Are you saying they lived before?"

"I am saying we live always."

I stared at him. "That's not true. My mother died."

"Lerys died to you," he said, "but not to your father."

"She could not be both dead and alive!"

"Why not? Because you say so? You are not in charge, Joss—nor am I, for that matter. What we see here and now is only the visible part of an invisible whole. Thislife, lastlife, nextlife—all rivers flow into the same sea."

I lost patience with the Dagda and his answers that answered nothing. Did he not realize how much it hurt to talk about Lerys? "I saw my mother's body," I said angrily, "and I know how much she suffered! No one could have survived what happened to her."

"What happened to her body did not affect her spirit," replied the Dagda. He extended his left arm with the palm facing me. "Push against this."

I was strong and angry and I shoved my fist into his open palm with all my weight behind it.

He offered no resistance. Yet he did not yield.

Caught off-balance, I staggered.

"You pushed against my body, but not my spirit," said the Dagda. "Both exist here and now. Only one is permanent."

I still do not know if ants can think, but I can think. The Dagda taught me.

The ability to think is no good unless you use it, so I did.

Considered individually, the bats were beautiful in their own way and very interesting. They neither harmed nor threatened us, but I did not want to live with them for the rest of my life, nor did I want my baby sister and my cousins to grow up with the odor of bat manure clinging to them.

We would have to leave our caves by the river sooner or later. Sooner would be better, providing we had a safe place to go. During the day, I braved the light and went searching for a new sanctuary. I had to—no one else was doing it. The remaining members of the tribe were sinking into a quiet resignation, content to stay where they were even with its drawbacks rather than make another change.

Change was beginning to feel familiar to me.

Shinann was the only other Danann who frequently left the caves during daylight. She was looking for something too. She never told me what she sought, but I knew the signs.

I am sure she was warned, as I was, to "be careful." The warning was unnecessary; we both knew the dangers.

✥ TWENTY-TWO ✥

THE GAELS WERE SETTLING down on Ierne.

Mighty oaks and graceful ash trees that had been growing for hundreds of years were sacrificed in a day to the
human urge for construction. Forests were cleared, cause-
ways laid across bogs, walls and timber palisades erected as
one region after another was claimed by the New People.
They were all calling themselves Mílesians now, wearing
success like a crown.

Emboldened by their victory over the Túatha Dé Danann,
as they moved into new areas, the Mílesians did not wait for
the primitive tribes to attack them. They sought them out to
batter them into submission.

The natives fought back.

The Iverni, weavers and potters and tellers of extravagant
tales, slowly bowed to the superior force. The Fír Bolga, a
warrior race that had occupied large swathes of the island for
many generations, were not as readily vanquished. The accommodation they had achieved with the Túatha Dé Danann had been one of expediency. The Fír Bolga were fierce

fighters with simple bronze weapons but had never faced anything like the mysterious capabilities of the Dananns. A single terrifying demonstration of the Earthkillers had been enough. In the interest of their own self-preservation, the Fír Bolga had accepted peace.

But it had never satisfied them. When war with the Mílesians presented itself, the Fír Bolga were happy to oblige. They too spread out across the country, placing scouts wherever they could, watching for any signs of vulnerability on the part of their enemy.

As long as they did not have to face the Earthkillers again, the Fír Bolga believed they had a good chance of winning.

Mílesian guards armed with iron swords and sharpened spears were posted outside houses so new that they still smelled of raw wood. Beyond the firelight, the Fír Bolga prowled like wolves in the forest, watching.

"We were here first," they reminded one another. "We will be here after the invaders are gone."

As soon as they exchanged their marriage promises, Éremón moved Taya into the house being built for him within his stronghold. A low wall with a little wooden gate set it apart from the other structures, reflecting its prestige. No effort was spared in preparing the chieftain's hall. A whole deer could be roasted on the stone hearth. Piles of furs provided luxurious bedding. Éremón requisitioned the best household goods from Ír's widow and the other women for the use of his second wife.

The other women fought back.

One morning, Éremón was disgusted to find that some disrespectful female had emptied her night jar into his chariot.

Sakkar used his skills as a shipbuilder to erect a stronghold for himself, which he called Delginis, then went hotfoot to Soorgeh's new fort to make an offer for the tall girl with red hair. As soon as his offer was accepted, he hurried to tell Amergin.

Druids were not assigned landholdings, which were individual territories to be held in the name of the clan but considered the property of the landholder. Under Gaelic belief, the earth herself belonged to the druids. Amergin was also a bard and therefore entitled to the perquisites of his rank. A balance must be struck. After giving the matter serious thought, he had claimed just enough land to build a house in the southernmost part of Éremón's territory. Near the hill of Tara.

Éremón offered Amergin the use of as many freemen as he needed to build the house, but when Sakkar arrived, he found his friend alone, using ax and adze with considerable skill. "You never told me you could do that," Sakkar said.

"Bards have hands, Sakkar, and we can use them for more than stringing a harp. I could hardly stand around and watch other men building my house. It would not be mine then, but theirs."

"That's how I feel too. Here, let me help you level that beam . . ."

"I can do it myself," Amergin grumbled. Then he laughed.

They worked side by side until the sun lengthened their shadows and their stomachs growled. Amergin rummaged among his supplies and produced bread and meat and a tiny packet of precious salt. "You'll stay the night, Sakkar? Another day like this, and my house will be ready to thatch."

As they ate, Sakkar remarked, "You had better not let Éremón know you have any salt, or he'll demand it as his right."

"Let him distil his own from seawater like the rest of us."

"He never will. He doesn't make; he takes."

Amergin raised an eyebrow. "Surely he isn't that bad?"

"He's getting there," Sakkar replied. "We hoped his new wife would improve his attitude, but she's made it worse. He's going to incredible lengths to impress her."

"Taya is easily pleased. I doubt if she requires a mighty effort from him."

"She doesn't, Amergin. He requires it of himself. It's as if Éremón doesn't believe he's entitled to the position he holds, and he needs to keep proving it."

"Has anyone else challenged him for the chieftainship of the north?"

"Not yet. I suppose the only person who could do that would be Éber Finn, and he seems to be content with what he has."

"Ah." Amergin tore a bit of bread off the round loaf and touched it lightly to the salt. "There you have the whole problem with Éremón: he has never been content with what he has. He would take a bone out of the mouth of a starving hound."

"And bite the dog before it could bite him," Sakkar added. The two men chuckled together.

Turning serious, Amergin asked, "How about you, Sakkar? Are you content with what you have?"

The former Phoenician sighed. "More than I ever dreamed possible. My red-haired woman . . ."

While Sakkar described in fulsome detail the many charms of his red-haired woman, Amergin slipped Clarsah from her case and began to summon music from the soul of the harp, music to express the way a man could feel about a woman.

A man who was not Sakkar; a woman whose hair was not red.

Later he would unfold a blanket for Sakkar, and the two men would make their beds in the unfinished house, ready to work together in the morning. Until then, Sakkar would dream of Soorgeh's daughter.

And Amergin would dream.

By the time Sakkar returned to Delginis, Amergin's new roof gleamed with golden thatch.

ལྦ

Odba was not dreaming. She was wide awake and extremely uncomfortable.

In spite of his original inclination, Éremón had built a good house for her. On reflection, he realized that giving his first wife an inferior dwelling would make him look petty when he was trying hard to look like a king. Odba's new house was within a short walk of the one Éremón shared with Taya—but so far he had never made that walk.

Recently, Odba had ventured out into an icy rain to pay a call of honor on Taya, who was swelling with child. Odba wanted to show Éremón how a woman of the chieftainly class should behave. Her noble gesture had resulted in a fever that was tormenting her now. Her head was pounding and her hearing had become preternaturally acute.

She could hear faint but curiously disturbing noises outside.

Éremón had taken a hunting party to spend several days in pursuit of wild boar. They had left men to guard the gates of the fort . . . but where were those guards now? And who was running across the ground inside the palisade?

What caused the sound of timber smashing?

Then Taya screamed.

Odba forced herself to stand up. She swayed on her feet.

The room was spinning around her. The two freemen's wives who served as her attendants attempted to put her back in her bed, but she would not go.

Taya screamed again.

Odba shrugged off her attendants, grabbed a spear from the rack near the door, and staggered from the house. Her women followed her. They were more terrified of the punishment they would receive if they left her than of anything else.

Dizzy, stumbling strides carried Odba across damp grass and packed earth to the house of the chieftain and his second wife. The wooden gate in the wall was smashed. The sturdy oak door of the house was standing ajar. Light from the fire on the hearth flooded the scene inside.

Odba belonged to the chieftainly class; she refused to be afraid. Even when she saw Taya lying unconscious on the floor while a man in the clothing of the Fír Bolga was about to drive his engorged penis into her helpless body with brute force, Odba felt no fear. The courage that had enabled her to smuggle herself on board one of the galleys and follow her husband across the sea, even though she was unwanted, did not desert her now.

Éremón had married Taya. This made Taya part of her clan. A chieftain's wife understood these things.

Odba hurled the spear with unerring accuracy.

While their leader was in his death throes, the men who had accompanied him threw themselves on her.

∾᯲

The hunting party returned to the fort tired but happy. Several days of skillful work with spear and javelin in the dense forests of Ierne had resulted in carts piled high with game; they were bringing enough meat to provide a sumptuous feast. Éremón expected a rapturous welcome from his clan.

Instead, Amergin came out alone to meet him in a chariot ornamented with ravens' feathers.

The news the bard brought was more than his brother could comprehend at first. "They killed her? *Who* killed her, Amergin? That's not possible. There must be some mistake. You say raiders killed my wife? I don't believe it." Stepping down from his chariot, Éremón walked in a small, erratic circle, like a boat without a rudder. Then he rested his hands on the side of Amergin's chariot and looked up into the bard's grave face. "They killed *Taya*?"

"Taya and your unborn child are alive." Amergin reassured him. "She was badly shaken, but she will recover."

He left his chariot and took Éremón by the elbow. "Walk with me," he suggested.

Éremón wiped beads of sweat from his forehead. "That wasn't so bad, Amergin; why did you startle me like that? Why come with every appearance of bad news? You played a cruel trick, and I will remember it."

"You have not asked about your first wife," the bard said. He tried to cushion his next words, but there was no way to make them any easier.

Éremón goggled at Amergin like a fish on a hook. "Odba? Dead?" He spoke the two words separately as if they had no connection. In his mind, they did not, could not. Wounds and fever and a vital, living woman suddenly dead and gone . . . it was too much to take in.

"I cannot believe any of this," said the chieftain of the northern Gael, staring at the spoils of the chase heaped in wicker carts. The carts were still leaking blood.

A change took place within Éremón that not even a druid could have predicted. Before the sun had set, he was referring to Odba as "my beloved wife." During her funeral, he wept copiously. After she was buried under a cairn built specifically for her, he talked endlessly of Odba's exceptional beauty, her noble grace, her incredible courage.

While Taya recovered from the near rape and gave birth to a healthy infant, she had to listen to comparisons with Odba that made it sound as if Taya were the poor second choice. Which in Éremón's mind, she was. After Odba was gone.

There was no doubt now that the natives on Ierne must be exterminated root and branch, once and for all. Éremón summoned every warrior in his command and sent a message to Éber Finn to do the same.

A fresh army of the Gael was required.

Éremón's instructions were unambiguous. "Search the hills and scour the valleys, look behind every tree and under every bush, drive out the savages who murdered my mother and dear wonderful Odba. Slaughter them. Slaughter every one, even the smallest child. Pups grow into hounds."

❧ TWENTY-THREE ❧

THE TÚATHA DÉ DANANN LEARNED about the new Mílesian campaign in a roundabout way, as they had learned most things since the Day of Catastrophe. During her ceaseless wanderings, Shinann observed a fully armed war party marching through the fields with deadly intent.

She followed them from a safe distance. Like many warriors, they were arrogant, never looking back, always assuming their enemy was in front of them. When they found a small Ivernian settlement—only three families—they killed them without mercy. Including the children.

Shinann returned to the caves to report what she had seen. She came to us first because, in spite of his protestations that he would not be our chieftain, everyone brought everything to the Dagda. The mantle of true authority becomes like one's skin; it cannot be tossed aside.

The inhabitants of our cave that day included innumerable sleeping bats and wide-awake children who were desperately bored. When Shinann appeared unexpectedly, they made her welcome. Little Piriome even seized her by the hand and would not let go.

The youngsters crowded around us while Shinann related the fate of the unfortunate Ivernians. Because my cousins were hanging on every word, she turned her narrative into an adventure story to entertain them. She wisely omitted the more gruesome details, but the younger boys were enthralled by her description of warriors carrying brightly painted shields and gleaming weapons.

I was reminded of my misplaced delight in the word "rebellion" at my first Being Together.

Among the children, only Rimba realized the implications of Shinann's information. In a voice that was not quite steady, he asked, "Are those men going to kill us too?"

Piriome burst into tears.

Melitt gathered the little girl to her bosom and glared at Rimba. "Have you no sense at all? Now look what you've done; you've frightened your sister to no purpose."

Rimba asked innocently, "Would it be all right if I'd done it for a purpose?"

Our laughter disturbed the nearest cluster of bats. They did not fully wake up but rustled their wings in soft protest. Our gentle, accommodating companions.

It might be best to stay where we are, the Dagda said in my head.

I concentrated my thoughts. *We cannot remain here. This is no life for the children.*

Glancing at him sideways, I saw his sparse eyelashes flutter. He had heard me, then. *And what about you, Joss? What about your life?*

I want one! I replied silently, but so fiercely I startled myself.

The old man turned and smiled at me. *If you want a life, you must go out.*

He stated a fact I had been avoiding. Knowledge comes to us in one of two ways: either from outside or from inside. Inside myself, I knew what I should do but was unwilling to acknowledge it. In the caves, I could be an adult to the children while still feeling like a child with Melitt and the Dagda. I wanted to be both.

Under the circumstances, "going out" involved radical change. If I chose to make a life for myself outside the cave, I would have to take the others with me—all of them, not just the children and the elders. The surviving Túatha Dé Danann could not be left alone in the dark without leadership. We were a tribe or we were nothing at all.

But if I was willing to take on the responsibilities of a chieftain, I would have to set my own doubts and vulnerabilities aside. Give up being a child, when the child within me was still alive.

In addition, I would have to convince the other Dananns to accept me. When I gazed into a pool of still water, I could see the reflection of a man looking back at me, but did everyone else still see me as a boy?

Was I the only person to face such a dilemma, I wondered, or did it come to others too?

Some questions are so personal we can never ask them.

That night we went foraging as usual, those of us who were old enough or strong enough for the task. The best foragers were the women, who were well aware of hungry mouths back in the caves waiting to be fed.

As usual, Droma was in dreadful pain from his back, but he put on a crooked smile and did his share of the fishing. Droma could wade into the river and tickle a trout's belly until it jumped up on the bank. Agnonis carried baskets for the rest of us to fill. As soon as one was filled, he produced another. Even without hands, Saball excelled at gathering soft fruits. When he brushed his one good arm along a bush, a rich harvest fell at his feet.

Tamal, who would give a violent start if a single leaf rustled, was assigned to be our lookout. Fortunately, we did not encounter any Mílesians, but I kept expecting them to leap out at us.

We collected all the edibles we could find and returned just ahead of the bats. After we had distributed the food, I ate my portion, then wrapped myself in a couple of blankets woven by my mother—oh so long ago—and fell into a fitful sleep.

When I awoke, the decision was made.

I lay rolled in my blankets, snug and comfortable. The bats and the children were asleep; not a sound out of any of them. By stretching time just a little, I could remain where I was and postpone the uncertain future. The smell of bat manure was not so unpleasant after all. I could still be a child if I wanted to, trembling on the brink but never quite becoming . . .

No. That is not who I am.

I threw my blankets aside and stood up.

"Joss? Are you awake?" Melitt's voice was breathless. "I need you!"

I found her farther back in the cave, where my head almost touched the roof. Melitt was crouching beside the Dagda. He lay on his side with his arms tightly clasped against his chest. "He fell down, and I can't get him up again," Melitt told me apologetically.

I knelt on the floor of the cave with my knees on dry bat excrement and put one hand on the old man's shoulder. It felt surprisingly thin; that broad shoulder that once had carried me so easily. "What happened?"

"I am quite all right," the Dagda replied. His voice was strangely distorted.

Melitt said, "If you were all right, you would get up!"

"I will when I can. Stop fussing over me, woman."

Although it was daylight outside, in that part of the cave there was perpetual twilight. I could not make out Melitt's features, but I knew her eyes were pleading with me.

"Can you put one arm around my shoulder?" I asked her husband. "Then I can help you stand up."

He replied as if we were having a casual conversation. "I cannot move my arms. Or my legs. It's too bad really."

Melitt gave a little gasp.

In that moment, I became totally calm. It was an odd sensation, growing deaf to the clamor of anxiety within me. If I let either of them know I was upset, it could make the situation worse. "Don't try to move," I told the Dagda. "Let me do all the work. I can lift you on my own."

I did lift him. The ease with which I raised him from the floor of the cave told me how strong I had become.

His legs would not hold his weight. He sagged against me. Melitt led the way to his bed—blankets spread on dry grass and leaves, like my own—and we eased him down. Quietly, so as not to wake the children.

His wife and I looked at each other across his supine body.

Without the Being Together, is there another healing ritual that would help him?

Melitt did not answer; obviously, she could not hear me.

However, the Dagda mumbled a few words aloud.

I bent down and asked him to repeat them. His eyes were closed and so were his lips. But to my relief, the rise and fall of his chest told me he was still alive.

Leaving Melitt to sit with him and care for the children

if they awoke, I made my way to the other caves in search of help. Surely one of the Dananns would know what to do for the suffering man. The calmness that I had assumed stayed with me, sank into me like sunshine. The decision that had been made in the night was irrevocable. My dearest wish was for the Dagda to wake up so I could tell him.

I discussed his condition with the others as if it were a minor mishap. Only one of them had seen it before. Cleena, Samoll's widow, told me that something similar had happened to her father. "He had become quite frail, so we were not surprised when he fell ill. We kept him warm and fed him like a baby, and he recovered a little, but he was never himself again. He just faded away. There was nothing anyone could do."

Faded away. Mongan had faded away. My heart sank; the Dagda had limited time left with us.

He had made a wise choice in having Melitt for his wife; she took bad news without flinching. An old woman herself, she must have given more than a few thoughts to mortality.

"When it was too late, there were so many questions I wanted to ask my father," I told her. "If the Dagda gets some strength back, I need to know." The scale of what I needed to know was daunting, but Melitt understood. "Ask him," she said.

"Will he give me simple answers?"

From within a net of wrinkles, her bright eyes twinkled at me. "That man does not know how to give simple answers, Joss. But I'm sure you can understand what he tells you."

I hoped her faith in me was justified.

When I ran my hand across my jaw, I could feel my growing beard; it was sprouting soft and springy.

❧ TWENTY-FOUR ❧

THE BRIEF PEACE OF IERNE was shattered again, but many of Éber Finn's men were unwilling to join Éremón's army. Their land had been plowed and their grain committed to the care of the earth. They declared the climate as ideal for barley; extravagant forecasts were being made as to quality and size of yield.

Meanwhile, the ewes were lambing; the majority of them gave birth to twins. A few even had triplets. Soon the cows would begin calving. What wise man leaves his holding at such a critical time?

As if that were not enough, their womenfolk had long mental lists of the things they wanted done—more than a man could accomplish in a lifetime.

"At the end of the day," Éber Finn declared, "it does a man a power of good to sit with the feet up and a bowl of beer in his hand and listen to the birds sing. We did our fighting already, why should we do any more? I'm sorry about Éremón's wife, but he still has a perfectly good one. Let him stay home and enjoy her."

The few southern warriors who traveled north conveyed these sentiments to Éremón. He furiously replied that Éber Finn was betraying him. "Just wait until those tattooed savages turn on him and he needs my support! He can appeal to me all he likes, but I won't help him. Never again. I hope they burn his grain in the fields and drive off his cattle."

This unfilial attitude had a strong influence on his followers. Men who greased their chins at their chieftain's feast knew it was politic to adopt his views.

In the south, Éber Finn's followers felt the same.

The border areas where the two factions met responded predictably. A man from the north claimed that one from the south had come across the river at night and taken his seed bull. A southern woman insisted that a northern man had tried to steal her from her husband.

There was no way of proving any of it. He said, she said, and witnesses were prejudiced. The lack of brehon judges among the Mílesians was deeply felt. Now that there was no going back, the settlers realized there were a number of things they had neglected to bring from Iberia—including more people who had memorized the law and could recite it word for word.

Twenty years was required to train a brehon judge.

For every problem that was discovered, someone had to be blamed. Like ice cracking, fissures of discontent spread. When one of Odba's sons met Taya in the chieftain's hall, he said coldly, "My mother would be alive if it were not for you."

Amergin was in the hall that day and heard him. The bard was well aware of the underlying angers. The brothers had quarreled in Iberia too, but until Mílesios died he had been able to control his fractious sons. The Gael were like their hot-blooded horses: they required a light touch but firm hands. A pair who pulled in two different directions would overturn the chariot. The damage could be irreparable.

As Amergin made his way homeward, he thought about the souring situation. The Mílesians had left Iberia as a close-knit family. Since arriving here, they were degenerating into enemies, yet the land could not be blamed. Ierne—Eriu—was lovelier than they had imagined, and her bounty was greater than their expectations.

Laying the blame at the feet of the sacrificer was no good either. Colptha had done appalling damage for his own satisfaction, but his wicked tongue had been addressing a receptive audience.

Amergin had carved a number of harps for himself before he made Clarsah. None of those earlier instruments had been able to sing as she did, though the hand that shaped the wood and strung the strings was the same.

The flaw was in the timber.

Lost in thought, the bard allowed the chariot horses to slow to a halt. They stretched their necks. Lowered their heads. Gratefully began cropping grass. One by one, the birds in the trees concluded their bedtime songs. The only sound remaining was the contented munching of the horses. Amergin started to take Clarsah out of her case and capture the moment but decided against it. Serenity was precious.

Serenity was the color of Shinann's eyes.

While he stood dreaming, a gentle twilight descended, a silvered darkness that was not darkness. Under the wondering gaze of the bard, Ierne began to shimmer and glow from within like the vanished Túatha Dé Danann.

He fully expected to see her coming toward him. A little woman no higher than his heart. "Shinann!" he cried, reaching out to her.

There was no reply.

At last, he gathered up his reins and drove home.

Shinann returned to the Dananns' current refuge. Some of the tribe already had gone foraging, but Melitt stood in the mouth of one of the caves, cradling Drithla. "If you want to come up, we have extra food," she called down to the young woman on the riverbank. "My husband is not eating his."

Shinann hesitated. It would be cold in the Dagda's cave. The Dananns relied on light from the outside during the day, and at night they lit a single candle made of beeswax, but for the sake of the bats, they never built fires inside the caves. The little flyers whose apartments they shared were too sensitive to wood smoke.

On this particular night, Shinann, who rarely reacted to the weather, felt cold. In her cave, she had an extra cloak among her belongings, a deliciously warm cloak she could hug around her body. But the Dagda had become central to their lives. Although healing was not her gift, she wanted to see him first.

As she walked along the narrow spine of limestone that gave access to the front of the caves, she was not thinking about the old man. Lost in thoughts of someone else, she let her foot slip. Weathered limestone crumbled under her heel. Shinann flung out a hand to catch herself.

In the twilight, a much larger hand closed over hers long enough to steady her. Then it was gone.

Melitt saw Shinann lose her balance and start to fall.

Tucking Drithla under her arm like a loaf of bread, the

Dagda's wife rushed forward to help the young woman. The effort was wasted; Shinann made a recovery that was astonishing even for one of the agile Túatha Dé Danann. "Where is he?" she gasped.

"My husband? He's inside with Joss. Come along now, and watch your step; you nearly tumbled into the river."

Little Drithla chose that moment to scream in protest at her undignified handling. Melitt had to stop long enough to readjust the baby. While she waited, Shinann scanned the rapidly deepening twilight but saw no one else, neither on the path behind her nor on the riverbank below.

The Dagda and his bed were in the center of the cave. There had been considerable discussion between Melitt and Joss as to the best location for the stricken man. Melitt wanted him close to the cave mouth, where she could see him better. In order to keep the sufferer warm, Joss thought he should be at the rear of the cave, away from any draught.

His bed's location was a compromise.

When Shinann entered, Joss was sitting crosslegged on the floor beside the Dagda. The bed was piled with blankets and cloaks. Near the old man's head was a beeswax candle stuck to the top of a stone with melted wax. The pale light falling across his features revealed stark bony prominences and deep caverns. At first glance, Shinann thought he was dead. She made an inadvertent sound of distress.

Joss got to his feet, flexing his legs one at a time. "It's all right, Shinann; he's only sleeping. You can sit beside him if you want to. I need to move around a bit anyway. Melitt, why is Drithla squalling? She'll wake him up."

The old woman pressed the baby into her bosom to comfort her. "If only she could wake him up."

"He'll come back to us when he's ready," Joss assured her.

I am not ready yet, said the voice in his head.

I know that.

Just give me a little peace.

We will give you anything you want if you stay with us.

The Dagda tried to censor his next thought, but Joss heard him anyway: *I do not want to stay.*

≈❧

One of Éremón's advance scouts, a young Mílesian called Ruari, had unusually keen eyes. This was his first time to carry battle weapons; he was taking part in an expeditionary foray into Éber Finn's territory to identify hidden pockets of the Fír Bolga. While the others were setting up camp for the night, Ruari made an interesting discovery.

As the last light faded, he saw a faint trail crossing open ground. Silvery, delicate, it resembled the track a snail might leave on a stone, but snails meander aimlessly. Whatever left this had been moving in a straight line. Going forward with a purpose.

Ruari called the strange trail to the attention of Gosten, his commander. In the Gaelic style, the army of the north was composed of a number of small companies provided by the clans who followed the chieftain. Each company was led by a commander whose loyalty was beyond question. Gosten hoped to be rewarded for his with a house inside Éremón's fort.

"What do you make of this?" Ruari asked him.

The older man scratched his head. "I don't know what it is, but I don't like it. This is a dangerous land, and we need to keep our wits about us." Almost as an afterthought, he added, "Follow that trail, Ruari, and see where it leads."

"Me?"

"You are the only one around here who's called Ruari, aren't you?"

"Can I take someone else with me?"

Gosten snorted. "Why? You are a warrior of the Gael. Show some courage!"

The scout gave a sullen nod. Fortunately for him, Gosten could not hear his unspoken thoughts.

With his eyes firmly fixed on the ground and his hand on the hilt of his sword, Ruari began to walk along the shining trail. After a few paces, he inadvertently touched it with his foot. The strange light faded. Within a few more steps, it was gone.

The baffled scout halted and looked around for new instructions. However, Gosten had issued his orders and marched away, back to the comforting light of a blazing campfire.

Ruari was alone and very young. In the gathering dark, in a dangerous land.

He could throw down his spear and run; the idea had strong appeal. But where would he go? Whatever was out there would surely get him.

If he returned to Gosten with nothing to report, the older man would berate him savagely.

Ruari sat down on the cold damp ground and wondered if he was too old to cry.

ॐ

I was not trying the keep the Dagda's condition hidden from him; I am sure he knew it better than I did, though I did not think he would care to hear it described to someone else. After Shinann sat with him for a while, she and I went outside the cave to talk. I repeated what Cleena had told me about her father's illness.

Shinann's eyes glittered suspiciously, but she did not cry. "We have to accept the fact that the Dagda is very old, Joss."

"No one can say how old," I agreed. "I'm not even sure Melitt knows."

"And he's not in any pain?"

"I don't think he is."

"He may recover, then." She looked at me hopefully.

I did not give her the reassurance she was seeking. Better to accept the pain now, I thought, than to be ambushed by it later.

My father climbing the burial mound. Me expecting him to come back down.

After an uncomfortably long pause, Shinann said, "The Dagda would be a great loss; there are so few of us left now."

"Did you think he and Melitt were going to add more children to the tribe?"

She smiled; she could not help it. "You must admit he is a remarkable man."

"You will get no argument from me."

"I suppose anything is possible," Shinann remarked. "Melitt is not even his first wife; the Dagda was married before, you know. To a princess of the Iverni."

My face must have shown the astonishment I felt.

"Does that surprise you, Joss?"

"He never mentioned it to me."

"Why should he? The only reason I know is because one of my grandmothers told me. When she was a girl, she had hoped to marry the Dagda herself, but he married the Ivernian to encourage peace between our two tribes."

I was not only astonished but fascinated. "What happened to her?"

"She grew old and died," Shinann said casually. "Her people don't live very long."

"I thought we only married other members of the Túatha Dé Danann."

"The Iverni are not that different from us, Joss; we can have children together. We might even have children with the Fír Bolga, but who would want to do that? Ugh." She gave a delicate shudder.

A shocking thought occurred to me. "Do you suppose we could have children with the New People?"

By the light of the moon I saw a blush creep into her cheeks. "I would not know," said Shinann.

But her eyes were dancing.

≈

"There are times when you remind me of your mother," Melitt said to me the following day. She had been spooning a broth made of mushrooms and thyme into the Dagda's resistant mouth and looked up to see me watching. "You have her eyes, Joss. And the same span of forehead."

"Was my mother Túatha Dé Danann?"

My abrupt question took her by surprise. "Of course she was."

"What did her name mean in the old language?"

"Lerys?" Melitt's wrinkled old mouth softened as it shaped the name. "It means "starbird." We knew the girl ever since she was born, and from the time she could talk she babbled about the stars. She dreamed of them every night, she insisted; dreamed that we were birds who had flown here from the stars. Her parents began calling her Starbird. I don't remember what she was called originally, but Starbird was a lovely name that fitted like her skin."

The dreams of children are dismissed as fanciful. I have now lived long enough to understand that some of them are not dreams but memories, carried into thislife from Before the Before.

❧ TWENTY-FIVE ❧

THE MYSTERY OF THE SHINING TRAIL preyed on Gosten's mind. He went to tell Éremón, whose interests were elsewhere. "This is a strange land, and strange things happen here, Gosten," he said dismissively. "There is something more important for you to do. My wife is about to bear my child, and I'm having all my fortifications doubled. Higher walls, deeper ditches, more guards on duty. Fortunately, one of the druid samodhii who oversee birth has survived, but I don't want to take any chances. No more native incursions to upset her. See to it."

Gosten interpreted these orders as permission for a band of warriors to investigate the shining trail. He had no doubt that some of the natives were involved.

Young Ruari was summoned as the only witness. That evening, he showed the other men exactly where he had been standing when he first saw the trail and indicated the direction he thought it had taken.

"Right!" said Gosten. "Let's go. Come along, Ruari, don't just stand there staring at me."

৩৬

The Dagda did not recover, but he did not appear to be failing further. I was spending a lot of time with him. I had learned a lesson when Mongan died; I wanted to ask all my questions of the Dagda while he was still with me.

He could speak a little, but he preferred not to; if he spoke aloud, others would talk to him, which was a strain for him. He was quite content for me to sit beside him and engage in a silent conversation.

Now the gift of memory that I had received from Mongan came into its own. When I shared my deepest concerns, the answers the Dagda gave would stay with me forever.

If the others will accept me, I am willing to take my father's place, but I am unprepared.

We are always unprepared, Joss. Every day we awake is a journey into the unknown.

They may say I am too young to lead them.

You are as old as the way you think.

If you go, who will I have to help me?

We only have ourselves. From birth to death, we only have ourselves.

I cannot imagine you dying.

Death and birth are but the change of the seasons. If we want another spring, we must endure another winter.

You will go somewhere else? And teach someone else?

The achievements and discoveries of a great but dying society can bring light to a young and growing one.

Was that what happened to the Túatha Dé Danann in the time Before the Before?

I waited eagerly for the answer to that question—but the Dagda had fallen asleep. If I woke him up, Melitt would make my life a misery.

≈❧

Ruari was sorry he ever mentioned the shining trail. His quiet father, married for a lifetime to his loud and argumentative mother, often advised, "Whatever you say, say nothing." Now Ruari could see the wisdom of those words. Against every instinct in his body, he was part of a warrior band hunting something unknown through the mysterious night. With no hope of finding it. Whatever it was. And no idea what it might do to them if they found it.

Stumbling over rocks and roots. Jumping out of his skin every time an owl hooted. And the older Mílesians laughing at him, teasing him about seeing things.

It was easy to "see things" in a land where every tree and bush had an unfamiliar shape and any large rock might be a crouching enemy.

At the outermost edge of Ruari's vision, a pale shape glimmered briefly and was gone. "There!" he shouted. "Over there, look quick!"

His directions were far from specific. The little band scattered to search the immediate area, but nothing unusual was found. Gosten was not pleased. "If you are making this up for some reason, Ruari, you had better admit it now. We have a bard to tell us tales; we don't need a beardless warrior to waste our time with fanciful notions of his own."

"It's not fanciful," insisted the young man. "I really saw that trail and just now I've seen a . . ."

"A white cow," one of the warriors interrupted. "There is a large one over the brow of the hill. Your sharp eyes saw her and made a monster of her."

The other men roared with laughter.

The evening's entertainment over, Gosten led his men

back to camp for a meal and a good sleep. Ruari slunk along at the rear, feeling humiliated.

Gosten did not sleep well. He kept thinking about Ruari. The lad was young but no fool, and his words had the ring of truth. Gosten had faced the Túatha Dé Danann on the battlefield; he knew that much of what they did was inexplicable by normal standards. If enough of them had survived after all and were planning an attack on Éremón, this might be the way it would begin.

On the following day, Gosten assembled a much larger company to undertake an extended search. Should they be successful in finding the Dananns and putting an end to them once and for all, Éremón would be exceedingly grateful. And generous, no doubt. Gaelic chieftains traditionally showered rewards on followers who rendered exceptional service.

Being decisive had made Gosten a commander in Éremón's army, but the full benefits of that position had yet to reach him. Éremón was still too occupied with consolidating his own position.

A short, stocky man with a proclivity to warts, Gosten was not the material of which champions were made. Women were not attracted to him; in Iberia, it had been said that he had a face like a lizard. He would have to do something exceptional in order to acquire the sort of wife he wanted. If he was given a house in Éremón's fort, it would improve his status, but more was probably needed.

He would begin by following the only clue he had: the shining trail. If Ruari was to be believed—and Gosten chose to believe him—the trail had pointed south and east.

Supplied with adequate weapons and enough provisions to last for several days, Gosten and a substantial company of men set out.

They had not gone very far before they began to find the detritus of death and conflict; some of it new, some of it ancient. The damaged hilt of a bronze sword, several flint arrowheads in mud cut up by the galloping hooves of a chariot team, a human thighbone sticking out of the earth, a pair of broken spears lying side by side, pointing in opposite directions. One spear was broad and thick, with the top rounded but sharp-edged. The other was long, narrow, and graceful, with a very sharp point.

Fír Bolga and Túatha Dé Danann.

"We aren't the first warriors to travel this ground," Gosten remarked, adding confidently, "but we will be the last. Pick up that sword hilt and those spears and bring them along, Ruari; we can repair and reuse them."

They spent the better part of the day finding nothing more interesting, but Gosten was determined to press on. He could almost *smell* the Dananns now. They had been here; they were still here. Somewhere. Ever since that final battle, he had a sense of them that made the hair rise on the back of his neck.

As twilight fell, the company approached a wide, shallow river. Their commander decided it would be a good place to camp for the night. They could make a fresh start in the morning. Meanwhile, the river would supply fresh water, and there were abundant trees nearby for firewood.

Before they settled down for the night, Gosten's company scouted the area. Ruari braced himself, determined to be bold and brave and not made to look a fool again.

Until an enormous cloud of bats came swooping along the river course.

The young man threw himself facedown in the shallows with his arms folded over his head.

After being momentarily startled themselves, his companions jeered and shouted.

The Túatha Dé Danann were alarmed. Mothers snatched up their children and took them to the very back of the caves just vacated by the bats. The darkness was all-encompassing, but no one suggested lighting a candle.

In our cave, Melitt took care of the children while I remained with the Dagda. The commotion below did not disturb him. I almost wished it would. He was lying so still and his sockets had sunk so deep that I wondered if his eyes would ever open again.

They have found us, Joss.

I gave a start. *No, I don't think so. At least not yet. If they had found us, they would be up here by now.*

Go and look.

As softly as a fall of dust, I crept to the mouth of the cave and peered down. On both sides of the river, I could see the figures of men moving about. They were clumsy in the twilight, but I was well accustomed to it. Living as we were had substantially increased my night vision.

I was observing a large company of unwelcome strangers: the New People. None of them were looking up. By the time they arrived, there had not been enough light left to reveal the caves above them. If we stayed quiet, they might leave in the morning without ever knowing we were here.

I needed to warn the others as quietly as possible, but only a very few were capable of silent talking. Like myself, those few routinely kept their minds closed to unwanted noise from outside. It was a skill that the Dagda had taught me and I valued highly.

In a situation like this, it could be a liability.

That is a pity, said the voice in my head.

Do you have any suggestions?

You spoke of being their leader, Joss. You need to find the solution yourself.

I would not allow myself to be angry at a dying man, but the temptation was strong.

How, I wondered, could I travel from cave to cave in absolute silence? Only dust and smoke could do that.

And members of the Danann nobility.

I smiled. Gifts are passed on in the blood.

Mongan. Changer of Shapes.

Buried in my memory and rising to the surface now was that moment at the temple, when I realized that I had changed. Something in my flesh and bone had . . . altered, ever so slightly. I did not know when or how, but I felt the difference.

Shinann knew how to change shape too; she had told me how to become like a tree. How to *become* a tree. I must recall her exact instructions.

The noise continuing down by the river was an impossible distraction, so I shut it out. And emptied my mind. I did not think about emptying it, which would defeat the purpose. I simply let it go blank as if I were falling asleep.

Smoke. The immolated spirits of trees. Soft, formless smoke. Moving through me. Weightless, bodiless, yet obedient to my own spirit for as long as I could hold my concentration.

"Just let it happen to you," Shinann had said. "To you, in you. Accept the tree."

Accept the smoke. Silently billowing, carrying an urgent message.

In the caves above the river, there was no sound at all.

≈❧

I awoke exhausted with no sense of how much time had passed, but the bats were back, clinging to the walls of the cave.

"The Mílesians broke camp with the sunrise," Melitt informed me. "They never knew we were here."

I sat up, aching in every muscle. What I had accomplished was not only mental but terribly physical. In the aftermath, my disrupted body was expressing its displeasure. "And the Dagda," I asked Melitt. "How is he?"

"He never stirred all night. I think he is awake now, though; his eyes just opened."

I went to his side. *Can you hear me?*

"Of course I can hear you, Joss," he said aloud. "There is no need to shout."

❧ TWENTY-SIX ❧

THE ENEMY HAD COME too close. The Túatha Dé Danann knew they should move as far away as possible, but it would not be easy. They had been in the caves long enough to feel safe there, almost long enough to feel at home.

Piriome confided to Trialet that she was going to be a bat when she grew up. Trialet echoed her intention, adding flourishes such as massive wings and fur that glowed in the dark.

When he heard them, Joss said, "Don't talk like that, children; you must never say such things. Don't even think them."

"Why not?" asked Trialet. "It would be wonderful to fly."

"And live on insects? Is that what you want?"

The children looked dubious, but Joss began to worry about his cousins.

Gifts are passed on in the blood.

Following their near discovery by strangers, the adult Dananns discussed the possibility of moving somewhere else. Those whose territory had been forested thought it would be best to seek another forest "where the trees can protect us." Mountain dwellers spoke wistfully of blue hills and long vistas. The clans who came from along the coast yearned for the sounds of the sea.

While they accepted the necessity for relocating again, they could not agree as to where. And no clan was willing to attempt it by themselves.

The survivors were fully aware of their limitations as a tribe. A strong tribe required a variety of individuals who could perform the many functions necessary to the body as a whole. It would be possible to continue without some of them, but not without a head, not for long.

The once-powerful Túatha Dé Danann had been reduced to a straggle of survivors who were clinging to a life that had lost its shape.

Conversely, the Mílesians believed they were in an excellent position. Although they had lost valuable members of their tribe to the Green Wave and the great battle, they still had adequate numbers to guarantee future generations. And instead of one head, they had two.

They had yet to discover that this would have a profound effect on future generations.

≈≋

In the descending twilight of his life, the man who had been the Dagda thought about the people he would soon leave behind. He was indifferent to the problems of the New People, but he was deeply concerned about the Túatha Dé Danann. To have come so far and achieved so much and then to melt away like frost without leaving a trace behind seemed too cruel.

Something would remain, however. Something tangible.

Like many a keeper of cherished secrets, the Dagda had clutched his to his heart. The deep esteem in which he was held by the Túatha Dé Danann depended upon his being the guardian of the mysteries. In a distant past, he scarcely remembered he had been instructed by others like himself, the last living members of the tribe that had come to Ierne Before the Before.

As a child he had listened to the narratives of the dispossessed. Had tried to capture their fragmented memories of their original home. Could not even imagine the obstacles they had overcome in making their incredible voyage.

All murky and twisted in his mind now.

But he had kept the faith. Pearl by pearl he had passed their treasures to the next generation, and the next, and the next, giving each a part of the whole. Had he been too slow in sharing? Did any of them truly understand what set Ierne apart, or why it was sacred?

Too late now, and he was too tired.

He had watched with pride as generations of young Dananns exhibited the unique talents of their ancestors. No one had all of them, which was as it should be. Nuada had come closest, but even he . . .

Memories of Nuada of the Silver Hand squeezed an opaque tear from beneath the Dagda's closed eyelids.

"Are you in pain?" Melitt called from very far away.

No.

"Are you in pain?" she shouted in his ear.

"No, I'm not in pain." His voice sounded like a rusty hinge.

Melitt sat back on her heels with a relieved sigh. "Don't frighten me like that. I thought I had lost you."

"You will not lose me."

"I understand, but I do get frightened."

Dear little woman, he thought. There had been other

women, not so tender; queens of fire and fury. Gone out now. Leaving him with this gentle spirit who was all he wanted at the end. Melitt and a boy called Joss . . .

"Joss!" the Dagda called in the voice that used to be his.

A grown man knelt beside him on the floor of the cave, a man with sky-colored eyes and a soft, springy beard. "I'm here," he said.

"You wanted to ask me so many questions . . ."

"They can wait."

"They cannot wait. Let me tell you what you need to know while I have the strength."

"If you rest now, Dagda, you will be stronger tomorrow."

"I shall, but not here. Listen to me. Do you remember the temple on the hill?"

"I do, of course."

"I told you there were other temples, and I intended to take you to them when you were older."

"I am older now."

The Dagda managed a faint smile. "Sadly, you must go on your own. But I want you to understand what you find. Come closer . . ."

His voice grew so labored that Joss could not make out the words. *Think to me,* he said to the Dagda.

As she watched the two of them together, Melitt saw the young man's eyes widen. His face became a study in intense concentration.

When the bats left the cave, Joss was still sitting beside the Dagda, listening to a voice that Melitt had never heard. She was not jealous. Over the long span of their lives together, her husband had said everything she wanted to hear.

She did not go foraging that night. There was nothing she could do but care for the children and wait. Patience was one of her talents.

I listened closely to everything the Dagda told me, and re-membered. Not one word escaped me; neither did the in-structions I did not fully understand. He was pouring his wisdom into me, and I must not spill a single drop.

Weave a tender network of those you care about, and who care about you. The path they light will guide your spirit.

Seek balance; from the mightiest sun to the tiniest insect, all must be in balance. What we do will, in time, be done to us, although we may not recognize it.

There are three questions that only you can answer, but you must answer them all, in thislife or another.

Who am I?

Why am I?

Where am I going?

And this above everything: have courage. In the end, we are perfectly safe. All things are one and part of the same Word.

❧ TWENTY-SEVEN ❧

THE DAGDA LOOKED UP at me, but I was not sure he could see me. His eyes were clouded and rheumy, the whites yellow. *Do not grieve, Joss, there is no need. It is my time, I have put it off for far too long.*

"I don't want you to go! What about the tribe? How can we . . ."

Ask yourself, he replied. He raised a shaking, skeletal hand and put his forefinger on my breast. "Elgolai," he said clearly.

I thought he meant that he was going out, which I already knew. But tears sprang to my eyes anyway.

You. Elgolai.

❧

He had gone out. Between one breath and the next, the Dagda had left us. I sat beside the emptied shell of him and tried to imagine my life without him.

Melitt pushed me aside so she could put her ear against his nostrils. Then she put the flat of her palm on his chest. Her eyes met mine. She shook her head.

The children knew. They silently gathered around us. Demirci was carrying my little sister in his arms. Drithla reached a tiny hand down toward the man who lay at their feet.

Take her hand! I willed with everything in me.

The Dagda did not move.

He had gone out.

A few at a time, the other Dananns came to the cave to see him. No one had summoned them. I stood on one side of the Dagda's bed and Melitt stood on the other while they walked in a slow circle around us. Sunwise, the sacred direction.

A few of the women murmured their sympathy to Melitt or lightly stroked her hand. No one tried to comfort me; I was thankful. I needed to be alone in that space he still occupied within me.

The tender network, he had said.

The Dagda had been more than a king. In a race of exceptional people, he had been the most exceptional. His funeral rites must befit his status. But how could the appropriate ritual be performed by a small band of refugees hiding in caves with bats?

In the end, we are perfectly safe. All things are one and part of the same Word.

I knew then what I had to do.

We covered the Dagda's body with the finest blanket we had and carried him to the coldest part of the cave. Then I asked everyone to join me on the riverbank. I was not sure they would come; it would be the first test of my leadership. No one had conferred the honor on me, and I had not requested it. But the space was there. And I stepped in.

In the same way they had come to bid the Dagda farewell, the Dananns arrived in twos and threes to hear what I had to say. Wounded warriors, weary mothers, feeble elders. And the children too; I had requested the children in particular. What was going to happen would become part of their memories. The children should not be shut out—I felt strongly about that.

When I announced what I planned to do for the Dagda, the Dananns protested. "The Mílesians will discover and slaughter us all!"

"We still have one protection," I said, "their fear of the unknown. If you will trust me and we work together, I believe we can create an illusion they dare not approach."

No one was totally convinced, but no one was willing to relinquish the funeral of a great king either.

We traveled by night, carrying the Dagda's body wrapped in blankets and with our wounded warriors acting as lookouts. Once or twice, we almost ran into a band of the New People—perhaps searching for us—but they did not live in caves and were unsure in the dark. They did not know the land as we did. Shinann knew it best of all. She danced on ahead of us, leaving a faint silvery trail that we could follow . . .

. . . all the way to the temple on the hill.

Along the way, we gathered firewood and enough material for a torch.

As a parting gift, the Dagda had shared the secrets of three temples with me—not all of the secrets, however. "Some you must learn for yourself," he had said. When we reached the mound on top of the ridge, I lit a single torch. With great effort, we opened the heavy doors behind the Guardian Stone. Then we carried the Dagda's body up the narrow passageway to the central chamber.

In the recess that had held my mother, the same stone basin waited for him. Just beyond the triple spiral.

I left Melitt with her husband's body and went back outside to give instructions. First, we had to remove the heavy plugs of quartz blocking the aperture over the entrance. Combined with the open passageway it would be sufficient to create a draft.

There were not enough of us to surround the mound while holding hands. So we pressed our hands onto the mound itself, onto the layer of white quartz. Wounded warriors, weary mothers, feeble elders, and the children too, connecting with each other through the temple.

"Now," I said as loud as I dared. "Think of the stars. Enter the stars. Become one with the stars."

The people on either side of me passed on the command.

The faintest ripple ran through us—or perhaps I was imagining it. "Again," I said urgently.

I was beginning to hear what sounded like voices approaching in the distance, shouting to one another in the accents of the invaders.

"Become the stars!" I cried. "Now! The stars!"

The faint ripple intensified. An icy heat ran up my arms and into my body. Jolted through me. Through us. Ignited the quartz covering of the mound until it emitted a radiance I could see reflected on the faces on either side of me.

The temple glowed like the moon.

It would have been a terrifying sight to any unsuspecting Mílesians.

When we removed our hands, I did not know how long the light would last, so we had to act quickly.

We could not all crowd into the central chamber to view the ritual, but we could all chant the invocation the Dagda had taught to me. The Dananns filled the other two recesses and the passageway and gathered around the Guardian Stone outside while I lit the fire in the large basin. It only smouldered for a few heartbeats before blazing up around the body of the Dagda.

The billowing of smoke, the crackling of flames, flesh and bone and fabric burning—yet what I shall always remember is the haunting fragrance of ancient stone dust.

We waited with the Dagda until the fire died down.

The last thing we did before leaving the temple was close and seal the heavy stone doors. I adjured the Guardian Stone to block any attempt to enter until I returned.

As we made our way down the ridge, the unearthly glow of the quartz was just beginning to fade. We traveled all the way back to the limestone caves without being molested.

❧

Éremón was furious. "You found some of the Túatha Dé Danann, but you let them get away? How could that happen, Gosten!"

The stocky warrior squirmed under the withering gaze of his chieftain. "I didn't say we found them and I didn't say we didn't. The shining path Ruari claimed he saw would only be visible at night, so we've been trying to find it at night. Blundering around in the dark like idiots," Gosten added under his breath.

"What did you say?"

"Hunting in the dark. Not easy to do, Éremón."

"Surely you've hunted game in the dark before."

"Deer and wild boar, yes, but not people. I'm not sure that what we were hunting this time could be described as 'people.' The Túatha Dé Danann are . . ." Gosten tried to think of the right word.

Éremón said impatiently, "Did you find them or not?"

"A couple of times I thought we had, but we never actually got our hands on them. We did follow them to a bend in the river below a ridge and . . ."

"And?" Éremón was drumming his fingers.

"They just weren't there. But we could see this huge white light . . ."

"White light," Éremón repeated sarcastically. "In the dark. You were looking at the moon, you fool."

"It wasn't the moon. This was entirely different, a sort of mound at the top of the ridge. Personally, I think the place is haunted. My men spooked like frightened horses and refused to go any closer. To avoid outright rebellion, I had to bring them home."

Éremón's face was turning red. "You should have stayed where you were and ordered them to thoroughly investigate it, whatever it was! What's wrong with you, Gosten? You had your orders!"

The dwelling within the walls of the royal fort was fast vanishing over the horizon, but Gosten struggled to keep his temper. "There's nothing wrong with me. I'm as loyal and obedient as anyone in your command, but I can't do the impossible. I would like to see you march a company of warriors up a hill that glittered brighter than the stars."

Éremón momentarily closed his eyes, trying to imagine the scene. Recalling some of the other incidents that had happened since they came to Ierne.

In his heart of hearts, he knew he would not have gone to investigate the glowing mound either.

He opened his eyes and looked at Gosten. "Haunted, you say? By evil spirits?"

"That's what I think. A druid might be able to explain; someone like Colptha."

"We seem to be a little short of such druids at the moment," Éremón replied drily. "For now, Gosten, stay away from that area and keep your men away too. We don't want anything to weaken their resolve. If the Dananns do still exist, we will discover them sooner or later and wipe them out."

Éremón spoke with the confidence the Gael expected of their chieftains, but his bravado did not reach to the marrow of his bones. He would never admit it to anyone, but from the beginning the Dananns had unnerved him. They were able to speak in his own language—albeit with a trace of an accent that strangely reminded him of Sakkar's—although they lived on an island that had never been visited by Gaelicians. If it had been, surely the event would have become part of tribal history.

There were other things that bothered Éremón too. No matter how hard he stared at the Dananns, he could never see them clearly. They were always at the edge of his vision, as if about to flicker out of sight. When they spoke to one another, they sounded like birds twittering. Oddest of all, they had come to battle with songs on their lips and flowers in their hair.

There was something very wrong about the Túatha Dé Danann.

Gosten had referred to the ridge being haunted. By what? And how malign were its intentions?

Although Taya complained, Éremón began taking his sword to bed with him. Cold iron had worked against the Dananns before; it might protect him again.

⁂

We had returned safely to our friends the bats, but the future looked bleak. The New People were actively hunting us, and they had come too close already. I was convinced that our best protection would be to move as far away as possible.

Shinann suggested we go beyond the Wide River. She had grown up in the west of Ierne, and her descriptions of the territory at the edge of the Cold Sea were as lyrical as a bard's. "We would be safer there," she assured me, "because the New People would never travel that far."

"They have already traveled the length of the land," I reminded her. "If they are so determined to get us, even the Wide River won't stop them."

"But they won't know we are there, Joss! Who will tell them? The wind? I don't think so; the breezes are our friends, not theirs."

No one had said anything to me about formally accepting the leadership of what remained of the tribe, but one by one the others came to me to discuss my plans.

My plans, for them.

The weight of responsibility settled on shoulders I thought were too young to bear it, but what options did I have?

I asked Shinann to describe those western caves in detail. Then we prepared for the journey.

❧ TWENTY-EIGHT ❧

ONCE AGAIN, we would travel by night, at least until we reached the Wide River. Shinann said the river that ran below the limestone caves was one of its tributaries, so we followed it like a pathway. The forests clothing much of Ierne were so dense that in places the only way to get through them was along the bank of a river or a stream. In other places, we had to pick our way across rough terrain or skirt dangerous bogs.

Ierne could be hospitable; she had been hospitable to us Before the Before. She had taken us in when we were broken and given us a home.

But the arrival of the New People had made her wary. They were not gentle and respectful of the land, and her defenses were up now.

My little sister wanted to hold my hand as we walked. I was carrying both my belongings and hers in a pack on my back, and her arms were so short I had to stoop to take her hand. But if I let go, she cried.

Drithla's tears were like a knife through the heart.

Remembering how the Dagda had once carried me, I swung her up onto my shoulders. To my surprise, the burden was much less than I expected.

Love lightens burdens.

Then too I was growing stronger day by day; taller, heavier, becoming a man as quickly as a fledgling becomes a hawk. Necessity was the magic. My people needed me.

Shinann was changing too. As we drew nearer the Wide River, I began to notice aspects of her that I had never seen before. Her light and sparkling voice was becoming deeper, more melodious. She no longer danced; she flowed.

I was growing into a man, but Shinann was already a woman, with a woman's power.

When we made camp for the night, it was always in the heart of the forest and we did not light fires. A fire might draw unwanted attention to us, but more important it could damage our friends the trees. The trees who protected us, who lowered their branches to shelter us and turn the rain away, who sang lullabies to the children and perfumed the air to comfort the weary travelers.

In order to keep the little ones warm at night, we wrapped them in their blankets and placed them in the center while the adults crowded close around them. I slept on the outer edge of the circle. Watchful, always.

During the night, I was increasingly aware of the bodies lying next to mine. Touching mine. Pressing against me. Other hearts beating. Warm breath on other lips.

I began to have disturbing dreams.

My people.

My ties of blood with most of them were very close. If not for the invasion of the New People, I would have begun traveling on my own soon, seeking a woman who was not kin to me. Someone light and lovely, from a distant clan. We

would marry in the custom of the Túatha Dé Danann and in time there would be a child; maybe even two. Because of us, the tribe would continue.

But what if . . .

On the morning before we reached the Wide River, I asked Shinann, "What will happen to us if there are no more children?"

She did not hesitate. "There will always be children."

"Born to the Túatha Dé Danann?"

She stopped walking and turned to look at me. "Carrying the blood of the Túatha Dé Danann," she said slowly.

I heard her thoughts. They were so deeply personal that I changed the subject. She was not thinking of me.

The Wide River ran like a mighty artery through the heart of Ierne, dividing east from west. The reliable rains of leaf-spring had swollen the river to a torrent. We had to search for a long time before we found a ford where we could cross. As sunseason advanced, the level of the water was dropping, but we could not wait. We needed to find a new sanctuary now.

The river was strong and cold. The riverbed contained a number of deep holes that could swallow anyone who took a misstep. At the suggestion of Agnonis—who thought about such things because he could not see—we used ropes and vines to link us to one another. The smaller children rode on the shoulders of the adults. Once or twice, I stumbled but dare not fall; Drithla was perched on my shoulders with her tiny fingers locked in my hair.

Besides, Shinann had assured us the river would not harm us.

By the time we reached the opposite bank, the light had changed. Later, I would observe that the light always changed from east to west; two parts of a single whole.

From the Wide River we had a considerable journey to reach the caves Shinann had told us about. Pockets of primitive tribes flourished in the forests of the west, but they did not bother us. They did not even see us; we made certain of that. Hiding in plain sight was one of our arts.

We were still the Túatha Dé Danann.

At last, we reached the cliffs at the edge of the Cold Sea. According to Shinann, the entire region was studded with caves, and the women were eager to find them. Yet I could not help lingering to gaze in awe at the majesty of the feral waves crashing against the coast. Too wild ever to be tamed.

My father had claimed descent from Manannan Mac Lir, the unconquerable spirit of the sea. Manannan's chariot was pulled by a team of white-maned horses. In the far west of Ierne, I stood on a rocky beach in a blowing gale and watched the white-maned horses come galloping in.

Are you here today, Mongan? I asked. *Can you see this?*

I trusted the wind to carry my words to him.

As we traveled along the coast, we observed crevices in the shoulders of the land. A few opened into little caves that were not large enough for our purpose, but their existence encouraged us. "Where there is an egg, there might be a chick," my mother used to say.

Like the dwellings we had shared with the bats, the western caves were made of limestone. Carved out by the drumming fingers of rainwater and the restless travels of underground rivers.

Water is life.

From far away, we could see a truncated mountain that resembled a giant table. We hurried toward it with Shinann running on ahead, lightfooted and laughing. But the mountain was not as close as it appeared to be. By the time we reached it, the children were exhausted and peevish, so we made camp and prepared to spend the night.

Halfway up to the plateau on top, I observed a perpendicular rock face like the wall of a giant's fortress. The surface was badly eroded by weather but held in place by ivy and pierced by numerous cave openings.

Shinann waited with the other Dananns while I climbed up to explore.

The caves were clean and dry and devoid of bats, to my surprise and perhaps even disappointment; I had grown to like the little creatures. But these caves were not large enough for us either.

The following day, we went on.

Near the northern edge of the range that included the flat-topped mountain, we finally caught a glimpse of what we sought. Wearily, we climbed a steep, grassy slope overlooking a deep valley. At the top of the slope, we had to pick our way across a dangerous talus of loose stones and a slanting rock face in order to reach the immense natural arch that had attracted our attention.

Before we could explore any farther, we stopped to light torches.

The initial cave was more than large enough, and it led to a cavern of immense proportions and astonishing beauty. Flashes of torchlight illumined sharply jutting rocks high above our heads—much, much higher than the domed ceiling in the temple on the ridge. Higher still were patches of unfathomable blackness that indicated still further heights.

"Mind your feet," commented Droma, who was always looking down because of the injury to his back. Lowering the torches, we discovered unsuspected abysses lurking in the floor of the cavern. Falling into one of them could be worse than falling into a hole in the bed of the Wide River. At least we knew what drowning was.

Exploration ceased abruptly while we used all the ropes we had to link ourselves together again. Those who were not adequately secured were ordered to "Wait right here!"

And I meant it.

The enormous cavern had other secrets to reveal. We were amazed to see giant spearheads of ice hanging down from the darkness above, bunched together like frozen fruits and many other improbable shapes. Walls and overhanging ledges were festooned with giant icicles. The entire cave glittered in spite of its permanent dusk.

When we examined the ice with cautious fingertips, we discovered it was not ice at all but stone. In the torchlight the stone gleamed like the quartz at the temple on the ridge.

That association prompted Cleena to exclaim, "This is like a palace. We should have brought the Dagda here!"

"No," I said quickly.

Saball chimed in with, "We could never have carried his body this far."

"Even if we could, it would have been a mistake," I replied. "There is one duty yet to perform for the Dagda, and it can only be done where we left him."

"What are you talking about, Joss?" Melitt asked.

"A final request he made of me."

"I didn't know anything about it," she said with pain in her voice.

How easy it is to hurt someone without meaning to; even in death, the Dagda was teaching me. "This was a burden he did not want to put on your shoulders," I told her, "because I am the one who will have to carry it."

Actually, I don't know if that was what the Dagda was thinking—but I hope it was.

To my astonishment, I heard myself add, "What I do for him I shall do for you, Melitt, when your time comes."

We continued to explore the huge cave system. To the right of the main cavern, we found a narrow but lofty chamber. Gradually, the walls contracted to form a gallery of sorts. Close to the entry was a curious mass of the icelike material, forming a colossal female form. Beyond this, the gallery continued to narrow until I had to crawl on my hands and knees—only to discover that it led again to the entrance cave.

To the left of the giant arch we found another gallery, wider than a tall man, with a winding pathway of stone rubble that eventually opened out on the face of the cliff. From this vantage point, we could see a magnificent panorama of the entire countryside. No enemy could approach us undetected. As the Dagda had said, we were perfectly safe.

We had come home.

❧

The western caves exceeded our highest expectations. At first, I had thought they might be too hard to access, particularly for the crippled and the elderly, but they were part of a vast network with many openings, including a well-concealed entrance in the valley below. We did not even have to leave them to find water. Rainwater poured through holes in the limestone ceilings of the caves and was easily collected.

The deep valley was a haven for plant life. We discovered not only those things that were familiar to us but other herbs and roots we had never seen before. After testing to make certain they were edible, the women harvested them with glad cries. A variety of soft fruits were found with only a little searching. Streams and streamlets crisscrossed the region, providing an abundant supply of fish.

We could live here indefinitely and forget about the rest of Ierne and the enemies who hunted us. They would never find us here. Our future was secured—though not the future we once expected. Now severely limited in number, the Túatha Dé Danann who had roamed freely across the island for many generations must now limit themselves to hidden sanctuaries.

We would become the voices on the night wind, the tales mothers told to their children at bedtime.

Yet in my dreams at night I kept hearing the last word the Dagda had spoken to me.

Elgolai.

🍀 TWENTY-NINE 🍀

THE DREAMS OF SHINANN were haunted too. She had thought returning to the west would make her happy, and it did, yet she discovered there were different shadings to that emotion. Her heart leaped with joy when she recognized the pellucid light originating from the Cold Sea and knew she was home at last.

She had ached for a companion to whom she could say, "Oh look, do look! Here we are!" But who would understand that something as ephemeral as light could bestow happiness? And that the lack of someone to share it with caused pain?

Shinann loved Ierne. Simply because it *was*. By existing, Ierne satisfied her spirit. The green land filled her eyes and the moist air was sweet on her tongue and the birds sang songs she knew and the hills were the shape she needed them to be.

Why, then, did she still feel such longing?

As the Dananns settled into their new homes—for

every clan had its own crystalline spaces now—Shinann was happy for them.

And yet . . .

❧

Both branches of the Mílesians and their followers now occupied great swathes of land. Most of it was mantled with forest, but they were confident they could clear enough to provide adequate grassland for their livestock and arable land for raising grain. Unlike Iberia, which suffered recurrent plagues of drought, on Ierne there was no shortage of rain. Summer was not too hot nor winter too cold, and the island remained green all year.

Yet neither Éremón nor Éber Finn was content. Each man thought the other had got the better deal.

Both blamed Amergin. He began trying to avoid them as much as he could, but it was a small island and through attrition Amergin had become the chief druid of the Mílesians. If his services were required, he had to provide them. His brothers were more anxious than ever to ameliorate their relationships with the unseen world. Births and deaths and dwellings being built and milk cows that went dry and quarrels over property all required the abilities of a druid in one way or another.

When a band of Éremónians came upon members of Éber Finn's tribe building a fishing weir within the borders of the northern territory, a furious battle ensued. Men from both sides were killed. A runner was sent to find Amergin and advise him of the possibility of war. He was intercepted on his way to visit Sakkar—who now wanted to be known as Sétga, a name that sounded more Gaelic to his ear and pleased his new wife.

Amergin had no intention of cutting his visit to the couple short. He would not deny himself the pleasure of seeing the peace and fulfillment the former Phoenician had found at last. The red-haired woman was a perfect mate for him. She was genuinely interested in the stories he told about his colorful past and equally interested in sharing his future. Which, as Amergin the druid foresaw, would include the birth of twins.

They were overjoyed when he told them. He stayed with them for several days, and they pleaded with him to stay longer, but he did not want to intrude. They needed time alone together before their family expanded so dramatically.

Amergin was returning to his own home when he heard the pipes in the hills announcing a royal death.

Odba's son Moomneh arrived at his door with a message. "Éremón bids me remind you that the chief bard must sing the eulogy for a chieftain's wife and the chief druid must preside at her burial. As you are both, Amergin, you are doubly needed."

Amergin could not imagine Taya being dead. A simple accident while she was drawing water from a well; her foot slipped; she overbalanced; it could have happened to anyone. If he had married her himself when they were back in Iberia . . .

But if was no answer to anything.

On the Hill of Tara, the bard stood beside the newly constructed tomb of Taya, honored wife of Éremón, and sought to compose a eulogy that would remind the Mílesians of their brotherhood. The words he needed would not come. In the end, he played Clarsah by herself, letting the harp create a vision of beauty and loss. As usually happened when the bard played his harp, people were deeply moved. Except for Éremón; it was hard to tell what he felt. His features might have been chiseled out of stone.

After the funeral ended and the tomb had been sealed, Amergin spoke briefly with him. He did not mention the incipient warfare, but both of them were aware of it. "You are a courageous warrior, Éremón," Amergin said, choosing his words deliberately. "There is a new war for you to fight; win back the unity of the tribe. That would be a fitting memorial for Taya, who loved peace and amity."

Éremón nodded, stepped into his chariot, and drove away with his head bowed in thought, but his contemplative mood did not last long. All too soon his brain was preempted by the plans/worries/irritations/angers/passions that could dominate the mind of a chieftain.

By the time he reached his stronghold, the words of the bard were forgotten.

When the other mourners had departed, Amergin was reluctant to leave Taya's tomb. He had not loved her the way she wanted, but he had loved her, and she was his friend. He felt diminished without her.

Again, he experienced the desire that was familiar to all druids: a longing to move beyond the walls of flesh that imprisoned spirit. To soar across time and space, to be as light and free as . . .

. . . as Shinann was, running up the hill to meet him. Holding out her hands.

ᏗᏭ

When I learned that Shinann was missing, I did not worry about her, not at first. The Dananns from the western clans were not overly concerned either; we all knew that she wandered. She had come home, we reminded one another, so she was simply reacquainting herself with the scenes of her childhood. Who would not do the same after a long absence?

But when Shinann failed to return by the time the seasons changed, her kinfolk appealed to me to search for her. That request more than anything else confirmed my position as their leader. The problem was, I had no idea how to start. She could be anywhere. It would be as easy to trace the path of a leaf blown by the wind.

I decided to search in a wide circle spiraling out from the caves and took several of our less-damaged warriors with me. As a precaution, we carried swords, although we knew how little use bronze was against iron.

We had traveled for quite a distance before we came upon the first settlement of New People. Careful to stay well out of sight, we stopped long enough to observe them.

The dwellings they had built for themselves did not seem to grow out of the land, as ours did, but were set on top of it; heavy, circular structures of timber and sod sealed with mud and roofed with thatch. Aside from a single door, there was no allowance for letting light into the interior.

The barriers they had erected around their houses— walls and banks and ditches—added to the overall impression of permanence.

Outside of these barriers, the land was divided into individual holdings separated by low stone walls. The ground had been torn open by iron ploughs and planted with foreign seeds. Instead of collecting the abundant rain on the surface, the Mílesian settlers had punched holes deep into the earth to provide water. It was sickening to see the soft flesh of Ierne abused.

Yet the actions of the New People were not totally alien. On the grassy uplands where they brought their cattle to graze, we were surprised to discover that the herders had built little shelters for themselves much like the dwellings of the Túatha Dé Danann. Lightweight and easily constructed, they were the ideal solution for people who frequently traveled from one pasturage to another.

Some of the Mílesians must have observed ours and copied them. It was a good sign; at least they could learn. Perhaps.

The Dananns knew all there was to know about living in and with this land: which native plants were good to eat and where they grew, the wide array of herbs that could kill or cure, the way to nourish hungry soil or refresh weary water.

We also could taste the weather. It was our intimate companion. We lived on an island in the sea and the wind came to us from all directions, telling us everything we needed to know. The lessening weight of the air on our skin prepared us for storms. From one moment to the next, the clouds wrote and rewrote their language in the sky for us to read. Rain in all its myriad forms sang the songs of prophecy. Without touching a finger to the ground, we knew exactly how warm or cold the earth was and how soon it would waken the sleeping seed.

The New People knew none of these things. We could have told them savage measures were unnecessary. Our sacred island would provide as bountifully for them as she did for us—if they were kind to her.

Our observations soon proved they were not kind. The invaders who believed they had conquered Ierne were trying to beat and bludgeon her warm body into submission with their cold iron tools.

With heavy hearts, my companions and I resumed the search for Shinann. If the Mílesians had captured her . . . I could not bear to think about it. Nor did I want to go home without her. At least my people were in a safe place and would be able to fend for themselves until we returned.

୨⅜

Amergin's horseboy came to Éremón's stronghold with troubling news. "The bard has not returned his team for my care since he drove them to Taya's entombment," he reported, "and I am beginning to worry."

Éremón was worried too. As chieftain of the north, much of his prestige rested upon his having the loyalty and the physical presence of the chief druid. As soon as he could, Éremón hurried to Amergin's house. It appeared to be unoccupied, although some of the bard's belongings were still there. A few well-worn cloaks and tunics hung on pegs; domestic fowl scratched holes in the earth beside the door to create dust baths for themselves.

But Clarsah was missing.

Éremón immediately sent out search parties. He led the largest one himself.

The men who had been unable to find the Túatha Dé Danann were unable to find the bard either. Reluctantly, Éremón came to the conclusion that the Fír Bolga must have seized and killed him. He gave orders that every Fír Bolga settlement his men could find should be put to the torch.

Some of his people had doubts. A warrior who had not received sufficient recognition from his chieftain told a swordsmith that Éremón and Amergin had been overheard quarreling. Whispers gained volume; rumors grew legs.

When Éber Finn was informed of the suspicions against his youngest brother, he was appalled. He sent messengers north to inquire as to Amergin's exact location and current state of health, which infuriated Éremón. "How could Éber think I would do anything to the bard! It's the end to any friendship between us."

≫

After the Túatha Dé Danann vanished, time on Ierne had assumed a predictable pattern. Day followed night without exception, each of a measurable length. Except for twilight. A trace of magic lingered in the twilight.

≫

As if responding to the growing enmity between the Mílesians, Ierne became less accommodating. In the season of leaf-fall, rivers burst their banks and valleys that had never flooded before were inundated. Healthy people fell ill; sick people died. Cattle strayed and children wandered off into the woods, never to be seen again.

Some claimed the Túatha Dé Danann had stolen them.

Éremón and Éber Finn blamed each other for their misfortunes.

Surreptitiously, warriors of the Gael who had gone too long without a battle to fight began sharpening their weapons again. A man needed victories to feel like a man.

≫

The winds had a message for us.

Disheartened by our inability to find Shinann, we had decided to return to the western caves. Darkseason was waiting over the horizon, and I had arrangements to make before I could obey the Dagda's final instructions to me. But as we approached our new home, we encountered a startling change in the weather. The prevailing wind off the Cold Sea was swirling around us as if it had lost its sense of direction.

Dark clouds were piling up to the north . . . *and* the south. Normally gentle air currents were roiling like water.

Like war.

The portents of a major conflict were unmistakable. They must mean that the bloodthirsty Mílesians were going to fight each other. Good! I thought. Let them. We could wait safe and secure in our glittering chambers. When the foreigners had exterminated themselves, we would reclaim Ierne; we would repair her injuries and heal her wounds.

Yet what of Shinann? Was she out there in the middle of it? She had survived on a battleground once, I knew, but could she do it again?

ᘒ✺

An uneasy peace existed between Éremón and Éber Finn, a peace necessitated by the never-ending work of trying to civilize their conquest: fell enough timber to build more houses and clear land for planting grain, haul countless rocks and boulders out of the fields so they would not break a plowshare, dam the streams and drain the bogs in the constant struggle against the overabundant rain. Men labored until their hands bled and their muscles ached. For a warrior race, it was emotionally unsatisfactory.

Only a small spark was needed to ignite a flame.

In the south, Éber Finn's freemen had been digging into the mountains in search of iron ore. What they found were substantial quantities of gold and copper. The skilled craftsmen of the Gael transformed the precious metals into spectacular jewelery—for Éber Finn. And his wives. And his children.

Envious observers of this flamboyant display reported it to Éremón, who declared that the island had been unfairly divided and he wanted his share of the wealth.

Éber Finn laughed at him.

The increasingly rancorous dispute between the two brothers should have been adjudicated by Amergin. But he had disappeared.

❧ THIRTY ❧

WE PREPARED TO MAKE another journey across the face of Ierne. Not all of us, of course—only those few Dananns who were physically able to travel again and old enough to take part in the ritual. The rest would stay safe in the caves.

Every day was shorter than the one before and every night was longer. The seasons were about to change. Our journey would be dangerous, but we had a great advantage over the New People. We could travel at night. The invaders could barely see in the dark, even with torches.

I like to think our enhanced vision was a gift from our friends, the bats.

Before we set out, I explained what the Dagda had explained to me. The older Dananns knew part of it already, but for some it was new. "Before the Before, our ancestors came to Ierne from a very different place," I told them. "It was not easy for the ancestors to settle here, not at first. They needed to align themselves with their new homeland and its seasons, which also meant aligning themselves with the stars in the sky.

"For this purpose, they employed the arts and sciences of their ancient race. They erected three great temples above the valley of the cow goddess. The temples comprised chambers built of massive stones covered by mounded earth and encircled with more stones. The interior design of each temple was unique because each was to serve a different function. The structures were situated according to precise patterns carved onto the stones. Other inscriptions recorded and compared the movement of the stars or depicted the journey we had taken and the place where we found ourselves. Many stones faced outward to instruct future generations. Others faced inward, identifying us to the mother earth."

My cousin Sinnadar spoke up. He was always the thinker. "You said the temples served different purposes?"

"Yes and no." As soon as I spoke, I realized it was the sort of answer the Dagda might have given. I could not resist a wry smile. "All three temples celebrate the Great Fire of Life by marking the passages of the sun. One salutes its birth on the shortest morning, when the days are about to lengthen again. The second marks sunset on the longest day, when the darkseason begins to return. The third temple observes the occasions when day and night are of equal length. Acknowledging the passages of the sun is vital for people who rely on the earth to feed them.

"Each temple serves multiple purposes, however. For now, we are only concerned with the one that welcomes the rising sun in midwinter, because it is the most important. If the sun did not rise on the shortest day and force the dark to retreat, life would not be possible. And life is the purpose of the ritual we will perform for the Dagda. For many generations he has been the keeper of the flame."

I kept watching for Shinann. I could not accept that we had lost her. I imagined her dancing forward to meet us when we reached the bend of the river below the temples. I envisioned her laughing face and called to her with the silent speaking.

But she never answered.

The two Mílesian chieftains did not go to war against each other that autumn. A persistent and exceptionally cold rain afflicted the season of leaf-fall, pummeling Ierne with such force that the earth was turned to quagmire. Warriors could not practice the killing arts when they were mired to the knees in mud. Or slipping on ice, because that was what happened next. An island accustomed to moderate temperatures was bombarded with sleet and hail.

The weather improved at night, but the Gael did not give battle at night.

As he sat close to the fire roaring on his hearth, testing the edges of weapons that needed no further testing, Éremón muttered that Ierne was cursed. His sullen attitude began to affect the other inhabitants of his stronghold. It spread outside the walls and widened to influence the larger settlement of Gaelicians, until they were no longer happy with the land they had won. They counted its flaws but dismissed its virtues. The many flaws they saw they blamed on the island. The few virtues they were willing to recognize they credited to themselves.

"Our chieftain needs a new wife," Sétga commented to his own new wife. "Éremón has buried two within a year, and that makes a man sour."

"Your friend Amergin has no wife, but he doesn't appear to be sour."

"He doesn't appear at all anymore," Sétga replied gloomily. "I asked about him in Éremón's fort the other day, but no one had seen him for a long time. A bard who never entertains his chieftain is failing in his responsibilities, and that's not like Amergin."

"Perhaps he has other responsibilities that are more important to him now," Soorgeh's red-haired daughter suggested. When Sive smiled, she had a dimple in her chin.

Her husband loved that dimple. "What sort of responsibilities?" he asked with wide-eyed innocence.

The dimple deepened. "This," she said, extending a searching hand. "Or this. Maybe something like this?"

We reached the temple on the ridge in the dead of night, in the dead heart of darkseason. The rain that had fallen as we traveled had abated; the quartz on the mound glittered in the light of our torches.

I approached the Guardian Stone with a remembered feeling of reverence.

It was watching me.

In front of my people, I folded my hands in supplication and knelt on the winter-chilled earth. Under the stars.

The Guardian Stone was my silent witness.

The hackles rose on the back of my neck.

The Stone knew why I was there.

Four of us were necessary to push open the heavy stone doors that blocked the entrance to the passageway— the doors the Dagda had once opened by himself. Four more Dananns removed the quartz plugs from the aperture above, leaving the light box open.

The Guardian Stone waited. When we were ready, it allowed us to enter.

Inside, all was as we had left it. The scent of ancient stone dust was as sweet and haunting as I remembered. In the basin within the small chamber at the rear, beyond the triple spiral, the ashes of the Dagda lay undisturbed. Holding my torch aloft, I gazed down at them. "We have come as you instructed," I said softly. "Your wife wanted to be with us, but she is no longer strong enough for the journey. When it is her time, we will bring her here. Melitt was the keeper of your flame."

There was almost enough room in the temple for all of us if we crowded together. The few who could not fit inside the chambers stayed outside with the Guardian Stone.

The passageway had to be kept clear.

I extinguished the torch.

The dark inside the temple was darker than the blackness between the stars.

We waited.

For a timeless time, we waited until . . .

. . . A thin finger of light from the rising sun entered the temple through the roof box. Almost as one, we held our breath while the narrow line progressed along the inclined passageway like a living being. It came to rest on the front of the basin in the chamber behind the triple spiral.

Gradually, the glowing beam widened until it filled the central chamber, illumining the carved details within all three recesses. Honey-colored light reflected from every stony surface, from the spellbound faces of the Túatha Dé Danann.

Sacred light bathed the interior of the temple. Blessing us.

We stood transfixed until the golden light narrowed again and was cut off by the configuration of the light box.

Then and only then did I approach the basin where the Dagda's ashes lay.

They had gone with the rising sun.

❧ THIRTY-ONE ❧

IN THE SEASON of leaf-spring, Éremón and Éber Finn went to war at a place remembered as the Hill of the Oxen. Both men brought their full complement of warriors together with oxcarts laden with extra swords and spears and shields and helmets and body armor.

Sétga—he who had been Sakkar the Phoenician—marched with the army of Éremón. On the morning he left home, he confided to his wife, "I don't like going to battle against Éber Finn. I always liked him."

"Then don't go," said the red-haired woman.

"I have no choice. Or, rather, I already made the choice to be one of the Gael and follow the banners of Éremón, so . . ."

She put her hands on her hips. "So?"

He shrugged both of his healthy shoulders. "I'll be back soon; don't worry. I cannot believe that two brothers would actually kill each other and expect the rest of us to follow along like sheep."

She stood in the doorway and watched him march away

over the hills. Proudly wearing his Gaelic tunic and cloak, with his pack on his back and his sword in his belt. Her good-natured, kind little man whose only dream was to see their twins born.

They were due any day.

∾❧

The two halves of the Gaelician tribe crashed together with a scream of trumpets and a thunder of drums. Éremón in his chariot led his men; Éber Finn led for his. Even from a distance, the brothers recognized the fury in each other's faces. Nearly identical faces.

The cacophony of battle carried a long distance on the wind. A dying echo reached a modest dwelling of wicker-work and thatch in a secluded woodland where the smell of cooked fish lingered. Earlier in the day, the lanky, graying man who lived in the cottage had collected enough windfall to feed the fire in the outside pit. His woman would not allow him to cut down a living tree.

The small dwelling was neither as sturdy nor as well-furnished as a bard was entitled to, but he loved it dearly.

Today he was repairing a battered copper pot. His harp leaned against the cottage door. When Clarsah detected the dissonance of war, she emitted a warning hum.

Amergin abruptly put down the pot. "What was that?"

The face that peered at him from the cottage doorway was small and saucy, with enormous eyes and a pointed chin. She recognized the sound as quickly as he did and understood its ramifications. The little woman hurried to the bard and put her arms around him.

"It's Éremón and Éber Finn," he told her. "I must go to them; perhaps there is still time for me to intervene."

She shook her head until a lock of pale hair tumbled

across her forehead. "They do not want you to intervene; they *want* to fight. I cannot understand it."

"My people are warriors, Shinann; that's what they are and what they do. Just as fish swim, they fight. If there is no war, sooner or later they will create one; they simply cannot— or will not—help it."

"But you're not a warrior."

"No. I'm like a hound born without a tail. Fortunately for me, there is a place in life for those who won't fight; druids have other talents to contribute."

"Stay here and contribute them to me." Shinann of the Túatha Dé Danann ran one tiny hand across the slight swelling of her belly.

"I'll come back," the Mílesian promised. "I give my word."

After putting Clarsah into her protective satchel, he harnessed his chariot team. He drove them hard, harder than he liked, for he was gentle with his animals. But the druid in him was aware of disaster.

Yet could not prevent it.

By the time he reached the Hill of the Oxen, the ground was trampled and bloodied, testament to a battle fought without mercy. Man and ox and chariot horse had been struck down in a frenzy. The longer the war was postponed, the more rage had built up, until it exploded like a thunderclap.

Amergin was heartsick. There was no visible difference between what had happened here and what had been done to the Túatha Dé Danann.

He found Éber Finn lying on his shield with his empty eyes staring at the sky. Seeing nothing. Ever again.

Amergin leaped from his chariot and gathered his dead brother into his arms.

There were no words for what he was feeling. In the beginning, Ierne had been a dream for him, the embodiment of a fantasy that had lurked in the depths of his heart for as long as he could remember. When he found Shinann—or she found him—the dream had acquired flesh and blood and a future.

Then flesh and blood had littered the earth and his brothers were dead—with the exception of Éremón, who was responsible for this latest war, this unforgiveable crime.

The best and the worst had happened, and Amergin was caught between them.

Still holding Éber Finn's lifeless body, he called out to a blood-smeared warrior who was gathering up weapons. "Who did this?"

The man would not meet his eyes. "Éremón, with his own hands."

Amergin wished he could return to his chariot and drive away at top speed, but he had no choice. His druid obligations were a gift of his birth. He laid Éber Finn back on the trampled earth so he could remove Clarsah from her satchel. Then he began to sing his brother's eulogy. He needed no time to compose it; the words came from his heart. He sang of the cheerful boy and the energetic youth; the bold adventurer and the tender father. All the parts that went together to form a complete man. An irreplaceable man.

The other Mílesians—Éremón's Mílesians, since Éber Finn's had fled when their chieftain was killed—gathered around the bard to listen. Many of them had tears in their eyes. But there was no sign of Éremón himself.

When Amergin finished the eulogy, he gave orders that Éber Finn's body be treated with dignity and returned to his wives and children as soon as possible. Then he searched among the other dead, seeking and mourning friends. He found Gosten. And Soorgeh. And a small swarthy man who was lying facedown in the mud.

Amergin felt as if he had been punched in the stomach. He crouched beside the body and turned it over. Wiped the face clean.

In death, the features of Sakkar the Phoenician might have been mistaken for those of a Gael.

Amergin pressed his lips to the familiar forehead. "I will care for your family like my own," he whispered. "I promise they will want for nothing, my friend."

My friend.

Before he returned to Shinann, Amergin went to see Éremón in his stronghold. It was where the bard had expected to find him, typically ignoring the consequences of his actions. Leaving others to bury the dead and raise the orphans.

Éremón welcomed Amergin enthusiastically without noticing the expression on his brother's face. To Éremón, the arrival of the bard was simply the perfect opportunity to boast of his battlefield prowess and relate his plans for further dividing Ierne. His loyal followers were entitled to receive additional rewards.

All of this must go into the praise-poem that Amergin would compose in his honor. Éremón made a great point of stressing his generosity; he was going to give part of the southern portion to Éber Finn's sons. Only a part, but it must be commemorated. A victor did not have to surrender any of his winnings to his defeated opponent. Éremón wanted future generations to admire his magnanimous gesture.

Amergin listened to this recital with folded arms but made no comment. Nor did he eat any of the food Éremón offered him. Or drink any of the honey wine.

When Éremón started talking about the territory he intended to give to the future sons of Amergin, the bard could no longer contain himself.

He denounced his brother in a voice like thunder. "You have no right to carve up this island with your bloody sword! I tell you this, Éremón; the poets I sire will never stand with hands outstretched for your favors. My children will celebrate life instead of death, and one day all Ierne will be theirs. Bard land. *Bard land!*"

Amergin turned on his heel and strode from the hall with his red cloak billowing behind him.

Éremón's followers gathered around their chieftain, wringing their hands and asking if the bard would come back. One declared, "If we have lost the chief bard, we are truly cursed!" No druid diviner was needed to interpret the portents. The atmosphere in Éremón's fort went from celebratory to funereal.

The singing wheels of Amergin's chariot whirled him away down a road Éremón would never find, and Clarsah rode on his shoulder.

᠍᠍ᱭ

Shinann knew the Dananns must be looking for her; when she opened her mind, she heard a familiar voice calling her name. But she had found what she was seeking and wanted time to savor it. She did not intend to break with her tribe forever, although Amergin had broken with his.

For a while, it was enough for them just to be together.

Their isolation ended when Amergin brought another woman home. "Sive was married to my friend who died in battle," the bard explained, "and I vowed to take care of his family. As you can see, she is with child. Children," he amended with a nod to the red-haired woman's swollen belly. "Sive is carrying twins."

Shinann chortled with glee and touched her own stomach.

Amergin smiled too. "Now we have the seeds of our clan."

❧

They knew their little wickerwork dwelling would not be adequate for an expanding family, but they could build a larger one. Or consider other options.

When Shinann made the suggestion Amergin started to reject it—then thought again. The Mílesians had come to Ierne seeking a new beginning. What new beginning could be more propitious than the one she proposed?

"Do you think your people would accept us?" he asked Shinann. "We were the enemy. Not me myself, and not Sive either, but our tribe. The Túatha Dé Danann must hate us."

"Hate destroys," she said flatly. "There has been too much destruction already. Only a few of my tribe are left, and we never have enough children. Adding three at one time would be a cause for great celebration."

Amergin raised an eyebrow. "Are you sure?"

❧ THIRTY-TWO ❧

WHILE I WAS WAITING in the dark of the temple for the coming of the light, something wonderful had happened to me. I had become Aware.

Wisdom dwells in the sacred places of the earth.

As surely as if I had seen it with my own eyes, I knew that at the moment of creation, the Great Fire of Life had blazed across the abyss. Suns and stars had been born of dust; living sparks had seeded empty space. Life in its myriad forms had been granted immortality.

In the end, we are perfectly safe. All things are one and part of the same Word.

The ritual we had performed in the temple was an echo from Before the Before. When the narrow bar of light penetrated the womb of the earth, it had replicated the union of male and female, flesh and spirit. By harmonizing opposing forces—keeping everything in balance—existence was assured. Our celebration had summoned our yesterdays and carried them into the future.

For the Túatha Dé Danann, the midwinter sunrise had been a Being Together.

By the time we left the ridge above the river, darkseason was receding. Minimally at first, but surely. Life would return day by day, warming the earth. We would need to be cautious on our way west, but we felt much stronger than when we arrived, and more confident. Revitalized.

I could sense excitement running through the other Dananns like sap in leaf-spring. As we traveled westward through the forests, I recalled how it felt to be a tree. Shinann had the gift, but so did I. When no one was looking, I stepped away from the others and concealed myself behind a majestic oak crowned with mistletoe.

A few moments of intense concentration and . . . it came easier this time. The weight and power of the massive trunk, the incredible grip of the roots sinking into the earth. The magical tingle of the mistletoe with its healing properties . . .

"Where are you?" an anxious voice called.

I had not meant to worry them. My little experiment had been selfish, and a leader should not be selfish. There was a brief flurry of branches and bark while I restored myself, then another flurry while the Dananns crowded around me, wanting an explanation. Most of them had never seen shapechanging before.

"My father had the gift," I told them, "and I inherited it from him."

"Show us!" "Teach us to do it too!"

We were halfway home by then, in an area settled by the New People. It was not the place to stop and attempt new magic. "When we reach the caves I shall try," I said, but I was careful to add, "if you possess the gift." They were so eager that I wanted them to succeed, but how could they? The ones who desired it the most might have the least ability.

The Dagda stirred in my mind like a gentle shadow. He had taught me many things that I did not believe I could learn.

The ability to teach might be a greater gift than silent talking.

We hurried westward until we came to a lonely farmstead at the edge of a dark lake. Soon the sun would drop below the hills. A small herd of black cows was penned near the lake, waiting to be turned out to graze during the night.

The prospect of warm, foaming milk was irresistible.

Leaving the others hidden in the woods, three of us went to fetch the cattle. They were not upset by our approach. They knew the Túatha Dé Danann were no threat to animals. Three placid cows allowed us to lead them away.

We warmed our hands in our armpits before we began milking.

No meal ever tasted better than that hot milk. We had drunk our fill and were taking the cows back to their pen when someone emerged from the farmhouse nearby: a woman carrying two wooden buckets. I could see her clearly in the light of the setting sun.

The shape of her head identified her as a Mílesian. A cluster of ringlets clung to her temples and fell into blue-black waves that rippled over her shoulders. Her skin was fair, but her eyes were as dark and bright as those of a raven.

If the ages of the Mílesians had corresponded with those of the Túatha Dé Danann, she would have been a little younger than I was, a girl just ripening into womanhood.

We stared at each other. I don't know what she saw, but her eyes grew very wide.

Her body was neatly made and high-breasted, with a lovely curve to the hips. Apart from that, there was nothing to captivate a man, yet I looked and looked and could not look away.

She could feel my eyes caressing her. Smiling, she said, "What do you want of me?"

Not smiling, I said, "Everything."

⊱⊰

Her name, she told me, was Alana. Her parents had died of an illness that the Dananns could have cured, but it baffled the Mílesians. She was left to raise two little brothers by herself on more land than she could ever work. One of her neighbors would take over the land whenever he liked. "Perhaps tomorrow," she said sadly. "Or the next change of the moon, at the latest. I shall become his servant, and if I'm very lucky he might let me keep one of the cows so I can feed my brothers."

When she asked my name, I was surprised to hear myself say the last thing the Dagda had said to me. "Elgolai."

"What does that mean—Elgolai?" Alana tasted the unfamiliar word with her lips and tongue.

"It means 'He goes out,'" I replied. "As in, 'he goes out looking for a wife.'"

She looked at me from under her eyelashes. "And are you? Looking for a wife?"

"Not now," I said. "I had to go out to find one, though." As the Dagda had known I must.

The night was cold, and Alana insisted I bring my companions into the house. It consisted of one room built of timber and caulked with mud, with a fire pit in the middle of the earthen floor and a sleeping loft above.

My company of Dananns filled the little house to overflowing. Yet there was enough room for all of us.

I brought in some wood from a stack outside the house

and helped Alana set it alight. The smoke could only escape from the open doorway; the Mílesians did not understand the necessity of a smoke hole in the ceiling.

But the fire was warm and merry, and Alana's eyes were merry and warm.

Her little brothers watched from the loft while she fed us dark bread—not as good as Melitt's—and golden honey sweeter than I had ever tasted.

When we left in the morning, we took Alana and her brothers with us.

I, who remember everything, do not recall asking her if she would come. Perhaps it was not necessary.

Hand to hand and heart to heart, we married in the way of my race. The Dananns witnessed our vows to each other. When they sang the song of wedding for us, it sounded like summer wind.

As we neared the western caves, I tried to prepare Alana for the life she would live with me. "My people are not like yours," I began—but she laughed.

"I know it already, Elgolai. None of us have pointed ears."

That distinction was the last thing I would have noticed.

The tribe waiting in the caves must have been astonished to see me arrive with a young woman and two little boys.

They were no more astonished than I was a few days later, when Shinann joined us bringing a very tall dark-haired man called Amergin, whom she introduced as the chief bard of the Mílesians. They were accompanied by a member of his tribe called Sive, a widow who expected to bear twins very soon. "In fact," Shinann said laughingly, "I'm surprised we made it this far."

Darkseason was over. The light had returned in full measure. Our tribe was growing.

On his first night with us, Amergin played the harp. The

golden voice of Clarsah rang through the caves of crystal-like music from the stars. We watched spellbound as the bard's fingers caressed the brass strings of his instrument. How could I ever have thought the Mílesians were clumsy?

The following morning, Amergin began collecting the stories of our race. They would come back to us as poetry to be remembered for generations.

I began to understand why a bard of the Gael was the equal of a prince.

My Alana had something in common with the Dagda's wife, Melitt. Not only did she bake bread—Melitt taught her to add fruit and other secret ingredients—but she also adjusted well to changed circumstances. Life in a cave with total strangers was not what Alana had expected when she and her family came to Ierne, but soon she was pointing out the advantages of cave living to me and teaching the Túatha Dé Danann the exuberant dances of Iberia.

Sive gave birth to healthy twins, a boy and a girl. The boy had black hair and almond-shaped eyes that she said were shaped like his father's. The girl entered the world with a bright cap of red curls. There had been no twins born to the Túatha Dé Danann in living memory, but we were quick to claim this pair. In the caves above the deep valley, two very different races had come together like two rivers flowing into one lake.

Our children would belong to one tribe.

On the day our daughter Cara was born, Alana and I wept tears of joy. Her ears were only slightly pointed—you would not notice unless you were looking for it—but her eyes were enormous.

The Túatha Dé Danann had been defeated in battle and almost obliterated, but the infusion of Mílesian blood would make a substantial difference to our race. The sons of the Míl were fighters; the spark of life they carried was very strong. They would always seek the far horizon.

We had thought the western caves would be the last refuge of our tribe, but we were mistaken. Within a generation, the Dananns were spreading across Ierne again. They became a vivid but unseen presence in lonely glens and on the tops of mountains. Or in the fragrant countryside, where their music drifted over the nearest settlement and haunted the dreams of the Gael.

Or they went into the sea and shapechanged into the most magical of Manannan's creatures, the seals.

Amergin composed poetry about them too.

More Dananns took mates among the Gael. Instead of producing just one child, or two at the most, the marriage of the two races resulted in larger families. Their offspring rarely inherited the long life spans of the Túatha Dé Danann, but other valuable gifts came to them through blood and bone, so a balance was struck. These children of the new generation were never ordinary. They carried dreams in their eyes.

They loved music and loved words that made music. A glimpse of beauty could stop them in their tracks. Intrigued by overgrown pathways and unsolved mysteries, they walked in the rain and talked to the trees and stared at the stars. The hard-and-fast parameters of time could not hold them; they adapted time to their requirements and made it flexible. If the truth was unpalatable, they embroidered it to shape a better reality.

Gradually, they repopulated the sacred island.

Even today, you might meet some of them in Ierne. Or anywhere else in the world.

You may be one yourself.

ॐ

The Túatha Dé Danann called me their chieftain, and I did my best to supply the leadership they needed, but I was not a chieftain; I was a teacher. It is the nobler title.

I instructed my people in the art of shapechanging so they would be able to camouflage themselves if necessary. As I had anticipated, some learned more readily than others. A few found it addictive. Little Piriome gave herself to a willow tree so totally she never came back.

After that, I was more careful.

I dispensed knowledge bit by bit, as the Dagda had taught me, beginning with simple things that were easy to understand. A mind must be stretched before it can accommodate complexity.

And the history of the Túatha Dé Danann is complicated.

The information I imparted was, and is, regrettably fragmentary. Great gaps exist where those who knew a part of our history never passed it on. I have always urged my people to try to fill in the missing pieces if they could. Gifts are passed in the blood, and so is memory. A sudden recollection may supply another part of the puzzle.

Who am I?

Why am I?

Where am I going?

Even I cannot answer those questions to my own satisfaction. But I keep trying.

Of this much I am certain:

With the passage of time, truth can become myth.

Objects that appear to be solid are in fact permeable. Otherwise, shapes could not change.

The condition called death, meaning the end of existence, does not exist.

There is no material barrier between lastworld, thisworld, and nextworld.

When an infant is born, the spirit that animates its body is not new. The undying spark existed Before the Before and may occupy many forms during the long reach of Eternity.

And this I cannot explain:

After you have gone, I may still be here. Time swirls and spirals and reconnects itself in this enchanted place among the stars.

At night, I stand alone beneath the boundless curve and gaze upward. Calling silently, not expecting an answer yet knowing you are there. All of you, who are one. As I am part of the same one.

You can call me Elgolai na Starbird. Elgolai means He Who Goes Out and is the name given to me. Starbird is the name I gave myself.

Not only the stones survive.

ACKNOWLEDGMENTS

EVERYTHING BEGINS with an idea. You did. So did I. So did the universe. This book is the result of an idea that interested my late mother, Henri Llywelyn Price. From my earliest childhood, she read serious books to me and encouraged me to ask difficult questions.

Many years ago, my mother gave me a copy of *Until the Sun Dies* so we could discuss it together. In this book, Robert Jastrow explored two great mysteries: the riddle of life and the riddle of creation. The conversations this inspired between my mother and me eventually led me to the wide variety of books listed in the select bibliography.

Most of the questions—and some of the answers—behind *Only the Stones Survive* are to be found within those pages.

To all of the scholarly, questing, and/or imaginative minds who researched and produced this diverse totality of work, I can only say thank you. There are too many individuals to name, but, like the stars in the sky, you shed magical light.

Morgan Llywelyn
Winter Solstice, Ireland, 2014

A SELECT BIBLIOGRAPHY

Annals of the Four Masters. Dublin: Hodges, Smith & Co., 1854.

Baigent, Michael. *Ancient Traces.* New York: Viking, 1998.

Binchy, D. S. *Early Irish Society.* Dublin: Royal Irish Society, 1954.

Bonwick, James. *Irish Druids and Old Irish Religions.* New York: Dorset Press, 1986.

Brennan, Martin. *The Boyne Valley Vision.* Portlaoise, Ireland: Dolmen Press, 1980.

Carpenter, Rhys. *Beyond the Pillars of Hercules.* New York: Delacorte Press, 1966.

Chadwick, Nora. *The Celts.* London: Pelican Press, 1977.

Collins, Desmond. *Origins of Europe.* London: Thomas Y. Crowell, 1976.

Cunliffe, Barry. *The Celtic World.* New York: McGraw-Hill, 1979.

Driscoll, Robert. *The Celtic Consciousness*. New York: George Braziller, 1981.

Hapgood, Charles. *Maps of the Ancient Sea Kings*. Philadelphia: Chilton Books, 1966.

Harden, Donald. *The Phoenicians*. New York: Praeger, 1972.

Herity, Michael. *Irish Passage Graves*. Dublin: Irish University Press, 1974.

Herm, Gerhardt. *The Celts*. New York: St. Martin's Press, 1976.

————. *The Phoenicians*. New York: William Morrow, 1975.

Jastrow, Robert. *Until the Sun Dies*. Toronto: George G. McLeod, 1977.

Jones, Carleton. *Temples of Stone*. Cork: Collins Press, 2007.

Joyce, Patrick Weston. *History of Gaelic Ireland*. Dublin: Educational Co. of Ireland, 1924.

Kearns, Hugh. *The Mysterious Chequered Lights of Newgrange*. Dublin: Elo Publications, 1993.

Lebor Gabala Erenn. Dublin: Irish Texts Society, 1956.

MacCana, Proinsias. *Celtic Mythology*. London: Hamlin, 1970.

MacNeill, Eoin. *Celtic Ireland*. Dublin: Martin Lester, 1921.

Manco, Jean. *Ancestral Journeys: The Peopling of Europe*. London: Thames & Hudson, 2013.

O'Rahilly, T. F. *Early Irish History and Mythology*. Dublin: Dublin Institute for Advanced Studies, 1976.

O'Riordain, Sean P. *Tara*. Dundalk: Dundalgan Press, 1979.

Piggott, Stuart. *Ancient Europe*. New York: Aldine Press, 1966.

Powell, T. G. E. *The Celts*. London: Thames & Hudson, 1980.

Renfrew, Colin. *Before Civilization: The Radiocarbon Revolution and Prehistoric Europe*. New York: Alfred A. Knopf, 1973.

Robb, Graham. *The Discovery of Middle Earth: Mapping the Lost World of the Celts*. New York: W. W. Norton & Co., 2012.

Sandars, N. K. *The Sea Peoples*. London: Thames & Hudson, 1978.

Slavin, Michael. *Tara*. Cork: Mercier Press, 2003.

Trump, D. H. *Prehistory of the Mediterranean*. New Haven: Yale University Press, 1980.

Velikovsky, Immanuel. *Worlds in Collision*. New York: Dell Publishing Co., 1950.

Wood-Martin, William G. *Traces of the Elder Faiths of Ireland: A Handbook of Irish Pre-Christian Traditions*. 2 vols. New York: Longmans, Green, and Co., 1902.